When the sun came up the creature rose. Just as it did each morning, it began a litany of threatening roars and hisses. But this time, it was a little less robust, its tone a little more tired. Nimrod knew what it would do next, as it had done the mornings before. The beast would turn around and drag itself to the nearby spring, water itself and come back to roar again. But this time when the beast turned its head, Nimrod dropped down upon its back, plunging one of the stones right through its eye. The other stone missed and slammed into its nose, cutting a red horrific gash through the flesh and down to the cartilage below.

The creature reared up, bellowing its pain to the world as Nimrod locked his legs around its neck and held on to the stones lodged in its face. As it bucked and shook, the two children climbed down the rock face and took off running, just as Nimrod instructed them to do. But the boy, after running a short distance stopped to turn around.

"Let go Nimrod!" he cried. "Let go and run!"

The creature heard him and swung its good eye towards the sound of the boy's voice. As if strengthened by the thought of prey escaping, it reared up mightily and shook Nimrod off, throwing him against the rock face. The boy screamed, causing the creature to swivel back and forth, looking from the fleeing children to the prey before him. Then, with a swat of its huge claw, it gashed Nimrod's head to the bone, then turned and took off after the fleeing youths.

For Gabriel:

Peace.

Bro. G

9/8/18

NIMROD THE HUNTER
BOOK 1

By Gregory "Brother G" Walker

Published by Seker Nefer Press, a division of Seker Nefer Group

www.africanlegendsinteractive.com

Cover art by Eric Wilkerson

Interior Art by Mawuli Ahiekpor

First Printing 2011

Other Books by Brother G:

Shades of Memnon - Book 1: The African Hero of the Trojan War

Shades of Memnon - Book 2: Ra Force Rising

Shades of Memnon - Book 3: African Atlantis Unbound

Library of Congress Cataloging-in-Publication data:

Walker, Gregory Lyle

Nimrod the Hunter

ISBN 978-1494942564 (2014 Softcover Edition)

1, Mythology. 2, Historical Fantasy Fiction. 3, African Studies. 4, Martial Arts. 5, Spirituality

1 Title

NIMROD THE HUNTER
BOOK 1

AN AFRICAN LEGENDS ADVENTURE

BY

BROTHER G

NIMROD THE HUNTER

BROTHER G

Brother G (Gregory L. Walker), creator of the African Legends genre, is the researcher/author of "Nimrod The Hunter." A respected historian, journalist and spoken word comedy poet, Bro. G was awarded the 2009 Octavia Butler Humanitarian Award for the social and educational contributions of his Shades Of Memnon series, a history based African fantasy epic. To develop the African Legends genre and showcase his unique humor, Bro. G has expanded into transmedia production. Google his hilarious animated short "The Day Black Hair Stood Still!"

AFRICAN LEGENDS TRANSMEDIA

Brother G and actor/producer Jeffrey Poitier

Bro. G and Jeffrey Poitier (nephew of legendary actor Sidney Poitier with the same vocal regality)

Announcing the "Nimrod The Hunter" transmedia project to the world at Harlem Book Fair 2011. Jeff has agreed to sign on as the Nimrod's nemesis the "Flame Lord" in upcoming cinematic and multimedia adaptations now in pre-production. See the Nimrod The Hunter teaser trailer script in this volume and look out for the animated teaser coming soon.

Brother G and Yvonne "Shai" Hankins at Harlem Book Fair 2011. In Background: Jeff Poitier and Nimrod Interior Artist Mawuli Aiekpor

I would like to thank my beloved Yvonne "Shai" Hankins for supporting me and putting up with all it takes to produce work of this nature. To my family, friends and shemsu (followers): You have my eternal gratitude, love and appreciation.

Thanks also to Jeffrey and Ellie Poitier for your contributions, advice and contacts as we work together to make this project the multimedia powerhouse we agree it will be.

Thanks to Max Rodriguez for standing by me in stormy times and for the kind words about this book.

Thank you Mawuli Aiekpor of konsciouscreations.com for throwing down on the interior art and to Eric Wilkerson for bringing Nimrod to life on the cover painting. http://www.ericwilkersonart.com/

Thanks to Jarret Alexander for producing a hot script sample. And thanks to Ekowa Kenyatta for the great Nimrod essay.

And, as always, thanks to Ra Un Nefer Amen and the Ausar Auset Society for the divine teachings and inspiration. Lastly, but certainly not least, thanks must go to the Creator and the ancestors who paved the way for this work.

Sela, Amen, Salaam and Hetep,

Greg (Brother G) Walker October 2011

www.africanlegendsinteractive.com

TABLE OF CONTENTS

Reclaiming Nimrod: The Original Sacred Tradition

Thousands of years ago, Israelite scribes sat down to preserve their religious tradition in writing. These scribes succeeded in leaving behind a document now called the Old Testament, which they called the Tanakh. The books in this document concerning their traditions about the origin of the world, earliest created people and the birth of human culture are called The Torah.

Whether the scribes were divinely guided or not is a subject of constant debate. What is generally accepted is that what they wrote down mattered. The information was and still is taken seriously as an important chronicle of the Judeo-Christian tradition, which is a major part of the foundation of western civilization and three world religions.

The story of Adam and Eve, Noah and the ark, Cain and Able and so many more passages from the Old Testament have been used as tools to teach about God, human nature and destiny. Again, these stories and the traditions surrounding them are taken seriously and usually defended from slander, except those sections relaying stories concerning black people.

All of the tales in the early part of the Torah, the book of Genesis, concern groups and individuals who are neither Hebrew nor Christian, but nevertheless have serious, meaningful relationships with God. Noah, Enoch, Abel and others are celebrated constantly, but here are passages concerning one individual who, though praised in the scriptures, usually is not celebrated:

Genesis 10:8 "And Kush begat Nimrod: he began to be a mighty one in the earth."

Genesis 10:9 "He was a mighty hunter before the LORD: wherefore it is said, "Even as Nimrod the mighty hunter before the LORD."

Genesis goes on to say:

The first centers of his kingdom were Babylon, Uruk, Akkad and Kalneh, in Shinar. From that land he went to Assyria, where he built Nineveh, Rehoboth Ir, Calah and Resen, which is between Nineveh and Calah—which is the great city.

There have been a lot of terrible things said about Nimrod over the centuries and it all comes from extra-biblical sources and legends. The perpetrators took the original biblical tradition, turned it on its head, and pretended that what they were teaching was biblical and from God. This, of course, means they are liars. It is time these lies be laid to rest. But before we do that, let us take a look at what the most expert liar in the 20th century, Hitler, said about the art of lying:

"All this was inspired by the principle--which is quite true within itself--that in the big lie there is always a certain force of credibility; because the broad masses of a nation are always more easily corrupted in the deeper strata of their emotional nature than consciously or voluntarily; and thus in the primitive simplicity of their minds they more readily fall victims to the big lie than the small lie, since they themselves often tell small lies in little matters but would be ashamed to resort to large-scale falsehoods. It would never come into their heads to fabricate colossal untruths, and they would not believe that others could have the impudence to distort the truth so infamously. Even though the facts which prove this to be so may be brought clearly to their minds, they will still doubt and waver and will continue to think that there may be some other explanation. For the grossly impudent lie always leaves traces behind it, even after it has been nailed down, a fact which is known to all expert liars in this world and to all who conspire together in the art of lying."

—Adolf Hitler , Mein Kampf

Reclaiming Nimrod: The Original Sacred Tradition

Hitler's advice on the art of lying is exactly what happened to Nimrod. This article will prove that a once revered figure from the bible has been unjustly maligned by a few liars who have gotten away with it by playing on the "emotional nature" of the masses. In this case the "emotional nature" is racism against black people, which has kept the masses from questioning the liars even when it is clear that what they are saying goes against the biblical teachings. For centuries this combination of a lying tradition, scholarly deceit and institutional racism has kept the information that I shall reveal below about Nimrod from the public. And that is a shame, because these lies have had a tremendously detrimental effect upon the study of history and the standing of people of African descent in the world. Along with the so called "Curse Of Ham," this lying lore about Nimrod has been used to justify all manner of prejudice, oppression and genocide.

In order to get some real perspective on Nimrod's character as originally presented by the Old Testament scribes, we will first take a look at what the passages concerning his character really say. To do this, we turn to Young's Literal Translation of the Bible, a bible study guide compiled in the 1800s and published in 1862. For more than 100 years this biblical language tool has been considered the most reliable source to glean what the original scribes really said by Christian and Jewish scholars. Young's is considered an ultimate source to end debates about the meaning of the scriptures and here is what Young's translation says was really written about Nimrod:

[8]And Cush hath begotten Nimrod;

[9]he hath begun to be a hero in the land; he hath been a hero in hunting before Jehovah; therefore it is said, `As Nimrod the hero [in] hunting before Jehovah.

The translation of the passage in the King James Bible commonly says "before the lord" and that alone should have been enough to dispel any notions of an evil character for Nimrod. This is because the term "before the lord," if anyone cares to check, is used frequently in the scriptures and always has a very positive meaning. The King James edition also says that he was "mighty." But it is clear from the more accurate translation from Young's that Nimrod was not simply "mighty." Oh no, no, no! The original scriptures referred to Nimrod as heroic! And was he simply performing these heroics "before the lord?" Not according to a deeper analysis by Rev. Gerald Rowlands, a pastor and writer respected world-wide. Although in this essay entitled "Nimrod A Mighty Hunter," Rowlands does not come down firmly on the side of a heroic Nimrod, he thoroughly debunks the ignorant, lying notion that the scriptures say Nimrod was evil. Then, as we shall see, the pastor throws light on a more accurate translation that I believe actually proves the Kushite king was heroic. Rowlands wrote:

"If we study what the scriptures say in Hebrew, many people will be surprised. We need to remember that in Hebrew, the nuances of English grammar and punctuation do not appear. This is word for word what the Hebrew Scriptures say about Nimrod written in Hebrew; "Cush he generated Nimrud ... He started to become of masterful in the earth. He became masterful hunter to faces of YHVH ... on so he is being said as Nimrud masterful hunter to faces of YHVH." That verse is very surprising. Nimrod was closer than just being before the Lord, he was literally face to face with God. To be face to face with someone means to be close enough to be within visual range. Could a wicked man be face to face with God?"

So according to Rowlands, a close look at the exact words used in the passage in original Hebrew reveals not "before the lord" but "to faces of YHVH." The Hebrew word for "faces" Rowlands adds, is the plural word "phnim" which means there were multiple faces involved. This means that Nimrod was not just doing something "before the lord" but doing something "in the face of the lord" which we call today "face to face." *

Since I can't read Hebrew, I had an African American rabbi who teaches in Harlem check on these translations. His expertise indicated that there is wiggle room in the interpreta-

Reclaiming Nimrod: The Original Sacred Tradition

tion of "hero" vs "masterly" vs "mighty," but that the "faces of God" translation is very apparent, and grossly mistranslated.

So, the most respected resource for Biblical translations and one of the world's most respected pastors both say that the original scribes described Nimrod as a "heroic" and/or "masterful" man who performed his duties, according to Rowlands and my source, while dwelling close to God.

To back this up even further and as an example of how long it can take the truth to be widely known, I shall cite the work of an eminent Hebrew scholar named E.G.H. Kraeling. In an eye opening essay published in the peer reviewed American Journal Of Semitic Languages and Literatures in 1922 entitled "The Origin and Real Name Of Nimrod" Kraeling reached the same conclusion the scholarship led me to reach over 91 years later:

"From this point of view we may be able to determine the original meaning of the proverb which already at an early date caused the interpolation of verse 9 into the text of Genesis, chapter 10. An inveterate and successful hunter in Israel is said to be "like Nimrod, a mighty hunter before the face of Yahweh." Remembering the fact that the Assyrian Heracles was often portrayed as a giant, we may conclude that this expression originally meant very literally as "measuring up to divine size," therefore superhuman, extraordinary. Whenever the words "before the face of Yahweh" occur in a like connection the meaning "extraordinary" fits excellently." (AJSL - pg 217, April 1922)

Taken together, these more accurate translations and interpretations point to Nimrod being a masterful extraordinary hero who performed his duties of hunting and nation building while "face to face" with the creator due to his extraordinary high spiritual nature! Again, even though I cannot read Hebrew, I can view images with great precision, and there is a spiritual/iconic tradition that dovetails nicely with the conclusions reached by Rev. Rowland, my rabbi friend and especially Mr. Kraeling. To get a deeper perspective about this, we have only to look at the iconography of the ancient cultures of the Old Testament times, particularly the Middle East and north east Africa. On the walls of the temples in ancient Egypt, Mesopotamia and many other cultures you find pictures of people, almost always priests or priest-kings or queens, standing face to face with images of their deities, in some cases even close enough to kiss. As mentioned by Kraeling 91 years ago, other scholars and priests today say being eye to eye or face to face symbolized that the human beings had acquired the spiritual skills and knowledge to become one with the deity, existing on the level of the deity - thus achieving "God consciousness!" This is the cultural/historical context and I believe the meaning of this passage.

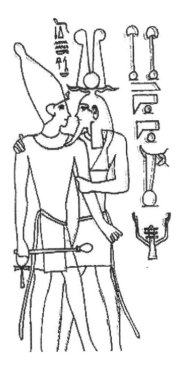

It is clear that the original scriptures described Nimrod as someone who had achieved a level of noted achievement that reflected upon his high character. This is a far cry above the usual translation of "mighty." Nimrod was not just simply strong or mighty, the scriptures clearly say he had achieved a status in life that allowed him to exist face to face with God. The fact that this is not commonly known is another example of sloppy scholarship or an outright lie to down grade the status of a black man the Hebrew scribes described as high in character. A mighty man can be a simple bully, but a masterful, extraordinary hero is almost always a learned person who has risen up as a part of a highly respected masterful tradition. In this case it would have been a Kushite, or African tradition, and this is a part of what the liars have been trying to conceal.

So, according to the original reading of the passages in Genesis concerning Nimrod in the Hebrew and with the historical/geographical context firmly in mind, Nimrod was a masterful hero who went about his duties not only with the approval of God, but with God's explicit blessing because he was one with the creator and living in a sort of "God consciousness." This spiritual achievement is the ultimate goal of all religions and is, I believe, the chief reason why the people who wrote the extra-biblical lies did so. I am sure that most of them could read Hebrew and knew full well the implications of the original scriptures.

What are these implications? What the scriptures imply is that Nimrod was a priest-king who worked with God to achieve God's will. And what is God's will according to the scriptures? It was always to build a spiritually uplifted civilization, which is what the Kushites were renowned for. Nimrod was also a great hunter, but it is never said what he hunted. According to comparative religion, sections in the bible and other sources, it was not regular animals that were the primary foes of people gathered in their efforts to create civilization. It was the animalistic tendencies in men, represented as spiritual metaphors in the form of monstrous creatures. The scriptures mention many times creatures called "leviathans," describing them as supernatural creatures devoted to the disruption of civilization and the desecration of the people who are trying to develop "God Consciousness." A familiar "leviathan" creature from the ancient Kemetic tradition would be Apep, a giant serpent who opposed those on the road to spiritual enlightenment.

The root word from which leviathan is derived is, "lavah," with means in ancient Hebrew "to join." Leviathan in Hebrew is "livyathan" which means "twisted." Clearly from an examination of the root words and the historical/cultural context, leviathan represent negative forces whose goal is to "join with" or possess the souls of men in order to "twist" them in demonic ways. Satan, Set, Apep or Mesopotamian demons like the Meshkem are all representations of the forces of evil and spiritual impediment. And who best to combat these evil forces but a warrior who has achieved "God Consciousness," a warrior saint who slays demonic creatures, similar to Saint George, who famously slew a dragon. Like these examples from ancient Mesopotamia:

Reclaiming Nimrod: The Original Sacred Tradition

This is why in my interpretation of Nimrod, he hunts leviathans instead of regular animals, which the iconography below indicates were his friends. This is the core meaning, purpose and internal construction of the "Nimrod The Hunter" book series: respect for and communion with the natural world and the defeat of unnatural forces that attack spirituality.

Now as hinted at above, one of the other hallmarks of a saint in traditions around the world is communion and communication with the natural forces, particularly animals. Saint Francis of Assisi and Saint Anthony in the Catholic tradition are great examples of this. African priests and shaman of all types worldwide share in this tradition too. It is said that once you achieve God Consciousness, you will be able to share in some of the creator's abilities and one of those is the ability to communicate with animals. Most people do not know that there is another iconic tradition arising from ancient, multi-national Kushite culture that not only points to such spiritual abilities and mastery, but says explicitly that Nimrod was one such master. This is it:

Reclaiming Nimrod: The Original Sacred Tradition

"Nimrod" means nimr (leopard or big cat) rad (subduer) -literally "big cat subduer" in the Elamite-Sumerian language of ancient Mesopotamia. This pre-dynastic artifact called the Gebel el-Arak Knife found in southern Egypt depicts one of the earliest representations of Nimrod from around 3,300 BC! The scholars point to it as proof positive that people from Mesopotamia interacted with people from the Nile Valley because the figure in the middle is dressed like an Elamite/Sumerian, not a person from the Nile Valley. Other representations of this multinational Kushite heroic tradition from the Sahara desert, Mesopotamia and Sudan are even older.*** Nimrod represents an African tradition going back thousands of years concerning high priests/hunters so at one with God that they could commune with nature, tame wild animals and combat unseen forces of evil that corrupt man and beast. These priests helped lay the foundations for civilizations by policing the natural order of creation and were thus "mighty hunters before the Lord!"

What you will notice in the above example is that the "Nimrod" character is "in the face of" the lions he is apparently subduing. Also note that there is not a hint of violence between the "Nimrod" personage and the felines, thus proving that what is being depicted is some sort of spiritually based communication. I believe this iconography says that after becoming one with the creator, just as the world traditions say, you can become one with God's creations.

Reclaiming Nimrod: The Original Sacred Tradition

Despite all the proof above, shrill voices keep shouting out the lies. A popular thing to do in defaming Nimrod is to claim that his name comes from the Hebrew word "mered" which the liars claim means "he who rebels" as in rebelling against God. Here is a quote from Alexander Hislop's "The Two Babylons," page 222. Hislop was one of the main slander mongers against Nimrod, making up all manner of stupidity about him, but even he knew better than relying on junk linguistics. This quote below from Hislop, who is no friend to Nimrod, is for those who argue that Nimrod's name means "to rebel" in ancient Hebrew:

"Nimr-rod"; from Nimr, a "leopard," and rada or rad "to subdue." According to invariable custom in Hebrew, when two consonants come together as the two rs in Nimr-rod, one of them is sunk. Thus Nin-neveh, "The habitation of Ninus," becomes Nineveh. The name Nimrod is commonly derived from Mered, "to rebel"; but a difficulty has always been found in regard to this derivation, as that would make the name Nimrod properly passive not "the rebel," but "he who was rebelled against."**

According to Strong's Concordance, another bible study guide compiled in the 1800s by a Dr. James Strong, just to back up Hislop, the word "mered" means "revolted against." As in done wrong, betrayed or in today's terms "dissed." So, according to the credible scholarship, even if Nimrod's name is derived from "mered"(which it is not!) it would mean someone rebelled against him! Not the other way around! I guess it turns out, ironically, that the word "mered" does have an attachment to this great hero: Nimrod has been "dissed" and his original character has been "revolted against" by liars! The fact that no one has popularly pointed this out means simply that no one has been willing to stand up to the liars, because it is easily discovered.

The original scriptures are clear, the fact that the nations the scriptures say Nimrod founded were separated by a thousand years make it clear, and the iconography found in the anthropological records of many ancient nations also make it clear that:

Nimrod was a title, not an individual. This is the reason why scholars can't find the person named Nimrod in the historical record and are lost on a merry-go-round of speculation.

The word Nimrod was like the word pharaoh. It was a title, in this case given for attaining a form of spiritual mastery that led to true civilization. As an individual figure for storytelling purposes, Nimrod is a historical/spiritual metaphor for the ancient Kushite people, just as the scriptures described him. ("And Kush Begat Nimrod!) If you know what to look for, you can find Nimrod related icons and traditions among the ancient Mesopotamians, Kemetic people and the Canaanites. These were all literate Kushite people whom the Israelites knew all too well, having sojourned in their lands for a long time as documented in the Old Testament. As the scriptures say emphatically, Nimrod was the subject of parable, ("wherefore it is said") thus he was so renowned that they dared not leave him out as the explanation for the foundation of world civilization. Leaving Nimrod out of their chronicle of the beginning of all things would have been akin to skipping over slavery in a study of the history of America: It would cause anyone who knows anything about real history to laugh at you.

The original Israelite scribes knew this, and after beating back the forces of racism, we now know it too. But later writers, far removed from the original authoring who apparently hated the Nimrod tradition for its implications, went on a long campaign of slander and misinterpretation. They feared a simple fact that was well known to ancient cultures like the Greeks, whose poet Homer called the Kushites "blameless Ethiopians, most favored of the gods" and said that the gods would come down off mount Olympus to dine "face to face" with the Ethiopians while everyone else had to go to the temple to commune with divinity. And the Greek writer Herodotus who said the Ethiopians were the "most long lived and the most just of men."

Reclaiming Nimrod: The Original Sacred Tradition

The evidence indicates that the Kushites were Godly people who possessed traditions that could actually develop you into becoming one with the creator, to be "in the face" of God just as the scriptures say Nimrod was. This is why Kushites were able to come up with things like animal domestication, mathematics, engineering, writing, laws and profound spiritual teachings. You know - that civilization thing. And they did this, according to most scholars, from out of thin air, while other nations were literally living in caves and eating what they could gather.

But it wasn't out of thin air. The anthropological records, if looked at without racist prejudice, easily tell the tale (Kemetic math existed in 23,000 B.C. in the Congo. Look up the Ishango Bones!).**** And there is another way of looking at things that has to do with divine inspiration. The traditional African view is that God knows how to do anything, and if you become one with the creator, if you live "in the face of" God, you can know how to do anything too. You can create civilizations like Nimrod did if you live like he and his people lived in communion with the creator.

Mentioning divine inspiration and other mysterious aspects of ancient history may make some laugh that this is all opinion and hearsay. On one hand some Jewish traditions claimed the Kemetians and other Kushites were devil worshippers, enslavers and sinners, which is partly why the lies about Nimrod have gone unquestioned for so long and why the "Curse of Ham" garbage has been so effective. On the other hand the Greeks said the Kushites were the most advanced and just people who communed face to face with divinity. This push and pull of hearsay could go on forever, unless we take a look at the way the ancient Kushites chose to tell their own story and prove who they were for all eternity.

There is a concept called "maat" from the ancient Kemitian (Egyptian) people that permeated the way they lived and related to the world. You will find some form of this concept all over the earth where other Kushites settled, and even among traditional Africans today. Maat, simply translated, means living, creating and reasoning in adherence to the natural structures of the universe as created by God. Any real study of it will reveal it to be the most sophisticated religious concept introduced to the world to date. But that is more hearsay, someone could argue, so I am going to point out objective proof that the ancient Kushites practiced what they preached, were divinely inspired and were indeed living in God –consciousness. And I am going to do it with a look at mathematics.

There is a sequence of numbers that underlie the structure of everything in nature called "Fibonacci numbers." *****These numbers are applicable to every living thing, from single cells, to plants to animals and even the human body. The ancient Kushites called them "divine numbers" and for centuries Egyptologists thought their mention was just egotistical superstition on the part of the ancient Africans. That is until they started to study the pyramids, art, city planning and other aspects of these ancient cultures as European math got better. Lo and behold they found that all of these Kushite creations were built according to the Fibonacci numbers, which the Europeans now recognized as the underlying mathematical structure of the universe. Somehow the ancient Kushites knew how to pattern their cultural artifices after the basic structure of creation! The Kemetians and others said they received the instructions on how to do this from the "neteru," which means "nature spirit messengers." Other Kushites had their own names for the neteru, which were promptly mistranslated as "gods" and the mistranslations used as a hammer to beat across the heads of all Kushite cultures in the undying efforts to accuse them of being pagans. But these beings are similar to the biblical angels; not gods, but carriers of God's information. Maat, the Fibonacci numbers personified in the tradition of Kemit, was one of them.******

Let me make this clear. While the rest of the world was just tossing one mud brick on top of another, it was important to the ancient Kushites to build according to the harmonious way God structured the universe. Leviathans, Satan and demonic forces represent disharmony, so how could those who worshipped evil, knew nothing of God and were pagans, build like this? Why would and how could those who knew nothing of God insist on being

Reclaiming Nimrod: The Original Sacred Tradition

surrounded by divinely inspired art and structures? If they worshipped "the devil," why would Satan tell the Kushites to build according to God's plan? In the biblical tradition the devil never tells anyone to follow God, so it should be clear by now that the "Kushite devil worshiper" trope has been a lie too.

The scriptures say Nimrod built cities before anyone else was mentioned as a city builder, so how did he know how to do this? This is how: God's mathematical foundation for creation was obviously intuited by the heroic/masterful minds of the ancient Nimrods because they had cultivated themselves to be able to receive it. These Kushites then systematically built civilizations using this information, making their art and architecture the ultimate proof that Nimrod lived, as the original scriptures said, "in the face" of God.

It is an impossibility to output materially what has not been input mentally first!

As the lawyer for the hunter and builder Nimrod I will now rest my case with confidence. I think that I have clearly established that liars bore false witness against our Kushite defendant, accusing him of immorally spreading evil. Nimrod's alibi, that he was busy communing with God to download divine numbers and using them to build just civilizations, has been confirmed by modern science, impartial ancient witnesses and accurate biblical translations. Evidence from ancient iconography and the bible have been presented that show the defendant possessed a level of spirituality that would cause him to befriend nature and hunt leviathan demons, so he could not have been a devil worshipping bringer of chaos as the liars have claimed. And the most damaging accusation, his supposed rebellious activity, has been booted from the court of history because no credible witness saw him doing it, those who were around during his time reported just the opposite and the false evidence of the Hebrew word "mered" has been proven linguistically impossible and therefore inadmissible. This phony charge was replaced by proof that Nimrod's activities were actually done on behalf of God, whom he has been notoriously and falsely accused of rebelling against.

The jury is in, the gavel has fallen and the phony trumped up charges against Nimrod have finally been disproven. Not guilty and case closed!

It has been a rough historical ride for this Kushite hero and for the depiction of ancient Kushite culture, but the time of the lies is now over. "Nimrod The Hunter," a multi-media, spiritual/historical adventure saga, is here. Finally the character of Nimrod is being depicted as the original scriptures described him and in his proper context as part of a spiritual and masterly/heroic culture. It is long past due, but I stand with Dr. Martin Luther King, who famously said when asked about the time it would take to achieve justice:

"How long? Not long: Because no lie can live forever!"

Dr. King defeated the leviathan of organized Jim Crow racism. All wise peoples should have storytelling traditions of mighty heroes defeating leviathans because these creatures represent the lie that man must live separate from God and that animalistic, demonic behavior must always rule the day. This big lie was then and is now being exposed by mighty warriors who dwell in the face of Yahweh like President Nelson Mandela, who came out of 27 years of racist incarceration, hugged his white jailer, and then went on to begin the hard task of forging a hate free South African nation. So let us be thankful for the Nimrods throughout history, both men and women, who dedicated their lives to fighting the good fight and stood as symbols against the leviathans. Let us never again allow our Nimrods to be taken from us by liars, including the original Nimrod, whom the Israelite scribes revered so much. And may the creator grant that the rest of us keep our heads to the sky, come close to the face of God, and make our own transformations into Nimrod! Let this be my humble contribution to that sacred purpose.

Selah, Salaam, Amen and Hetep!

Reclaiming Nimrod: The Original Sacred Tradition

Gregory "Brother G" Walker July, 2011

For the Nimrod The Hunter adventure ebook: http://africanlegendsinteractive.com/?page_id=9

 * http://www.bibleabookoftruth.com/NimrodAMightyHunter.pdf

** http://arcticbeacon.com/books/Alexander_Hislop-The_Two_Babylons-1853-MER.pdf

***http://content.yudu.com/Library/A1ikmg/MasteroftheAnimalsin/resources/index.htm?referrerUrl=http%

**** http://www.youtube.com/watch?v=CyduQYmlowM

*****http://jwilson.coe.uga.edu/emat6680/parveen/fib_nature.htm

******http://www.youtube.com/watch?v=WFNZeBtn3sY

Ben Underwood: A Young Nimrod

I dedicate this page to Ben Underwood, an extraordinary young black man, who in his short time on the earth represented everything that the "Nimrod The Hunter" series stands for. Stricken with ocular cancer at the age of 3, Ben's courageous mother Aquanetta had no choice but to have his eyes removed. In the face of despair, Aquanetta turned to her faith in God and was strengthened during what was then the darkest of times. Then this amazing mother told her blind son that he could learn to see in other ways, do anything he set his mind to and have a rich, fulfilling life. Little did Aquanetta realize how her words would empower Ben and lead to a modern day miracle.

It was from this positive environment of faith that Ben was divinely inspired and given the gift of echolocation. This is the ability to sense your surroundings by bouncing sound waves off objects that is utilized by bats, dolphins and other creatures. Human echolocation is very rare and developed by the blind as a substitute for sight. There have been a few extraordinary cases, but none nearly like the echolocation developed by Ben Underwood with his "clicking."

By clicking his tongue against the roof of his mouth to send out sound waves, Ben developed human echolocation the likes of which the world had never seen. He rode bicycles, played video games, skate boarded and practiced martial arts. Ben was a wonderful and profound inspiration to all who knew him: A true shining spirit of an

Ben Underwood: A Young Nimrod

almost angelic disposition, who carried hope like a golden beacon, a smoldering torch, or a feather plucked from the wing of a phoenix bird (The storyline will explain this later). Biological scientists were puzzled, social scientists were astounded and people who believe in the power of God were bolstered.

And this writer was absolutely inspired. That is why you will find much of Ben Under-wood in the character of Nimrod in this book series. I was trying to decide how to tell the story of an unjustly maligned African figure from the Old Testamant when I happened upon a TV show that featured Ben several years ago.   Suddenly, there it was right in front of me: A young black man who, with the help of an outstanding mother similar to Nim-rod's teacher Elder Eshri, defeated the leviathans of hopelessness and despair. Then God miraculously attuned Ben's spirit with the forces of the natural world, causing him to ob-tain a skill usually reserved for animals like Nimrod in this book series. Also like Nimrod, Ben is a symbol of hope to all people, but especially to people of African descent.

 Ben ascended to be with the Creator in 2009. He did not live past 16 years old due to the return of the cancer, but those of us who took notice of his message of hope, strength, faith and inspiration will remember him forever. That is why this book is dedicated to Ben Underwood, a true Nimrod living now in the face of the creator.

http://www.benunderwood.com/

Ben Underwood: A Young Nimrod

"I'm a rebel, soul rebel
I'm a Capturer soul adventurer"
Bob Marley-
"Soul Rebel"

Chapter 1: My Name Is Nimrod!

Somehow Albel knew he was doomed as he knelt to the grim task set before him. The throne room was hushed and dozens of eyes were watching as he grasped the long locks of the recently blinded, 3 year old Kushite boy. He pressed his razor sharp dagger against the little brown throat, drawing a tiny drop of blood. But instead of dealing the killing stroke as he had done so frequently of late, he hesitated. Gulping slowly, Albel's eyes flit back to the boy's eerily serene, eyeless face.

"Why does he not scream out!" the executioner cried out in his mind. "Perhaps, if he would just cry out, I could get this done!"

Albel thought again of the torturer Mutla, the man who had put out the boy's eyes and those of the rest of the royal family before they were executed. Mutla too had hesitated for some reason, but performed the deed regardless. The child had screamed, and then went eerily silent as he was now. Then, not 10 heartbeats later, the torturer was struck dead. Whispers of arcane forces surrounding the child began and priests were sent in to examine him. As they chanted to the Gods of Chaos for guidance, one of the priests howled in anguish and fell to the floor. The rest ran screaming from the room, never to be seen again. Albel had witnessed the fate of Mutla and the priests and had mocked them. But now, as an overwhelming feeling of dread washed over him due to his nearness to the child, he understood.

"Oh, for happier days when being Shamshi's executioner was a pleasure," Albel thought.

The fat, pasty-faced, short-bearded executioner had never been good at commerce, never been lucky in love. This was his calling and he had killed the rest of the boy's family with relish. But somehow he knew that if he pulled the blade across the throat of this little prince, he would be both doomed and damned. Looking up toward the throne, he saw the usurper, King Shamshi, devouring a tray of food set before him. A brown skinned slave girl dabbed his pale skinned, bearded face with a cloth, then he hoisted a leg of lamb to his teeth and took another bite. The slave girl dabbed Shamshi's mouth again and he slapped her hand away. Looking down at Albel, the new king's face twisted into a dangerous scowl .

"Albel!" King Shamshi shouted, causing everyone in the throne room to shrink. "What is the problem? Kill that boy and throw him to the dogs like the rest of his family!"

"But, my lord…" Albel cried, his hand beginning to shake violently.

All in the room gasped when Albel spoke back to the king. It had taken Shamshi nearly 20 years to murder and deceive his way to the throne of Elam and assume rulership from the grand capital Susa, and he had not done so by suffering insubordination.

King Shamshi angrily waved the tray away and stood up. Pulling his own dagger from the sheath, he slowly descended the steps towards the executioner and the boy.

"If that boy is not dead by the time I get there Albel…"

"I can't!" cried Albel, pulling the blade away from the child's throat and tossing it away. "Kill me if you must, my king, but I can't kill this child! Not this one! He is cursed! Cursed I tell you!"

King Shamshi hesitated as he hovered over Albel and the boy, pondering the situation. Never had he witnessed terror worse than the fear of death itself! As a man who had counted on that fear in his rise to power, and who would no doubt do so to maintain it, this greatly unnerved him. Of course, he did not believe the child to be cursed and considered the priests who had examined the boy to be a weak superstitious lot. He had already placed a bounty upon their traitorous heads. The death of his torturer Mutla was the most troubling, but Shamshi considered it a mere coincidence because Mutla was old. But this, Shamshi observed, this fear of a curse was real. Glancing around at the members of his court, he saw fear in most of their eyes too. Ever a man seeking ways to gain advantage, Shamshi decided it wise to find a way to work such fear to his favor. Sheathing his dagger, King Shamshi turned to his court and spoke out.

"It would please me to keep this one alive," Shamshi declared.

Everyone in the throne room sighed as if a collective stone had been lifted from all their backs. Everyone, except Albel. He knew the king could not afford to let public defiance go unpunished. No matter the fate of the boy, Albel thought his death quite imminent. Shamshi scanned the court as he continued.

"This boy shall be a living example to all those who choose to defy me. Once the heir to the throne of Elam, he shall live now as the lowliest slave of my court, a stable cleaner for the rest of his miserable blind life."

Then the king turned his glare upon his failed executioner.

"Stand before me Albel!" King Shamshi commanded.

Albel stood up nervously, expecting to be struck down on the spot.

"You are my executioner no more. You are hereby appointed stable master, with the task of looking after this boy and caring for my horses. Fail in this Albel and your eyes shall be put out also - and you'll join the child in his tasks. Do you understand me?"

Albel was both relieved and ashamed. He had his life, but stable master was the lowest title in the court. Executioner had been one of the highest. Lowering his head, Albel contemplated his future. Oh how he would be laughed at! All the debts he had accrued would now have to be paid, and women would no longer give themselves to him for free. And being consigned to watch over the blind child, the cause of his miserable fall, was a most bitter irony. For a second, Albel considered the fatal choice of declining, but then pushed the thought aside.

"Yes, my lord," Albel said with resignation.

"Then take the boy," King Shamshi said as he walked back up to his throne and sat back down. "And get you to my stables. "

The tray of food was pushed back in front of the king and he waved Albel away dismissively.

"Now…let the celebrations for my new rule begin!" he cried.

The room exploded with cheers as musicians struck up their harps and horns. Albel looked down at the eyeless boy. Grasping his little brown hand, he took a long last look at his former life, and then he led the child slowly from the room.

What's your name?" the little girl asked the little blind boy as she handed him her pony's bridle. They stood before the large double doors of the royal stables a short distance from the rear of the castle. Sheep bayed in the distance; the metallic pounding of a blacksmith could be heard too, along with other familiar sounds of castle maintenance. Above it all the boy could hear the sound of the little girl's foot tapping impatiently.

"I said: what is your name?" she asked again for the fourth time. She was a pretty little girl, with long black hair pulled into a pony tail, light olive colored skin and big sparkling green eyes. She ran one hand along her tiny waist, smoothing out her expensive riding skirt and pointed at the boy threateningly with the other. Frowning, she remembered he couldn't see and lowered it. "If you don't tell me your name, I'll tell my father you were being disobedient! You'll be beaten!"

Albel overheard the little princess from two stalls over where he was grooming King Shamshi's prize horse, a fine white stallion recently acquired. He and the boy had been working the stables for nearly 10 years and rarely had anyone spoken to the boy besides him. But since King Shamshi's daughter, princess Hamash, began taking riding lessons she had been looking at the boy with increasing interest. Now she indulged the natural curiosity of a 12 year old child and began asking questions. Albel sighed. She was a haughty child, and beloved by her father, so he knew he would have to deal with her carefully.

Albel emerged from the stall and strode towards the stable doors, noting the angry look on the girl's face and her hands upon her hips. He tried to disarm her with a gentle smile.

"He has no name my princess," Albel said carefully. "We simply call him "boy."

The princess looked back and forth at both of them. The boy tried to lead the pony away, but she grabbed the bridle and held it firmly.

"That's stupid stable master Albel," princess Hamash retorted. "Tell me his name! And what happened to his eyes?"

The boy tugged the bridle again and the princess tugged back. Albel gulped nervously.

"These are things we do not talk about princess. Now please let the boy tend to your pony and go back to the palace," the stable master pleaded. "This is no place for you…"

"You don't tell me what to do stable master!" the little princess snapped back. "Can't this boy speak for himself? Is his tongue cut out too?"

The boy suddenly spoke up.

"I can speak, princess Hamash…"

"Silence boy…" Abel said threateningly.

"Let him speak!" shouted princess Hamash. "How do you know who I am if you can't see me?"

"I…I have heard you. Even before you started taking riding lessons," the boy replied. "I know your voice."

"What happened to your eyes?"

"I…I do not know. I don't remember…it has always been this way. Please princess, I will be beaten."

Princess Hamash let go of the bridle and glared at Albel. Then she took a step closer to him and whispered:

"If you beat him Albel, I will say you tried to touch me," the little princess said coldly. "Father will chop off your head…"

Albel stepped back, his eyes widened in fear.

"Please princess, don't…!"

"Father won't let commoners into the royal compound and I need someone to play with," princess Hamash replied as she stomped away from the stable. "So when I come back Albel, you'd better give him to me."

As the princess walked away, her two personal guards followed and they disappeared around a corner. Scowling at the boy, Albel picked up a riding whip and started towards him. Hearing his approach, as well as the familiar swish of his master's favorite tool to beat him, the boy put up his hands defensively. Then suddenly Albel stopped and lowered the whip.

"Tend to the princess's pony boy," he said through grinding teeth and walked away.

The boy did just that for the rest of the day, spending hours rubbing the animal down and grooming its long mane. That night the boy slept in the stall near the pony and when the morning came he was awakened with a gentle nudge instead of the harsh kick he had grown accustomed to. With no eyes to open, waking up meant becoming aware of the sounds and smells nearby and he immediately heard the voice of the princess.

"Wake up boy, we're going riding," she said.

The boy pushed his straw bedding aside and stood up.

"I've never ridden a horse before…

"You mean you have tended these horses for all these years and never once got on one and rode around?" the princess replied.

The boy lowered his head.

"I tried once, but Albel beat me… he called me a blind fool."

"Well today you ride with me and I will teach you how to control a horse."

"But what about Albel," the boy replied fearfully.

"Forget him. I already told him we were going. He didn't like it, but so what."

The children placed the pony's saddle on its back and tied it under the animal's belly, and then the princess got on and pulled the boy up behind her.

Her two guards awaited atop their own horses as the children emerged from the stable. Albel stood nearby rubbing down a steed. Grinding his teeth, the stable master pretended not to be paying attention.

"To the small hill guards," the princess cried. "Ready boy?"

"Yes!"

As the pony started to gallop he held on to the princess with all his might. Never had the boy been so thrilled in his life. The wind rushed by faster and he clasped her waist even harder.

"Hey not so tight," the princess cried and his grip loosened. "There now…let's keep going."

The sun beamed down beautifully as they galloped across a fine grassy field towards a row of beautiful hills. The breeze felt wonderful and the warmth of the light made the boy smile. Suddenly he felt a tingle in his forehead, right between the eyes, and he felt like eating some grass. The boy wanted to stop right there, jump down off the horse and eat some grass. It was a most strange feeling and moments later he somehow realized that it was not him, but the pony they rode upon that wanted to eat the grass.

"Princess, stop, the pony is hungry…"

"What?"

"The horse wants to eat some grass. Stop here."

The princess pulled the reigns and they trotted to a stop. Then the pony wiggled as if he wanted them to get off. As they slid to the ground the pony looked back curiously at the boy for a long moment, then lowered its head and started munching grass with relish. The princess' guards got off their horses and their steeds too began grazing.

"How did you know he was hungry?" the princess asked.

"I don't know…I just did I guess," he replied. "This just happens some-times…"

"You do this all the time?" the princess gasped.

"Umm…sometimes," the boy replied. "In the stables…I have to bribe the rats…"

"You bribe rats?"

"I have to sleep in the stables," he replied. "Rats sleep there too and they were biting me. So I leave some food for the bigger ones and they keep all the others away from me."

The princess looked at the boy for a long moment.

"You are a very strange boy. You don't know your own name, but you talk to horses and pay rats for protection. Very strange…You want something to eat?"

"I don't get to eat until the evening when it starts to get cool. Albel never gives me food this early. And even when he does it's never enough, so I have to sneak and drink milk from the cows at night."

The princess just looked at the boy, a curious look in her eyes.

"I drink milk too, to help with my spiritual instructions." the princess replied. "My teacher says it helps to perceive the creators messages and can bestow gifts of the mind. How long have you been drinking it?"

"My whole life," Nimrod replied. "Ever since I can remember since I never get enough to eat."

"Hmm," the princess pondered. "Perhaps that's why you can speak to animals… well today you get lots of food my friend!"

Then she yanked a blanket out of her saddlebag, spread it over the grass before them and began pulling out little bundles covered in cloth. The boy immediately smelled the food and reached for it, but the princess slapped his hand away.

"Don't you have any manners?" she scolded. "Sit down like a civilized person and let's give thanks before we eat."

They sat down cross legged in the grass and the princess carefully separated the food. Then she clasped her hands together and drew them up towards her chin. Noting that the boy's hands were still sitting in his lap, she reached over and placed his hands together. Then she pushed his hands up towards his chin.

"Alright, now we can give thanks," she said, lowering her head.

"Thanks princess Hamash!" the boy cried.

"You don't thank me…"

"Well who do we thank?" the boy shot back. "You brought the food…"

The princess sighed.

"We thank the one who made the food…"

"You mean the cook?"

The princess looked flabbergasted.

"Has no one ever given you any spiritual instruction?"

The boy shook his head.

"What's that?"

"Just listen to what I say," she replied, bowing her head and closing her eyes.

"We thank the Almighty Mother Father Creator for giving us this meal and for the company shared as we consume it."

Then the princess looked up and tapped the boy on the knee.

"Now we can eat."

The princess nibbled on the fruit and smoked meats before her as the boy stuffed one handful of food after another into his mouth. Chewing loudly, he belched several times.

"This food is really good princess," he said between bites. "And none of it tastes stale or sour. Who is the Mother Father Creator?"

"The being that made the world," the princess replied. "The Creator of everything. You know…the great and only God."

"I hear Albel speaking about the Gods when he is angry," the boy said, licking his fingers. "He said the Gods wanted me to be blind and do as I am told…"

"Albel is wrong," the princess shot back. "The Creator doesn't want any such thing. I'll let you speak to the person who has been teaching me. She'll tell you all about it. Now I have something else for you, besides this food."

"What is it Princess?" replied the boy.

"I don't know how to put this, my friend," the Princess said hesitantly, "but where your eyes should be, there are only sunken in eyelids. It looks strange to people…"

"Oh, I'm sorry," the boy answered sadly, lowering his head. "I'm sorry that my ugliness makes you feel bad…"

"You are not ugly!" The Princess shot back with authority. "Someone did something to you, something evil that wasn't your fault. But it's just bad taste for everyone to constantly see it. Because it makes people feel sorry for you and not just treat you normally. But I have something I think can help…"

The Princess reached into her bag and pulled out a long, dark strip of cloth. Getting up on her knees, she scooted around to the boy's back as he continued eating. Slipping the cloth around his head, she positioned it over his empty eye sockets and tied it on. Then she sat back down in front of him and smiled.

"Now when people look at you," she said, "they'll see this pretty cloth with a nice message written on it."

Suddenly the boy felt choked up. This was the first time he had ever received a gift, the first time he could recall that anyone showed that they cared for him. Reaching up, he ran his fingertips along the thin strip of cloth wrapped around his head and covering his eye sockets. His keen sense of touch felt stitched letters that repeated themselves several times along its length.

"What does the message say, Princess?"

"Blessed by my Creator," she replied. "Now let us keep riding."

They packed up the saddlebag and resumed their morning ride. When they returned to the stable around noon, Albel greeted them with his familiar scowl. Noticing the fine cloth around the boy's face, the stable master started to say something about it, but a withering glance from the Princess made him hold his tongue. Albel comprehended that it was a kindness given to the boy by the Princess, so he dared not take it from him. But after the princess departed, Albel doubled up on the boy's work load just to show he still had power.

But the boy did not care. Life was changing for him. He could feel it. Albel could feel a change coming on also, and he did not know what to make of it. One thing was sure for the stable master about the situation, though: He knew he'd have to tread carefully when it came to the princess.

For several more days the princess came and took the boy away for morning rides, until she showed up one morning with an elderly Kushite woman who walked with a cane. They walked into the stable just after daybreak and the princess shook the boy's shoulder as usual. As he came awake, he heard an unfamiliar voice with a strange accent.

"Oh, so this is him…oh he's is bigger than I thought he would be…"

Princess Hamash looked up at the old Kushite woman who had come with her, noting the long grey locks wound and pinned elegantly atop her head and brown eyes that sparkled with a light much younger than her true age. Her dress was a simple garment of light brown that the princess would never lower herself to wear, but the elder wore it with great dignity. With a small, eight pointed star around her neck her only adornment, she looked very much the wise, humble elder.

"Yes, that is him," the Princess replied as she took the boy's hand. "Say hello to Eshri, my friend. She is my caregiver."

The boy stood up, brushing off straw and dust. Turning his head toward the unfamiliar voice, he could not help but ask a question.

"Greeting Eshri. Why do you sound so different from others I have heard?"

"Because I am a Kushite child. I am originally from a land called Canaan, but I have been here for quite a while. And that's Elder Eshri to you, son," the old lady replied. "Has no one taught you manners and protocol child?"

The boy tilted his head in confusion.

"Manners and protocol?" he replied. "What's that?"

"It means you address me as Elder Eshri because I am older…"

"But Princess Hamas called you…"

"The princess can do that because she is the princess!" Elder Eshri shot back.

A creaking noise interrupted them as the door swung open to the small shed just outside the stables. Albel walked out wearing a long grey sleeping shirt. The discussion woke him and he was rubbing his eyes with his pudgy hands. Walking into the stable Albel spotted the two children and the old woman.

"Here now, what's going on in my stables?" Albel asked, suddenly recognizing the little girl. "Oh, princess Hamash!"

"This doesn't concern you Albel," the princess replied. "Go back to bed… or go sniff a horse's rump!"

"Princess Hamash!" Elder Eshri scolded. "Such language!"

As the princess lowered her head shamefully, Elder Eshri bowed to the stable master.

"Please excuse the princess and her rudeness, stable master," she said respectfully. "But she told me about the deplorable condition of this boy and asked me to help. I am Elder Eshri, the appointed caregiver for the princess."

"This boy has been consigned to his fate by the king himself, "Eshri," replied Albel. "What business do you have with him…"

"It's my business!" snapped princess Hamash. "This boy is my friend and I'm here to see he is treated better. Like a person. Just because he has to work with horses doesn't mean he has to live like one. When was the last time he had a bath?"

The boy cleared his throat and raised a finger.

"I swam in the river about one moon ago…"

"Shut up!" the princess shouted at him. Then she turned back to Albel.

"I'm taking this boy twice a week to go to school with me and you are going to build him a shed like yours to sleep in. And if I ever catch him smelling this bad again you are going to be in trouble. I'll do what I said I would do and it'll be bad for you Albel…"

Albel gulped fearfully as Elder Eshri looked down at the princess, shaking her finger.

"What did you tell him you'd do princess?"

"He knows…" the princess replied. "And he knows it would mean his doom…"

"Princess!" scolded Elder Eshri.

"I am trying to help!" the little girl cried. "He has no one, just like me before you came along Elder Eshri! My mother is dead and father is never around. This boy is like I was, with no one there for him…and he is blind. Can't you understand that, Elder Eshri?"

"Yes, I understand dear."

The boy cleared his throat again and everyone looked his way.

"What is school?"

Princess Hamash looked at the boy with her mouth open. Then she turned back to Albel with sheer hatred in her eyes. Before she could speak Elder Eshri chimed in.

"School is a place where you learn things, dear one," the elder said gently. "It's where we teach you to be a productive person. You will learn to read and write and count, and some spiritual instruction also. Your lessons begin today, so let us depart."

Albel opened his mouth to protest, but the princess silenced him with a harsh stare. Shaking his head, the stable master turned around and walked back into his shed.

Princess Hamash seized the boy's hand and they left the stables, following after Elder Eshri. Walking briskly despite the cane she leaned on for support, the old lady had a considerable spring to her step because things were going just as she planned. After the princess had told her about the strange blind child, Eshri had experienced a dream. It was a prophetic dream, she knew, like the dreams she used to have as a priestess before she had indentured herself to Shamshi's family in order to save her temple from destruction.

She had helped raise Shamshi also, and watched helplessly as her young charge rejected her teachings and became a ruthless tyrant. Her heart was heavy because of it. There had been many times she could have walked away while out on a trusted errand, but something would not let her. She had thought it was because of princess Hamash, whom she was grooming to be the opposite of her father. But the dream had told her there was another purpose for her staying all those years.

They walked through the palace down long halls with walls covered in tapestries depicting Shamshi's family and their long line of conquests. There were great battle scenes and weddings, along with gory images of defeated enemies tortured and killed. Elder Eshri hated walking down this corridor, which Shamshi called the "Hall of Victory.' But the elder did feel a bit of satisfaction when she noted Princess Hamash glancing at the images with shame in her eyes.

As they came through the kitchen area, the boy started sniffing loudly, then he had to be pulled along by both of them.

"Wait!" he cried. "I've never smelled anything so good. Can I have some? Please?"

"You'll get to eat after your first lessons," replied Elder Eshri. "And after I see what the Creator has to say about you…"

Finally they entered a small room with three sets of tables and chairs. One table had a small jug of water, a row of soft clay tablets and the sharpened sticks used to write upon them. Princess Hamash sat the boy down at a table, then reached for a slab of clay and picked up the water jug to wet it.

"Not yet my dear," Elder Eshri said, waving for her to put the items down. "First we must find out something. I must look into your little friend's heart…"

"Huh?" the boy cried fearfully, clutching at his chest. "What are you going to do to me? Albel threatens to cut out my heart all the time…"

"No silly," princess Hamas replied. "She is going to see into your soul, to tell you who you are."

"Is it going to hurt?"

"No child," Elder Eshri said reassuringly. "Just take my hands and be quiet. Listen to your heartbeat, and be quiet."

Elder Eshri closed her eyes and held both the boy's hands as princess Hamash stood by watching. Suddenly a burst of white light rushed into the darkness of Elder Eshri's consciousness and she was confused. Then she realized the light was coming from the boy. The elder gasped in astonishment. Never has she seen anything like this. She had only heard about it, in the legends about high priests of her spiritual order. An idea came into her head and Eshri decided to pursue it. She decided to see if the boy could hear her, mind to mind.

"Child," she thought. "Can you hear me?"

The Elder almost jumped out of her shoes when two dark voids appeared before her in the form of eyes in the light. The eyes blinked, as the voice of the boy spoke out.

"I can hear you Elder Eshri," the boy replied as the eyes blinked again. "Is this you Elder Eshri? Is this seeing? Does everyone look like a glowing light?"

Now the elder was truly taken aback. Not only could the boy hear in the ethereal world, but he could see too. Who was this child? She had to find out, and quickly.

"It is hard to explain, my child. Follow me; I need to take you somewhere."

With that, the two lights called Elder Eshri and the boy began hurtling through what looked like a long tunnel. Finally they came to a realm of pure white light that was a million times brighter than the light coming from their own forms. Elder Eshri's light form was quivering before the sheer crackling power of pure creation. But the boy's light stood steady, comfortable, as if it belonged there. The Elder knew that she could not stand the brilliance for long, so she looked to the light and screamed out her question.

"Oh blessed Creator, please tell me: Who is he!"

The answer was so loud, so filled with sacred power that both their spirits were blown back down the tunnel and into their bodies. Elder Eshri opened her eyes and stared at the boy, who sat with his mouth wide open.

"Elder Eshri!" cried princess Hamash. "Elder please, tell me what happened?"

The Elder was breathing hard, gasping for air. She could hardly speak, due to her sheer astonishment.

"Huff…huff…His name is…"

"Huff, huff huff…"

"His name is,

huff, huff, huff…"

Smiling broadly, the boy took them both by the hand and said:

"I heard what the great voice said too elder," the boy declared. "It said my name is Nimrod!"

The royal bedroom was still and dark. King Shamshi's loud snore reverberated throughout the room. Suddenly a shimmering red light appeared above his bed. At first it was the size of a lit candle wick, then it grew torch sized, before finally blazing up like a generous fireplace flame. The crackle of the unnatural fire was familiar to Shamshi as he woke up, wearily cracking open his eyes.

"Shamshi! Awake and attend me my servant!"

The king sat up with an irritated groan.

"What is the meaning of this?" he whispered. "I have not contacted you…"

"We have come to secure a soul…" the crackling voice hissed.

A frightened look came over Shamshi's face. His hands clutched the bed cover.

"Surely it is not time? There should be a while yet before my payment is due!"

A hot finger of flame blasted towards Shamshi's face, nearly searing his beard. As he held his hands up defensively, the voice growled threateningly.

"We will take what we want when we want it, Shamshi! But no, that payment is not due for some time. There is another we want…"

"Who?" asked Shamshi.

"The boy! The blind Kushite prince of the realm you now rule. He has the gift of infinity, and attachments to things disgustingly…holy."

Shamshi rubbed his long beard.

"If the child has such abilities, why don't we just kill him? His kind is a threat to our goals, is that not true?"

"Noooo!!" the terrible voice rumbled and the flame crackled. "Do not dare to harm him Shamshi! His kind provides us with the sweetest victory of all, when we can turn them to our ways…"

"But how, Flame Lord?" Shamshi asked. "If he is already on the holy path…"

"He is young. The boy can be turned. We have chosen one for the task."

An image appeared in the flame of a little creature with pale, scaly snake-like skin, big floppy ears and large milk white eyes. The creature wore a little black cap and a garment that seemed to be made of patches of human skin. It looked at Shamshi, smiled evilly and started doing a little dance. Spinning to a conclusion, it doffed its hat and took a little bow.

"This is Squeekil," the flaming voice said. "He is the only member of the sacred race of little ones called the Anu that ever came over to our side, which means he has their gifts. His evil charm will pull the boy over to our ways. You have only to summon him."

"Now?" Shamshi replied.

"Now!" the voice commanded sternly. Then the crackling flame disappeared.

Shamshi got out of bed and walked over to a wall. Striking it twice in two strategic places, a panel slid up, revealing a hidden closet. Bending down, he reached inside, pulling out a small chest covered with symbols. Popping it open, he pulled out a black candle, a chunk of coal and several small clay pots with sealed corks. Placing the items on the floor, Shamshi contemplated the night's events. He hated the intrusion, but did appreciate the favor the Flame Lord had done him. By revealing the creature's name and letting him see it, the ritual should be quick and fairly safe. Usually opening up a portal to the infernal realm was a risky fishing expedition, with the price of catching too big a fish being the summoning fool's life, and all too often his soul.

Shamshi reached inside the closet again and pulled out an item rolled up like a carpet. Averting his face due to its particularly bad odor, he brought it to the middle of the floor and unrolled it, revealing a rug made of human skin. The vile thing was nearly circular, with different hues stitched together in a pattern. Lighter shades of skin formed a circle in the middle, with darker skin surrounded it to the edges. Shamshi lit the candle, and then used the coal to draw a series of patterns and shapes on the lighter section in the middle. Where the shapes intercepted, he poured a drop of liquid from several of the pots. Finally he took a knife and sliced the middle of his hand, dripping the blood all over the patterns. Repeating the name of the creature he was summoning several times, Shamshi dripped blood onto the flame of the black candle, causing it to leap up several times its size. Then suddenly the flame dissipated, a gust of wind cleared the smoke, and there stood the creature he had beckoned. Doffing its hat, it gave Shamshi an evil grin.

"Greetings Shamshi the damned," Squeekil declared in a squeaky, rat-like voice. "My fame, I know, precedes me ---so you know who I am! When it comes to spreading sin, with me you'll always win! Just point me to the child and I shall make him wild! Ha he ha he ha he ha he ha he!!!!

Chapter 2: The Prayer Of Yah's Way

For the next several moons littleNimrod became the most avid student Elder Eshri had ever taught. The boy proved relentless and it did not take long for him to begin reading by feeling the letters etched into the clay tablets with his fingers. Nimrod surprised both Elder Eshri and princess Hamash by volunteering to take some tablets etched with language lessons back to his shed to study at night, even after a day of brutal chores imposed on him by stable master Albel.

Nimrod was an outstanding academic student, but to the delight of Elder Eshri and often the jealousy of princess Hamash, it was at spiritual studies that he truly excelled. As a priestess of Yah, the one true Mother Father Creator, Elder Eshri taught the boy "Yah's way," the spread of balance, justice and love of all creation. Each morning the school session began with the consumption of two large cups of fresh cow's milk, followed by a meditation to become one with Yah, starting with the "Elelu-Yah," - the praise of Yah's Way:

"Blessed be the Mother Father Creator for infinity and eternity!

O Mother Father Creator give me will to love creation

O Mother Father Creator give me wisdom for my nation

O Mother Father Creator guide me to forgive my foes today

Elelu-Yah, Elelu-Yah - Yah's Way!

We thank you for creating us as mother: Oun-Yah-may-wah Asherah

We thank you for protecting us as father : Oun-Yah-may- El

We thank you for the spark of you that was born on our birth day

And May the Branches of Strength in Yah's defense stand by my side today

Elelu-Yah, Elelu-Yah - Yah's Way!

Nimrod especially loved the prayer of Yah's way and recited it many times a day, saying it helped his mood as he went about the copious chores heaped upon him by Albel. But little did the boy know that the prayer also had an effect upon an observer who watched him from the shadows. Squeekil the demonoid lurked near Nimrod at all times, and had almost approached him to begin spinning his web of deceit many times. But when Nimrod recited the prayer of Yah's Way, which was almost constantly, the boy's spirit vibrated with waves of holy power that proved quite painful to the denizen of the infernal plane.

The boy constantly carried the power of the prayers and if he started reciting them in earshot of the demonoid, Squeekil fled with his little clawed hands over his big ears. The infernal creature waited patiently, but the boy prayed at school, at work, at supper and before bed. Finally Squeekil hit upon a plan, deciding to use Albel to assist him. The demonoid had observed that the stable master was angry about Nimrod's progress, even refusing to call him by his rightful name, no matter how much the boy and his friends protested. And Squeekil also knew that Albel was especially annoyed by the boy's constant prayers.

One afternoon as Nimrod went about his duties after school, Albel walked by frowning as he heard the boy praying. This was the demonoid's chance. From the shadows of the rafters above the stables where he usually lurked, Squeekil projected power that intensified the anger in Albel's mind, then sat back chuckling to observe his handiwork.

"Cease with that drivel boy," Albel shouted, shoving little Nimrod to the ground atop a pile of stinking, fresh horse leavings. Burning hatred shined in Albel's eyes as he continued screaming.

"All this praying is making you slow boy!" the stable master shouted. "This stable is not a temple!"

"But master, please…"

"Give it a rest boy! If I hear any more praying while you work, I'll lock you up…and cut your food servings too. I am tired of hearing about this Yah! I'm sick of it!"

"But master if you knew about Yah's way…"

"You'll pay attention to my way!" Albel shouted. "The stable master's way, do you hear me?"

"Yes master," Nimrod replied with resignation. "I'll stop praying while I work…"

Albel glared down at Nimrod, raising his foot to stomp him, then put the foot down and began walking away.

"Don't let me have to tell you again, boy…"

Nimrod got up from the stinking muck and started cleaning it up with a wooden shovel. Angry at Albel's cruelty and ashamed of his own humiliation, he was about to recite the prayer under his breath. But suddenly he had a strange feeling- a feeling that someone was near, accompanied by a strange acrid scent.

"Greeting my boy," an eerie squeaky voice said. "Always cleaning up horse leavings – that can't give you joy!"

Nimrod stopped in his tracks. He had not heard anyone walk up to him. And his hearing was very good.

"Who's there?"

Squeekil crouched upon his perch, high in the rafters of the stable, like an owl looking down at its prey.

"Just another child of creation," the voice replied. "Who happened by in time to see an unjust situation."

Nimrod turned slowly, trying to focus on the location of the voice. It seemed to jump from place to place.

"Look, if you came about business you need to speak to master Albel…"

"My business is with you, hardworking boy so true!"

"Your voice sounds strange, and you smell strange…who are you?"

"If I told you my name, you may know of my fame…"

Nimrod sighed.

"Alright, so you are a thief," the boy concluded. "And don't want to tell me who you are. Why not just take what you came for and leave? Or do you enjoy taunting a blind person?"

"Taunting I do live for, but that's not why I'm here. If you let me be your friend Nimrod, you'll soon have cause to cheer!"

Suddenly Nimrod felt a little fearful.

"How…how do you know my name?

"It does not matter how I know, what matters is I do. If you let me be your friend, Nimrod, the world will bow to you."

"You don't sound right," Nimrod replied. "And I don't trust you.

"You'd trust me if you knew me, I am a friend with mighty power. I shall demonstrate my abilities on Albel just this hour."

Nimrod's fear increased at the mention of his master's name. If Albel found that he consorted with a thief he would be in serious trouble. He was about to shout out to summon the stable master when an intense feeling made him pause. It was Squeekil using his demonic powers. Peeking into the boy's mind, the creature sifted through years of torturous memories. Seizing upon some of the most painful instances in Nimrod's life in the stables, Squeekil pushed them to the surface of the tortured boy's mind.

"I can hurt the one who hurts you, of this you can be sure," the demonoid said with conviction. "Your life is humiliation, but revenge can be your cure..."

The years of abuse from Albel were swirling around in Nimrod mind. He clenched his fists at the thought of all of the beatings. The possibility of revenge was suddenly a very sweet idea.

"What can you do to the stable master?" the boy whispered.

"Keep hidden and stay close my potential new young friend," Squeekil replied. "The stable master's woes will start and fun for us begins."

Tituma, the warlord, strolled toward the royal stable to get his new horse. He walked proudly, his deep set, black eyes twinkling with pride. Physically large all his life, he was now a truly big man after being awarded the title of Shabra by King Shamshi for his role in recent military conquests. The fine steed that awaited him at the stable was a gift that came with his new station, along with land and a dozen new slaves. And for Tituma, the deal was that much sweeter because the stable master was Albel; once his rival for both the favor of the King and the attention of a woman the warlord once fancied. Albel had won out on both counts, but had since lost his position as court executioner and the favor of the woman. Now it was Tituma's time to gloat, and he prepared to do just that as he walked up to Albel's shed and began beating on the door.

"Stable master Albel," he shouted. "Awake from your dreams of making love to horses! I have come for my new steed!"

"Here is your horse, Tituma," the stable master shouted back from the far side of the stable. Then Albel ambled forward, leading a tall, beautiful black stallion. "I'm out here, no need to beat down my door."

Squeekil, lurking in the rafters, was observing the exchange carefully. Searching Tituma's mind, the demonoid found what he was looking for and quickly cast his spell. Suddenly the new Shabra found himself extremely annoyed by the mere sound of Albel's voice.

"That's Shabra Tituma to you, horse washer!" Tituma bellowed as he turned towards Albel. His gaze settled upon the stable master and the horse. Then his face twisted into an angry, confused expression. Where a healthy new horse should be standing, the warlord saw Albel giving him a broken down nag. In fact, it looked just like an old horse he once owned that had caused him a considerable amount of embarrassment.

"What is this?" the warlord shouted.

"Why, this is your steed, Tituma," Albel replied. "The horse awarded you by the king…"

"That's Shabra Tituma fool!" the warlord repeated. "And that is not the steed promised me. What are you about Albel?"

Albel looked at the horse standing beside him. It was one of the most beautiful creatures he had ever groomed. Yet Tituma looked at it as if it were a pig. The stable master shrugged and shook his head.

"If this horse is not to your liking, then you must take it up with the king. I'd be glad to keep such a fine animal myself."

Squeekil leaned forward grinning as Tituma's fists clenched in anger. Nimrod, hiding behind the door to the stable, smiled as he listened. The boy was almost breathless with excitement at the thought of the stable master being hurt and humiliated.

"You've always been jealous of me Albel," Tituma growled, pointing accusingly. "You've switched steeds on me, hoping to steal away from my glory! Now get my rightful horse out here, now!"

Alerted by the shouting, the blacksmith just across the way stopped beating metal and emerged from his building. Several other people stopped to look at the commotion also, until a withering glance by the new Shabra sent them all back to minding their own business. The onlookers hustled away and the blacksmith went back to his forging.

Albel's eyes darted back and forth nervously.

"Now…now Shabra Tituma," he said slowly. "This horse is a fine one, so please take it and go."

Tituma started walking toward Albel, a dangerous look in his eyes.

"Get me my real horse now, or I'll thrash you!"

Squeekil was giggling and Nimrod was smiling broadly as they both heard Tituma getting closer and closer to his master.

"But, this is your…"Albel began.

"I warned you!" Tituma shouted as he pounced upon the stable master.

Before he knew it, fists were pummeling Albel's face back and forth. The stable master had some warrior training and tried to put up a defense, but the much larger man was too big and battle hardened. Albel fell to the ground, barely conscious. Then he felt himself lifted off the ground, and then hurtling through the air. His flight ended when he smashed into the wall of the stable.

"You've hated me for a long time Albel," Tituma shouted as he stood over the groaning stable master. "And I have hated you. But to do this to me on my day of glory is just too much!"

"Please Shabra Tituma," Albel pleaded. "Let me be…"

"I'll stomp you down to the very depths of the earth if you don't produce my horse," Tituma shouted, looking back at the sound of the animal stamping its feet. Suddenly the spell wore off and he could see the real horse. "That steed is not…that steed is…"

Nimrod had come out from hiding and was standing near the door of the stable. Tituma looked back and forth at the boy and the horse. Then he strolled over and perused the animal closer.

"Well, it seems your slave has saved you by bringing out the real steed," Tituma said as he led the animal away. "Don't cross me again Albel. Next time I won't be as merciful."

As Shabra Tituma left, Albel groaned loudly. His face was swollen and blood poured from his mouth.

"Boy," he cried. "Come here…get me to my shed."

"Right away," Nimrod replied. "First let me get you some water…"

"Good, that's good boy," Albel replied weakly. "Yes, get me some water first."

As Nimrod ran to the back of the stable to fetch fresh water, he heard a giggle, then stopped and started laughing himself. Before he knew it he was joining with Squeekil in hardy, muffled laughter.

"Now you see what I can do," Squeekil said finally. "Will you let me be a friend to you?"

Nimrod thought for a minute, a wicked smile playing across his face.

"Will Albel get more of the same treatment?" he asked.

Squeekil smiled with satisfaction.

"Surely this demonstration has made my powers clear," replied the demonoid. "We shall gloat with satisfaction as they kick your master's rear!"

"Then I think we can be friends," Nimrod replied, grinning.

Squeekil rubbed his clammy little hands together, dancing around on the wooden beam he perched upon. But his deceit was not yet complete. Next came the real test.

"Before we go any further, my happy new young friend, there is another subject to which we must attend…"

"What subject?" the boy asked.

"For our plans to get you anywhere, you must cease with all the prayer…"

"What?" the boy replied. "What are you talking about? Praying make me feel good, gives me hope."

"What your praying friends have told you is just stupid and untrue," Squeekil replied slyly. "What feels the best: the praying, or the revenge I just gave you?"

Nimrod stopped to think, his mind filled with confusion and conflicting emotions. Some of those feelings were being subtly manipulated by Squeekil.

"It is apparent boy, who told you lies and who is speaking true," the demonoid insisted. "What feels the best: the praying or revenge I gave to you?"

Just then Albel's painful groaning could be heard and Nimrod smiled again. The boy could not deny that the groans were music to his ears. But his feelings of oneness with Yah conflicted with his lust for revenge. Squeekil read it all in the boy's mind and continued his enticement.

"Praying is for weaklings and for those who cannot do," the evil creature persisted. "Not for those like you or me whose wishes can come true."

"I don't know…" the boy began, but the demonoid cut him off.

"Stick with me and you'll be free and get power, children and wife," the creature hissed. "Stick with Yah and you'll be here, a slave for all your life!"

Nimrod bit down hard on his lip. He knew deep inside that there was something wrong about this strange person with the squeaking voice, but what he said sounded so good. It also seemed to make sense. Elder Eshri and the teachings of Yah had never promised anything specific. They had just promised a better future… somehow and at some time in the time.

But here Nimrod was being offered precisely things that he never thought he could have, starting with revenge against his cruel master. Finally Nimrod lowered his head and relented.

"All right," Nimrod said. "We shall do things your way. But if it does not work out, I'm going back to Yah…"

"It always works with me my boy, and you can call me Squeekil," the demonoid replied with triumphant glee. "I shall give you what you want my friend and soon you'll have no equal."

Albel called out again and Nimrod went to fetch water and help him to his shed. The stable master was not seriously hurt, but requested that Nimrod tend to him for the rest of the day. Every time Nimrod turned away he smiled at the pain and humiliation his master was experiencing. He knew this was not Yah's way, but rationalized it as justice that the Creator seemed slow in delivering. Squeekil sensed the continuing conflict in the boy and decided that more enticement was needed to continue to sway him. And the demonoid knew that food was the way to do it.

Later that night Nimrod began stirring in his recently built shed due to his grumbling belly. As he began gathering himself to creep over to the nearby cow shed to drink some milk, Squeekil transformed himself into a mist and seeped through the wall. Materializing into a solid form, he stood over the boy. Then the demonoid tapped his foot to get the blind boy's attention.

"Eh," Nimrod . "Who is there?"

"The time to get up is now my friend, despite your sleepy mood," Squeekil declared. "You got a little justice, now it's time to get some food."

"Oh," replied Nimrod. "It's you. I was about to get some milk…"

"One meal a day is unjust friend, it's time for them to pay," the demonoid said smoothly. "We'll sneak into the kitchen and get you more without delay."

With that, Squeekil waved at the door and it opened, then he took Nimrod by the hand and they walked away from the stable area. It was late and no one else was about as they walked stealthily towards the rear door that led to the palace kitchen. The guard that was posted there to curtail just this type of activity sat against the wall snoring and Squeekil cast a spell to deepen his slumber. As they crept past, the demonoid pried a large wooden cudgel from the guard's fingers and handed it to Nimrod. The boy ran his fingers over it.

"What's this…" the boy whispered. "A weapon?"

"We'll get you plenty of food my friend, but you'll need to watch my back," Squeekil replied. "If someone spots my pilfering, you must give them a good whack!"

With a wave of the demonoid's little hand the lock to the kitchen door came undone and they crept inside. Squeekil had scouted the place thoroughly earlier and positioned Nimrod at the corner of the hallway that led to the cook's quarters. Then the demonoid grabbed a sack and started towards the pantry. Glancing back over his little shoulder, he left Nimrod an insidious instruction.

"If the cook wakes up and comes this way, you must hit his head without delay."

Nimrod nodded. As he grasped the weapon in his hand and ground his teeth, he tried to reason it all out: It was time he received payment for all the years of misery and humiliation, he decided. The food they were stealing was nothing compared to what had been taken from him. He did not even know where he came from, had no memory before the darkness and working in the stable, and felt that it was all so unfair. He did not really want to hurt anyone, but this, he decided, was a day for retribution.

Squeekil sensed the goings on in Nimrod's mind and it made him smile as he stuffed the bag with food. He could sense a small seed of darkness inside the boy's spirit, a darkness he intended to help nurture and grow. Deciding that it was time to begin doing just that, the demonoid sent a nudge from his mind to the mind of the cook slumbering in a room just down the hall. Immediately the skinny little olive skinned man opened his eyes, pushed his bed coverings away and sat up. Consumed by a strong feeling that someone was in his kitchen, he rose and tied on a robe. Mumbling and cursing, he then swung open the creaking door to the hallway and stalked out.

Nimrod heard the cook stir, heard the man curse as he opened his door and started heading down the hall. Squeekil, continuing to stuff the bag, grinned as Nimrod raised the wooden cudgel high. Just as the cook walked into the kitchen and peered into the darkness Squeekil purposefully dropped a plate that loudly shattered against the floor.

"You thieves never learn!" the cook growled, snatching a big cleaving knife from a nearby shelf.

Before he took another step, the cudgel in Nimrod's hand came down, and with a little help from the power of Squeekil, struck the cook a solid blow on the side of his head. The man spun and dropped the knife, then crumbled to the floor. Nodding at Nimrod with evil satisfaction, the demonoid hoisted the bag over his little shoulder and took the boy by the hand. As they stepped over the unconscious body of the cook and stealthily made their exit, Squeekil praised his new friend.

"Well done Nimrod, your aim was true and you've earned your feast tonight. With lots more food and skull bashing, we'll soon increase your might!"

"But, what if he is hurt badly? Nimrod replied nervously.

"He surely would have chopped you, so care nothing for his plight," Squeekil replied. "Rejoice for all the food we have and no more hungry nights."

Later in his shed alone, Nimrod gorged himself like never before, falling asleep atop a pile of food. His belly extended, the boy snored the night away dreaming of the promises made to him by his newfound ally.

Meanwhile his new demonoid friend was on his way to make his report.

Behind the closed door of his private chamber, King Shamshi once again stood before the roaring manifestation of the demonic Flame Lord. A mist flowed beneath his door, swirled before them and transformed into Squeekil. The demonoid stepped forward.

"Greetings my masters Flame Lord and king," Squeekil said with a bow. "Winning for us this golden child is not such a hard thing."

"How much progress have you really made little one?" the Flame Lord hissed.

The demonoid giggled.

"I have made a natural priest give up on words of holy prayer. He turns away from Yah, convinced with me he'll get somewhere!"

Shamshi eyebrows raised and he nodded.

"This sounds most promising...," the king commented. "Just how much spiritual force does this boy carry?"

"Enough power for us to sense it in the infernal dimension," hissed the Flame Lord. "We must take this boy, and deny the holy wretches of Yah's Way a powerful ally."

"Yes the boy is very gifted, I have seen that this is true," Squeekil added, turning towards Shamshi. "But we can use his pain to twist him and we owe that, king, to you!"

The king smiled broadly. He knew there was a reason he spared the boy's life years ago. Now his revenge against the child's dead father would be even sweeter by corrupting the son and unleashing him to do the Flame Lord's bidding. Then Shamshi gasped as a thought came to him.

"Wait," the king exclaimed, looking at the Flame Lord. "Years ago, when the child was to be killed...was that you protecting him?"

"Ha ha ha ha ha ha ha ha!" both the Flame Lord and Squeekil laughed hardily. Then the roaring fire of the demon master leapt and flared.

"We see when you don't think we observe!" the Flame Lord declared. "We hear when you don't think we listen! And our will is done when you think there is only fate!"

King Shamshi bowed his head and dropped to his knees.

"Praised be the Flame Lord," he said. "And all who stand with him. What is next for our little blind friend?"

"I shall prod the boy to go our way with naughtier endeavors," Squeekil replied. "Then I'll test him in a final way and make him ours forever! Ha he ha he ha he ha he!"

The next day when Nimrod sat down at the table for school, Elder Eshri sensed something was wrong with the boy. He had forgotten to bring his homework for the first time. He refused to drink his milk and when the time came to start the day with prayer, the boy remained closed mouthed and seemed agitated.

"Is there some reason you are not joining us in prayer, Nimrod?" the elder asked as Princess Hamash looked on curiously. The boy's face was lowered and he hesitated to speak. The princess leaned over from across the lesson table, eyeing him closely. Then she noticed he was trembling.

"Nimrod," princess Hamash asked. "What is the matter?"

"I..I can do the prayer no more," he replied. "And I won't drink anymore milk."

"Why not dear," Elder Eshri asked. "Is it Albel? Is he bothering you?"

"Because if he is, I'll fix him good," hissed princess Hamash.

Nimrod gulped.

"No...it is not Albel," he replied. "The praying...I was told not to..."

Elder Eshri stood up and approached Nimrod slowly.

"Who told you not to pray?" she asked.

"My new friend, his name is Squeekil..."

Elder Eshri's eyes widened with concern. Her priesthood had taught her about a being by that name, but surely this could not be the same creature...

"Nimrod, this is very important..." the elder asked carefully. "Where did you meet this Squeekil?"

"He came to me several nights ago...in the stables."

"Did anyone else see him?"

"No...I don't think so. He goes away when other people come around..."

With a grave expression, Nimrod's teacher turned towards a shelf filled with small vials. Rummaging through, she finally picked one and uncorked it. Then she stepped towards Nimrod and held it under his nose.

"Did you smell something like this when he was around child?" she asked.

"Well...yes." Nimrod replied. "But you taught us it was impolite to mention when someone smells bad..."

"It's sulfur child, from a world of damnation! Oh, Yah, please save us!" Elder Eshri gasped. "Nimrod, take my hand."

"Are you going to make me pray? I told you I can't..."

"Just take my hand boy!"

Nimrod took the Elder's hand and heard her praying under her breath. Princess Hamash bowed her head and prayed silently also. A moment passed before Elder Eshri opened her eyes. She then looked down at Nimrod with a horrified expression.

"Elder Eshri," the princess asked. "What's wrong?

"Nimrod has been approached by a demon," the elder stated. The princess took a step back from the table.

"Oh, no!" the little girl cried.

"What? What is a demon?" asked Nimrod. "Why is everyone acting so upset?"

"Nimrod," Elder Eshri stated firmly, "you must not listen to this creature. Reject him!"

"No!" Nimrod cried. "He is my friend. He took revenge on Albel for me and got me some food..."

"I'm your friend, Nimrod!" cried the princess. "I made Albel treat you better..."

"But Squeekil does better things for me," Nimrod shot back. "He understands me more..."

"He is playing on your pain, my child," Elder Eshri replied. "I implore you! Reject him and save your immortal soul!"

"No, I won't," Nimrod cried, backing away from the table toward the door. "Squeekil told me you would say things like this, to get me to come back to your weak ways. He said so."

"Nimrod, for the love of Yah!" Princess Hamash pleaded. "I saw my father speaking to one of those things before...one of those...demons. It was ugly and mean and it spoke of hurting people. You don't have eyes so you can't see how evil they are. Nimrod, please don't do this!"

Elder Eshri walked over to a shelf and grabbed something. Then she walked towards Nimrod. The boy was nearly to the door, about to leave.

"I'm going now and I won't come back," Nimrod cried. "All you do is beg Yah for things and nothing ever happens! I prayed to Yah to get back at Albel for me and nothing happened! I prayed for better food and nothing happened. Squeekil says he'll set me free, while you and that praying are all weak. Your God Yah is weak!"

Elder Eshri sighed as she realized the boy would have to make up his own mind. She beckoned to the princess and they joined hands and came close to Nimrod.

"I understand that you have to see for yourself my child," the elder said. "But do not doubt that Yah loves you, that we love you. You do you know that we love you, don't you Nimrod?"

The boy hesitated at the sincerity of Elder Eshri's voice.

"I...yes elder," he replied. "I know you love me..."

"Then take this," Elder Eshri replied, tying a medallion on a leather string around his neck. "This is a token of our love for you. Even though you have decided to leave us, I would like you to keep it."

Nimrod felt the gift with his fingers. Tracing its shape, he found it was an eight pointed star. Elder Eshri tucked it under his shirt.

"It is made of silver," she stated, "which is very valuable. So keep it hidden from view."

Princess Hamash had tears streaming from her eyes. She stepped forward and hugged Nimrod, then stepped back with her hands on both his shoulders.

"We are still going to go riding, right?"

As he turned and walked out the door, Nimrod shook his head.

"I...I don't know." he replied. "I'll have to ask Squeekil."

As he was leaving he heard Elder Eshri call out to him:

"Yah loves you little one, no matter what happens or wherever you go. As long as you breathe and you live in the love of the creator, nothing is beyond or above you."

Later that night, after his chores were done and all was still near the stables, Nimrod sat eating on a pile of straw in the stall where he used to sleep. He could sense the minds of the rats nearby, so he broke off a piece of bread and tossed it to a corner. Several rats scrambled for it as he contemplated what Elder Eshri and Princess Hamash had said about his new friend. Squeekil lurked in the shadows, sensing seeds of doubt growing inside the boy. Determined to stamp out those seeds, the creature leapt down from the rafters, landing atop one of the wooden posts of the stall. Hearing his little feet, Nimrod turned his head in that direction.

"Squeekil, is that you?"

"Indeed it is I, your savior, my little tortured friend," the demonoid replied. "And tonight's the night that all your doubts forevermore will end!"

"What do you mean?" replied Nimrod.

"Now is the time for you learn the taste of true real power. Your greatest gift, my fine young friend, begins within the hour!"

Squeekil scrambled down from the post and leaned down, holding onto one of the stall's boards with one scaly hand and touching Nimrod's forehead with his other clammy claw. Immediately the minds of the rats came into clearer focus to Nimrod. Deeper still, he began to understand the motivations of the rodents, their hungers and fears. Then suddenly the multitude of feelings started to form a kind of language.

"Call to them and they shall come," he heard Squeekil say above the noise of the rats in his head. "Ask them what you will of them and see your will be done!"

Suddenly a series of squeaking noises emerged from Nimrod's mouth, and the stall began to fill up with rats. Dozens of them surrounded him like soldiers in formation, ready for orders. The boy knew that they would do his bidding and smiled. Then he imagined his master Albel being bitten and torn apart and the rats turned around and began marching towards his shed. Squeekil watched them go for a moment before waving his claw-like hand, causing the rodents to abruptly stop.

"Your thirst for vengeance is, my boy, a very worthy quest," Squeekil cried. "But first you have to prove yourself and pass the final test."

"What test?" Nimrod asked. "What do I have to do?"

"Before you destroy your enemies, you must sacrifice a friend. By this you'll prove your worthiness to let your strength begin."

"But," Nimrod began, "I only have two friends..."

Squeekil raised a finger and the smell and voice of Elder Eshri flashed into boy's mind.

"Noooo!" cried Nimrod in horror.

"Yes, she must go and go she must quick!" Squeekil cackled gleefully. "She is old, so it makes sense to me that she be your deadly pick!"

"This...this is not right! Elder Eshri is a good person!"

"Good or bad or innocent the woman has to go!" Squeekil replied. "Now tell your rats to tear her up! End your times of woe!"

Before he could stop himself, Nimrod imagined Elder Eshri being killed by the rats and they began marching away towards her quarters. Suddenly realizing what he had done, he opened his mouth and a loud piercing squeal came forth. The rats stopped abruptly, ran around in circles, and then began to disperse back into the shadows.

"I won't hurt Elder Eshri!" Nimrod cried. "I won't!"

Squeekil was livid with rage. He stamped his little feet on the top of the pole and then sprang forth like a cat, landing atop Nimrod. The boy fell back onto the straw as the demonoid raised his little claw-like hand into a fist.

"I have increased your gifts of power, so you will do as I say! Submit right now to what must be, or pain you'll feel today!"

"No, I won't!" Nimrod cried.

The demoniod's little fist came down, hitting Nimrod in the mouth. Blood poured profusely because the creature was stronger than it looked and the boy swooned. Struggling hard, he pushed the creature off and tried to crawl away, but Squeekil grabbed his ankle and pulled him back into the stall.

"Get off me!" Nimrod shouted. "Help!"

Albel, asleep in his shed, was awakened by the scream. At first the stable master thought he was having a dream, until he heard an eerie, squeaky voice reply:

"No matter how you cry my boy, there is no help for you," Squeekil snarled. "Give the sacrifice required! Only innocent blood will do!"

The demonoid clawed into the boy's leg and the howl of pain that followed made Albel leap from beneath the covers and snatch up a nearby sword. Slowly he cracked open the shed's door and peered out.

The agony in Nimrod's leg was overwhelming and so was his growing fear. During the struggle he had felt Squeekil's face, thus perceiving the creature's twisted and ugly features. He now realized that he had made a mistake; that he was dealing with a being of pure evil. Now, when it seemed to be too late, Nimrod finally had some conception of what a demon truly was.

Albel, who was now standing at the entrance to the stables looking on, knew immediately that Nimrod was struggling against a denizen of Hell. He had seen King Shamshi conjure such beings himself. The stable master stood transfixed and watched as Nimrod finally clasped his hands together in prayer.

"Oh Yah, please help me!" Nimrod cried. "I'm sorry o creator…please, please help me now!"

Squeekil winced at the prayer, then laughed as he wound up and struck the boy in the face again. This time there was a crunching sound that Albel could hear all the way to the where he was standing. Nimrod, reeling from the pain of his brutally broken jaw, suddenly felt a growing heat against his chest."Are you ready boy, to submit to me now?" Squeekil hissed. "Send the rats forthwith to chew up that old cow!"

Albel was terrified, transfixed to the spot as he watched Nimrod fall upon his back, helpless before the terrible little demon. The stable master did not know what to do, but interfering was the last thing on his mind. As the creature stepped onto the boy's chest, its claws raised and extended to strike, he thought it was the end for Nimrod. But the boy reached up, ripped open his shirt and a white light burst forth from his chest. Blasting outward with tremendous force, the light caught the demonoid like a feather in the wind, lifting the creature up and smashing it into the ceiling. Craning his neck, Albel saw that the creature was caught like a fly in a web, pinned by crisscrosses of light in the form of a radiant eight sided star.

As the light continued pouring from his chest, Nimrod continued praying with greater intensity, though his jaw hurt like no pain he had ever felt before. The creature thrashed and screamed, but could go nowhere. Then Nimrod shouted:

"In the name of Yah, I command you! Go back where you came from!"

"Aaaaa!" the creature shrieked in pain." Only a priest of the highest order can send one such as I back to my realm's own border!"

Undeterred, the boy raised both hands and pushed them palm up into the light. Then suddenly the demon screamed louder, its body seeming to flatten against the roof as if a great force pushed against it. Albel could not believe his eyes! The boy was crushing the demon with some sort of divine light!

"How are you doing this? You are only a boy!" the writhing demon screamed. "Please let me stay and I'll grant you your joy!"

"No!" Nimrod shouted. "Go away! You are not going to hurt my friends!"

"Have mercy on me and be a good boy! Please let me stay and I'll grant you your joy!" the creature cried again in utter agony. "Please let me stay… I'll grant you… your joy…!"

Nimrod pushed harder, though he felt the palms of his hands burning, as a small, dark circular void appeared behind the demon. The strong acrid scent of sulfur streamed out of the hole, indicating that this was creature's place of origin. The void grew until it was large enough to envelop the creature, then a strong suction began pulling it in. Squeekil clung on desperately as he was pulled all the way in, until only a grasping claw could be seen. Then the light flashed brighter and the portal snapped shut, leaving just the creature's claw behind. The scaly appendage wriggled slightly as it transformed into smoke, and then a light breeze flowing through the stable blew the wisp away.

Albel simply stood where he was. Mouth gaping, the stable master's mind reeled at what he was witnessing. The light emitting from Nimrod's chest finally dissipated, and curls of smoke rose from the boy's hands as he

clasped them in prayer once again.

"Praise Yah," Nimrod managed to mumble in a slurred, pain-filled voice, as he fell back onto the straw unconscious. Albel dropped his sword and fell also, fainting dead away from pure astonishment.

"I have spoke with the tongue of angels
I have held the hand of a devil
It was warm in the night
I was cold as a stone"
U2 – I Still Haven't Found What I'm Looking
For

Chapter 3: The Crippled Kushite Servant Girl

What Nimrod noticed when he woke up were all the bandages. He was swaddled in them, with one wound around his head and under his chin so tightly he could barely move his jaw. After trying he discovered it was best not to, due to the intense pain of his broken face. The bandage on his leg covering the claw mark left by Squeekil was very tight also, but most distressing was the cloth wrapped around his hands. This unsettled him more than anything, because he used them so much to get around as a sightless person. Rubbing his palms together, he winced at the pain of the eight pointed stars he sensed permanently burned into each of them. The only thing pleasant was the softness of the bed he was resting on. He had never felt such comfort. Then he heard footsteps come into the room, followed by a happy, familiar voice.

"Elder Eshri! Elder Eshri" princess Hamash cried. "He's awake!"

Nimrod heard someone else enter as the princess leaned over him and kissed his forehead.

"I was worried about you at first, Nimrod," the princess said. "But Elder Eshri said you would be alright. She says you have been blessed."

Elder Eshri approached his bed and laid a hand upon the boy's head. Feeling his temples, she gently ran her hand over his closed, sightless eyes, ending her inspection with a pat on his cheek.

"Indeed you have Nimrod," the elder priestess said. "And the blessing is mighty indeed."

Nimrod tried to speak, but the bandages were too tight for him to move his jaw. In frustration, he clicked his tongue against the roof of his mouth and something strange happened. He felt a small vibration in the center of his forehead, a burst of awareness occurred, and suddenly he could sense everything around him. The shapes and positions of all the objects in the room became clear to him. It was like he was touching everything in the room at the same time. It startled him so much he drew in a sharp breath.

"Nimrod," princess Hamash said, leaning in over him. "What's wrong?"

Nimrod could not speak, so he could not answer her. He turned toward the princess though, focusing on her voice. Clicking his tongue again, he could sense the outline of her entire body, as if he were touching her with his hands all over at the same time. He could feel the shape of her face and the texture and movement of her long hair. He could even feel her breathing. Concentrating harder, Nimrod clicked again and was absolutely startled: He could even feel the organs inside her body throbbing with life.

Elder Eshri clasped her hands together, smiling broadly.

"It is his blessing," she joyfully stated. "His show of faith in defeating the demon has earned him freedom from his earthly impairment. He can now see as a bat sees, and a bat can snatch a gnat from the air!"

"What do you mean, elder?" asked the princess.

"You will see," she replied. "Observe as he becomes acquainted with Yah's gift. Nimrod, do you want some water?"

The boy nodded and clicked his tongue again. He could sense the water jug on a table near his bed, along with a little cup sitting next to it. Before he realized what he was doing, he leaned over, reached for the cup and snatched it up. Princess Hamash gasped as Nimrod turned directly to her and held it out, gesturing for her to fill it up.

"Go on, princess," Elder Eshri said. "Give him some water."

The princess picked up the jug and poured. As she did so, Nimrod clicked his tongue again. Sensing the flowing, cascading shape of the water pouring into his cup, he leaned slightly to keep any from spilling. Then, with a bit of struggle, he pried open his lips, pouring the water down his parched throat. Effortlessly, he put the cup right back where he picked it up.

Princess Hamash put the jug down and stood staring at the boy, while Elder Eshri beamed with joy.

"Come princess," she said. "Let us leave him to himself now."

Nimrod clicked his tongue again as they walked from the room. He could tell exactly where they were in relation to the walls and each other, could feel their bodies moving, until they turned a corner down the hall. Nimrod pondered for a while, concluded that he did not know what to make of this oddness, and he simply went back to sleep.

Princess Hamash hugged Elder Eshri as they emerged from the hallway, then she turned left towards the royal quarters while the elder continued on about her daily duties. She had heard of some strange things in her short life, but could not believe what she had just witnessed. It was as if Nimrod somehow got his sight. But she had washed and retied his blindfold herself and knew he still had no eyes!

Continuing on, she walked past the hall leading to her father's study room and heard the king call out to her. This startled the princess, because her father rarely spoke to her lately. After hesitating briefly, she turned down the hall and found herself looking up at the king's bodyguard at the entrance to the room. With a courteous bow, he opened the door and she walked in.

The princess stepped inside to find it just as she remembered from the few times she had been allowed inside. The walls were lined with shelves upon which sat hundreds of slabs of inscribed clay documents. Works of art acquired after many conquests were everywhere along with rare musical instruments from lands near and far. A fireplace blazed against the far wall and her father sat near it at a table where a lit candle flickered. A stack of documents and books were stacked high before King Shamshi and he peeked up from behind them when his daughter drew near.

"Ahh, my dove," he said with flowery affection. "How is your little friend coming along?"

"What do you care father?" the princess replied. "He is just a slave who works in the stables to you..."

The king clutched at his heart in mock pain.

"My lovely, you cut me deep! I do care, because you do. He is your friend and I care for my only daughter's feelings..."

The princess looked at him skeptically. She knew her father well enough to know when he was being deceitful. He had done it so very often throughout her life. The princess sighed though and decided to play along.

"He'll be fine, according to Elder Eshri," the Princess replied. "And something has happened to him father. It is as if he sees, but without his eyes."

The king's eyebrows perked up.

"Really?" Shamshi replied. "Well, I must say, that is most interesting. Perhaps I should meet this child..."

The princess rolled her eyes.

"Can I go now father?"

"Yes dear one, you can leave. But tell you little friend that the king may be paying him a visit soon."

"Yes father," the princess said as she strolled from the room.

The king sat watching as his daughter left. He had used her as a spy to keep track of Nimrod for quite a while now, and this latest development was just one in a string of distressing events. After hearing about the child's defeat of Squeekil and his injuries as a result, Shamshi had come up with a plan to poison Nimrod during his recovery. But before he did it, he decided to get a report from his daughter, and then consult with his master, the Flame Lord. The former now taken care of, Shamshi now rose to see to the latter.

King Shamshi left the study and strolled down the hall to his private quarters. Once inside his bedroom, he tapped the hidden panel and took out the ritual implements. Moments later he had summoned the Flame Lord, who appeared once again as a crackling fire floating in front of him.

"We know of the defeat of Squeekil, Shamshi." growled the voice from the flame.

"Then we should destroy this boy now!" Shamshi declared.

"Nooo!" hissed the Flame Lord as tendrils of blue fire flared.

"Then what are we to do?" Shamshi asked, covering up his eyes from the intensity of the flame. "The boy will not be turned. And my daughter reports that he has received an extraordinary blessing..."

"Which only makes him more valuable to us," the Flame Lord replied. "We shall use him to achieve again something that was one of our greatest feats. We seek to once again twist that which is most sacred into that which is most profane!"

An image emerged in the midst of the Flame Lord's fire; a lifelike image of perhaps the most beautiful creature in the world. It was a golden plumed phoenix bird, standing in majestic splendor, surrounded by a halo of white light. Then the image became dark and twisted as the white halo of goodness turned a dark, sickly hue. The colorfully plumed feathers transformed into dark, leathery bat-like wings, its beak sprouting fangs dripping with blood. This, Shamshi recognized, was the fabled Zu, the demon bird which, according to the legends, was slain by a hero of old. But Shamshi never knew what he was now being shown, that it had once been a sacred phoenix bird, perhaps the most blessed animal in all creation. Somehow the demon lords had succeeded in transforming something nearly divine into the epitome of evil!

"Only one pure of heart can acquire an egg from the nest of a phoenix," the Flame Lord explained. "And only an egg will be useful for us. Bring the boy close to you Shamshi. Train him. Send him to get us an egg so that we can create our beloved Zu bird once again. Then we shall destroy the troublesome child!"

Shamshi smiled at the deviousness of the plan. He bowed down to his unholy master in respect to his malicious genius. As the fire of the evil one dissipated, the king spoke to the lingering smoke.

"Yes, Flame Lord. It shall be done."

Albel sat atop a barrel looking at Nimrod as he went about his chores around the stable. It had been nearly six moons since he had come back after healing, and the stable master marveled at the boy's feats. He ran to and fro, fulfilling every duty heaped upon him with fervor. And the most amazing thing was that he no longer had to feel around blindly. Now Nimrod ran errands all over the place as if he had full vision, always praying to that Yah god of his with impunity. Albel had tried to silence his annoying holy prattling, but attempts had proven fruitless because the child could now flee from a beating! And even when cornered, the boy would dodge his blows until the stable master collapsed from exhaustion.

These amazing developments, along with Nimrod's defeat of a demon from the infernal pits, had Albel grudgingly admitting that there must be something to this Yah worship. Without seeming too interested, Albel decided, he must find out more about this Yah god. The stable master's contemplations continued as the day went on, until just after noon when he heard words being shouted that he never expected to be uttered back near his lonely stables:

"The king approaches, make way, the king approaches!"

Albel sprang to his feet and ran to the stable entrance. It was his secret longing that the king would one day have mercy upon him and free him from his punishment. As he watched king Shamshi approaching, hand in hand with princess Hamash with a broad smile on his face, Albel dared hope that day had come. The stable master brushed the hay off his clothing and tried to scrape the horse dung from his shoes as the royal family, along with several elite bodyguards walked up to him.

"Greetings my king," Albel said, bending low on one knee.

"Greetings stable master," said King Shamshi. "And how are my steeds this day?"

Albel swallowed hard, his eyes twitching nervously. If this was some sort of inspection, he knew he was in trouble. There was much around the stable that needed repair. Some of Shamshi's prize horses had not had their hooves filed in months... The king noted his fearful expression and gently held up a hand to calm him.

"Fear not stable master," Shamshi said. "I come for a joyous occasion! I have come to grant freedom this day!"

Albel's fearful look changed to one of gleeful happiness. Leaping up and down like a child, his hands clasped together in joy.

"You have my king?" cried Albel. "You have come to grant freedom? Freedom at last from this stable?"

"Why yes," the king replied, pointing at Nimrod, who was carrying a saddle across the yard. "For him!"

Albel's expression changed abruptly to one of absolute despair. Princess Hamash looked up at him, giggling.

"You...you...you have come to free...the boy, my lord?" Albel sputtered.

The king nodded and let go of his daughter's hand.

"Fetch him, my dear."

As the princess ran over to get Nimrod, Albel looked after her. Then he turned back to the king.

"But, what of me, my lord," Albel asked. "What of my fate?"

The king grinned.

"My daughter tells me you are doing a great job back here and that you love it. She says she has heard you declare numerous times that you never want to leave!"

Tears were starting to form in Albel's eyes as he shook his head negatively.

"But...but…my king…"

King Shamshi squinted at Albel dangerously and two of his bodyguards placed hands on their swords.

"Are you calling my daughter a liar, stablemaster?"

"No, sire, no," Albel stammered. "It is a great honor to serve you in any way sire..."

Just then princess Hamash approached leading Nimrod by the hand. They stopped right in front of the king and the boy bowed down on one knee as the princess had instructed him earlier. The king nodded his approval, noting the cloth tied around his eyes and the clicking noise coming from the boy that the princess had told him about. This was the noise that had something to do with the boy's semblance of sight, and the king was eager to test it.

"Arise, Nimrod," the king said as the boy stood up. "Today I come to offer you a choice, young one. But first a test…"

Shamshi signaled one of his bodyguards and the man stepped forward holding a long wooden staff.

"There is a man standing before you holding a fighting staff used in our warrior training."

"I know my king," Nimrod replied. "And the staff is half a head taller than the man."

The king's eyebrows rose along with those of everyone else who heard the boy. He gestured for the man to stand the staff up straight. It was a half a head taller than the man. Princess Hamash beamed with pride. The king stroked his beard and pursed his lips.

"My daughter says that since you have healed from your injuries, you do things even those with sight find difficult. Prove it now. Keep the stick from hitting you long enough to impress me."

Nimrod stood back, clicking his tongue rapidly as the guard walked towards him. The king clapped and the man lunged with the staff towards Nimrod's legs. The boy effortlessly widened his crotch, causing the man to miss. Impressed, the guard looked back at King Shamshi, who signaled for him to continue. This time he tried an overhead strike towards the boy's head. Nimrod swayed backwards slightly and the staff swished past, almost close enough to touch his skin. The man tried again and again, each time missing by a mere fraction as Nimrod moved in an almost leisurely fashion.

"I told you father!" cried princess Hamash gleefully. "When he and I play sword fight, I can never touch him. And last week when Nimrod pulled me away as my horse tried to kick, he caught the steed's hoof with the other hand!"

"Enough!" the king cried. "I have seen enough! Step forward Nimrod!"

Nimrod came towards the king and got back down on one knee.

"Talent such as yours is wasted here tending horses. Come with me now and become a warrior in my service. Do my bidding, protect my daughter, and wealth and glory shall be yours. What say you?"

Nimrod stood up.

"I will get to protect the princess?"

"It is what she wishes," replied the king.

"Then I gladly accept."

Albel watched as they walked away from the stable. He was alone now. And felt as if he had nothing. As Nimrod disappeared around the corner to his new life of honor in the royal court, the stable master nearly choked on the irony. Albel also admitted to himself just how much he had come to need the boy. How much satisfaction it had given him to abuse and berate him so that someone else could be lower in the pecking order. Now that Nimrod was gone and that was taken away, he felt lonely and empty. As Albel crawled into his shed to weep, he knew he needed something. Perhaps, the stable master pondered, he would ask that Eshri woman about her Yah God...

During his first few weeks of warrior training, Nimrod came to know what it meant to be a Kushite in a land where they had become second class citizens. There were only two in the whole of Shamshi's training camp, Nimrod and a young girl who cleaned and served. The rest were all boys, older than Nimrod's 14 years, who teased the girl and played cruel joke on him at every turn. All where mountain tribe invaders: pale skinned and big boned, who relished berating anyone who was different.

One called Ulli was especially mean. A tall chubby boy of 17 with straw colored hair, he was King Shamshi's first cousin. Which meant Ulli was first in line for food, had his pick of the best practice weapons and generally did as he pleased in the training yard and sleeping area. But it was in the eating hall, where Ulli held court daily, where the worst of the teasing and bullying took place.

One day Nimrod was sitting in a corner eating alone as he did every day, when suddenly his ears perked up. He could hear Ulli and his cohorts whispering about him, though they thought him oblivious to their developing plot. It was mashed yam day in the eating hall, which meant, according to a whispered edict from Ulli, that someone had to be pelted with it. Nimrod, as usual, was the day's chosen target.

Forewarned, Nimrod clicked his tongue rapidly to sharpen his awareness. Then Ulli and four other boys rose, each armed with a spoonful of yam, and flung it at him. Nimrod liked the yam and had already eaten his, so he thrust up his bowl like a reversed shield. Moving his arm rapidly Nimrod caught each spoonful, splattering the yam against the bottom of his bowl. Then he casually placed the bowl back down in front of him and began spooning it into his mouth. All the young men in the room looked on with gaped mouth awe. Then they turned towards Ulli to see what he planned to do about it. Ulli stood up and shouted:

"Hey, I spat in that!"

The room exploded with laughter and Ulli smiled, nodding with satisfaction. As the noise died down, Nimrod licked his spoon calmly, finishing the last of the creamy vegetable. Then he turned towards Ulli.

"No, you didn't spit in it, because I would have smelled your stinking breath," Nimrod retorted.

The room exploded in mirth once again, but this time they all laughed at Ulli. This was something the big mountain boy could not take. Balling up one pudgy fist, he pointed threateningly at Nimrod.

"Who do you think you are talking to dung-skin?"

"I don't know what color dung is Ulli," Nimrod shot back, "but I do know what it smells like. It smells like Ulli."

The boys in the room were now rolling with laughter, while Ulli quaked with anger. Shoving several young men aside, he stomped across the floor to loom over the seated Kushite boy.

"I have a mind to thrash you right now," Ulli growled. "But we'd both get beaten for fighting in the eating hall. But just you wait. I'll get the last laugh, dung skin!"

"If you say so mighty Ulli," replied Nimrod. "Hey, anyone else want to throw some yam my way?"

Ulli backed away as several other boys flung yam at Nimrod. He caught it all just as he did before and feasted hardily. Ulli stalked out of the room, with smoke fairly rising from his ears.

After several trying weeks of individual drills and basics weapon training came the morning of the first sparring day. This was the day some were eager for and others dreaded, where the boys were paired off to fight with sticks tipped with cushioned leather. The contest took place in a huge tent made from hundreds of animal skins stretched over a wooden frame. The structure smelled bad, especially to Nimrod, but the trainees were told that the sparring hall was a tradition brought from the mountain tribe's snow swept homeland. It was a custom, like so many things the barbarian invaders brought with them, that they intended to maintain in their newly conquered land. Their instructor, Battle Master Kan, a pale, fierce looking, tall mountain man with a bushy head of white hair and equally bushy white beard, glowered at them with his usual disdain.

The brutal contest started early and went on throughout the day, and was like nothing Nimrod had ever imagined. Kan instructed them to be merciless or suffer beatings, with the clear intention of shaping monstrous warriors. Though the battle master encouraged the drawing of blood, he always chose sparring partners by size to keep the contest fair. But when Ulli and another boy his size were beckoned toward the stage, Ulli stepped in and whispered something to the old warrior that made him smile. Then the battle master called forth the next two combatants.

"Nimrod the blind," Kan shouted as he raised his hand, "and Ulli the fat!"

Ulli stepped forward, frowning at the instructor for the dig about his girth, while Nimrod, totally surprised, pushed his way in from the back of the crowd where the smaller boys awaited. Both combatants leaped atop the raised circular fighting stage and were handed their fighting staffs. After flexing the sticks for balance, Ulli and Nimrod squared off. "You know the rules,"the battle-master growled. "Get knocked off the stage and you lose. No mercy! Now fight!"

Bets were quickly placed, with odds very much against the much smaller Kushite boy. Ulli wasted no time in coming in with a wide sweeping blow designed to knock the smaller boy right off the stage. But Nimrod, clicking his tongue rapidly to sense the pace of the fighting, leaned back and the staff barely grazed him. Then he retaliated by stepping in close, delivering a solid blow that bloodied the mountain boy's nose and sent him reeling. Nimrod then aimed a low blow directly at Ulli's manhood, but stopped short, merely tapping him on the thigh.

"I will leave you with what little manliness you have Ulli," Nimrod cried as he snatched back the staff and twirled it, "for now!"

In answer to the taunt, Ulli bared his teeth. Wiping the blood from his nose, he came in charging. Thrusting the staff like a spear, he hoped to batter Nimrod off the stage with his greater weight. But instead found he was teetering at the edge after Nimrod casually pivoted aside. Ulli would have fallen off then, had not Nimrod seized him by the seat of his leather skirt and pulled him back in, causing the crowd to roar with laughter. Ulli turned back around, slightly nodding at a boy near the stage behind his

opponent. The accomplice uncorked a small vial, quickly splashing something behind Nimrod as Ulli charged again. But Nimrod could both smell and hear the devious act and sidestepped instead of backpedalling.

Ulli's thrust missed, his momentum carried him too far, and suddenly he found himself a victim of his own oily trap. His feet became a blur for one hilarious moment as the mountain boy frantically tried to regain his footing, ending when a swat on the rump from Nimrod sent him flying into the howling crowd. It took several moments to disentangle from the boys who had mercifully caught him, and then Ulli got up and slowly turned around. A dagger was in his hand and the room fell silent. Shaking with anger, his eyes squinting into two hateful slits, Ulli started toward the stage until the battle master seized hold of him.

"That will be all for today little lions," announced Kan as he pushed the boy's knife wielding arm down. Then he leaned in and whispered to Ulli: "He is favored by the king. But worry not little cousin, we will get him another way…"

Ulli and the battle-master kept talking in low tones as they joined the crowd flowing towards the exit, and Nimrod kept listening to them plot. It was lucky he never let on how well developed his hearing had become, because what he heard taught him several things he needed to know: he learned that his trainer and his worst enemy were related, that they were united against him and that they both hated Kushites. Which meant things could get very, very dangerous for a lone blind Kushite youth.

During the next 12 moons, just as Nimrod expected, there were plenty of tricks and attempted traps from his enemies. Their attempts to harm him included tampered weapons, unfair fight placement and even food tampering, which Nimrod luckily managed to sniff out each time. Detecting most of the plots, avoiding some, and viciously fighting his way through the rest put the blind, yet gifted Kushite boy through a trial of fire. Above all, the hardships transformed him from young boy to young man, prompting an unprecedented growth spurt in both size and skill. Whether it was access to a steady supply of nutritious food for the first time in his life, the grueling exercises, brutal contests or simply the will of the creator, Nimrod could not comprehend. What he could understand, when he flexed his sinews during workouts and battered opponents aside, were his newly developing warrior strengths and his equally astonishing increase in size.

Without the ability to see himself, Nimrod at first only noticed his growth spurts when he would grow out of the clothes. Then he began sensing his surroundings at a different angle when he clicked and the other boys began making way when he walked into a room. No one teased him to his face any longer because no one could beat him. Whether it was stick fighting, fist fighting, wrestling, sword practice or any of the contests the battle-master forced them into, Nimrod had advanced from tiring his opponents out by dodging blows to aggressively inflicting pain. But even though his prowess was becoming legendary in the training camp, Nimrod was an outsider. This meant that the hateful whispering continued, albeit buffered by a newfound respect.

There were also changes in the thinking for the former stable slave. Though his own life was hard, Nimrod began to develop a social and polit-ical sensibility, leading him to silently question the status of his conquered people in their own land and of his own role in the scheme of things. More immediately, Nimrod kept noticing something else that disturbed him more than his personal plight. This concern was about the only other Kushite in the training camp besides him.

There was one other that Nimrod had heard referred to as "dung skin." At first he paid little attention due to dealing with his own troubles. But now that he had gained some measure of respect, Nimrod decided to turn his at-tention toward an issue that has been nagging at him for a while: The issue of the crippled Kushite servant girl.

He did not know her name, did not know where she came from, but during the time he had been there, Nimrod could always tell when she was about. He recognized her footsteps because of her peculiar cadence-- the result of having one foot shorter than the other. This, along with other things that Nimrod could not see, but heard frequently referred to in cruel jokes, made him feel sorry for her. The situation came to a head one day in the eating hall, after Nimrod overheard a table full of boys hatching a plan to force themselves upon the servant girl and rape her. This, he concluded, was the final straw and Nimrod decided that something had to be done.

That day the girl went about her normal duty. Head bowed, silent and completely submissive, she went from table to table pouring water for the thirsty warriors in training. Suddenly, Nimrod heard the familiar sound of a hand slapping a body part, along with an equally familiar whimper from the terrified servant girl. Snickering and hardy laughter came from the boys near her as Nimrod stopped eating and stood up.

"What's the matter," hissed a tall redheaded boy as he yanked her by the arm. "Don't you like mountain men, you one-eyed dung skinned whore?"

Nimrod recognized the boy's voice as the leader of the rape plot. No one took notice as he began making his way towards them, because all eyes were on the poor tortured girl. Shaking with fear, she tried pulling away, but the cruel boy only twisted her arm harder. A tear rolled from one eye as the girl jerked her head back, causing her long locks to fall away, revealing a gruesome facial injury. Where her other eye should have been was a harsh, diagonal scar running from forehead to cheek. Yet the boys stared at her lustfully despite the wound, because her body was shapely and well defined. Her long locks were lustrous, and the unblemished half of her face was quite appealing. This made the poor servant girl an unfortunate object of lust, prejudice and revulsion. This was why Nimrod considered her plight worse than his own. And this was why he vowed to finally do something about it.

As the boys jeered, the girl continued to struggle, all the while trying not to drop the water jug in her other hand. But the jug proved too heavy and did indeed slip, right into the grasp of Nimrod. Placing the water jug on a nearby table, the large Kushite boy leaned over; wrapping his own hand around the same wrist the boy was using to accost the girl. He squeezed hard, locking the arm in a bone grating, iron hard grip. The bully groaned painfully, prompting his four friends at the table to stand up.

"Let go of her and tell your friends to sit down," Nimrod said in a low and dangerous tone. "Or I shall break it."

The boy looked up with a derisive scowl, spat in Nimrod's face, and then screamed out to his friends:

"Don't just sit there! Get him!"

The boy's nearest cohort, sitting on the same side near Nimrod, attempted to rise, but Nimrod's strong brown hand seized the back of his head, slamming his face down on the table so hard he was too dazed to move again. The three other boys at the table came charging as Nimrod twisted the wrist locked in his grip hard, causing the bully's fingers to let the girl's arm go. Shoving the Kushite servant girl out of harm's way, he then booted the first of the other attackers in the chest, sending him sprawling back into the others. Turning back to the ring leader, Nimrod punched the redheaded boy cross eyed. Then, as promised, he dashed the boy's elbow down upon his muscular brown knee. The arm snapped loudly, followed by the boy's bloodcurdling, anguished scream. Still grasping the whimpering boy's broken arm, Nimrod seized him by the throat, lifting him up from his chair. Drawing the bully's pain filled face almost nose to nose,

NIMROD THE HUNTER

Nimrod spoke clearly and calmly:

"Tell them to stand down, or I break your neck next."

The answer was a painful gurgling sound, but the bully didn't have to say anything to his friends. Nimrod's calm, dangerous demeanor, eerily serene voice and apparently deadly skills sent chills up the spines of all watching. To everyone in the room it was crystal clear that the imposing Kushite with the cloth covered eyes meant exactly what he said. As the bully's cohorts threw up their hands and sat back down, Nimrod carefully placed their friend on the floor to keep from further harming him. Then all the boys in the hall shook their heads in disgust, as the formally imposing bully curled himself into a ball and started weeping.

Just then the doors to the eating hall burst open and Battle-Master Kan appeared, along with several brawny, heavily armed guards.

"By the Demon Lords, what is going on here!" their instructor howled. "You all know there is to be no fighting in the eating hall! Who started this?"

All eyes turned from their instructor and toward Nimrod, who stood silently, looming over the weeping bully. With a gesture from battle-master Kan, the guards came over and seized him. The servant girl, who stood nearby observing it all, took a step forward to say something, but then stepped back, lowering her head fearfully. With great hesitation, and a final sad look over her shoulder, she picked up the jug and went about her duties. As Nimrod was being hustled out of the hall, battle-master Kan clapped his hands together for attention. Then he made a chilling pronouncement:

"You've all been told time and again about the penalty for disobedience. Well, it seems now that an example has to be made. This boy, Nimrod, so defiant of the rules, will have to spend time in the box!"

As Nimrod was being hustled away, he too heard the announcement. As a follower of Yah, who'd been taught to fear nothing but his creator, even he could not help the cold tendrils of terror creeping up his spine. "The box" had been whispered about since his arrival. It was apparently considered the ultimate punishment, because sometimes those who were taken to it never came back. This thought caused Nimrod to struggle, forcing the guards to strike him several times and even threaten him with drawn swords. They then took Nimrod out past the farthest point he had been since his arrival on the training compound. He was dragged through an old crop field, out past a tattered, unused stable and finally tossed down in front of a low wooden box. It looked to be built to hold a goat, with several square air holes and a door secured by two thick crossbar locks.

Nimrod was forced to strip naked, to kneel and then crawl backwards into the box. Then the door was pulled shut, the locks slid into place and the guards took his clothing and left. With room to neither stand up nor sit down, the boy had to draw himself into a twisted fetal position in order to get any relaxation at all. The box was very uncomfortable, but Nimrod was determined not to show weakness by crying or calling out. Steeling himself with nearly constant prayer, he made it to the middle of the night before despair started to set in. Because it was then, when the coolness of the arid, moonlit night began to creep in, that Nimrod began to truly understand his predicament.

The long months in the sleeping quarters with the other boys had made Nimrod nearly forget how cold it could get at night outside. And he also remembered how hot it would get during the day. He had endured a lot under Albel's cruelty, but nothing like this. Nimrod now realized, to his dismay, that this box was a torture device. Designed with no protection from the elements, crafted to cause discomfort, it was a device designed to break a man -- body and spirit. With no idea how long they intended to keep him caged, Nimrod prayed intensely to Yah to give him the strength to endure, before finally drifting off to a cold, uncomfortable slumber.

Chapter 4: You're Going To Die In That Cage!

Nimrod began to stir when a familiar scent wafted towards his nostrils. It was faint at first, but as it got closer his awareness sharpened due to the bad history associated with this particular body odor. Familiar footfalls came closer and closer, finally stopping right in front of Nimrod's torturous prison. By this time he knew exactly who was coming to see him, so when he felt a foot kicking against the side of the box, he was not at all surprised.

"What you want Ulli?" sighed Nimrod. "If you've come to gloat you'll get no satisfaction. I'd rather die than let you see me beg."

Ulli answered with a snicker, which made Nimrod click his tongue, extending his awareness to find out what was going on. Ulli stood over his cage holding a tray of food that Nimrod could now smell also. It was a hunk of bread, a piece of dried meat and a cup of water. Ulli sat on the ground in front of the box and snickered again as he lifted the bread and water to his lips.

"You know dung skin," Ulli said between bites and swallows, "the battle master plans to keep you here for ten days."

"Ten days?" Nimrod replied angrily. "But... but that's not fair. I've never heard of anyone being kept here for more than six days..."

"Yes, that is true dung skin," Ulli replied, smacking loudly. "But that boy who's arm you broke, well, he had to be sent back home. The healers don't think he'll ever be able to use it again... and the battle master was very angry. But don't you worry; you won't be spending ten days in this box..."

"What... what do you mean," Nimrod asked, the answer to his question dawning on him as soon as it slipped out.

"The battle master assigned me to deliver your food and water," the mountain boy replied with an evil grin. "And I will deliver it, straight to my own belly! Ha ha! You'll not last five days, let alone ten."

Nimrod ground his teeth in anger as Ulli sat in front of him eating his food for the next several minutes. Then he got up, tucking the tray under his arm, and began walking away.

"I'll see you tomorrow to share another great meal dung skin," the mountain boy shouted back over his shoulder. "And don't hope someone will come save you because no one else is allowed back here. Only the assigned "caretaker"... and that's me."

For two more days Ulli returned to taunt Nimrod as he ate his food and drank his water. And though his belly growled and he was thirsty beyond words, the Kushite boy held true to his word, neither begging nor crying out. Ulli could tell though, that Nimrod was weakening and that it was only a matter of a few days until his demise.

As he came back from the outer fields on the third day, Ulli passed the battle master drilling several advanced trainees in sword and shield formations. They exchanged knowing, evil grins and he walked on. Ulli's thoughts were filled with joy at how sweet his revenge would be on the day he found the wretch Nimrod dead. And he knew that it would be soon by the way the Kushite boy looked during his last visit. This pleasant thought put an extra pep in his step as he strolled back to the training compound's kitchen. But Ulli didn't notice that his happily evil demeanor was being observed. As he returned the tray to the kitchen area, the single eye of the tortured servant girl was upon him.

The rage swelling in her chest was hard to conceal as she picked up the tray Ulli put down and watched him walk away. This was the third day the mountain boy had returned the prisoner's tray and she now recognized a pattern: Every time Ulli came back from delivering food to the boy in the box there were crumbs around his mouth, and his fat belly seemed a bit more bloated. This, coupled with Ulli's look of evil satisfaction, indicated that he was eating Nimrod's food, which meant, of course, that Nimrod himself was starving.

Her rage was great, but guilt ravaged her even more at the thought of Nimrod dying because he had chosen to protect her. For years the servant girl has suffered in silence, doing whatever she could not to attract attention. This was because going unnoticed was essential, as she fulfilled her clandestine role as a spy for the underground movement gathering to oppose King Shamshi. She had tried her best, but in a camp full of young men her flowering female form had betrayed her, leading to the crossroads where she now stood. Her advantage, that the ignorant mountain invaders mistook her deformities as signs of a slow mind, remained intact, which was the reason she had not spoken up for Nimrod on the day he defended her. She knew exactly where they were keeping him though, having secretly mapped the entire area with a mind extremely gifted for both noticing and remembering details. This was what made her so valuable to the rebels, and what could be jeopardized if she took action on behalf of the boy who stood up for her.

Years earlier, during trips to the market and other errands, she had noticed people communicating via a series of subtle hand signs. As the
months went by she began to discern what the signs meant, recognizing
them as the fabled "Su" language, the secret means of communication of
the ancestors. Carefully, she reached out to the rebels by duplicating the
signs, which astounded them because no one was supposed be able to
notice them, let alone learn "Su" without being taught. They welcomed
her as a valuable asset to the cause and she planned to join them immediately. But they had begged her to stay in the training camp to gather
information about the king's military resources. Now the day was drawing near for her escape and new life as a rebel, which meant the situation
concerning Nimrod could not have come at a worse time.

At first she thought as her rebel training dictated, deciding that Nimrod
had to be sacrificed for the greater good. But images of his heroics in her
defense, coupled with visions of the poor blind boy suffering to death,
seized her and would not let go. And there was something else. Some
feeling that she could not put her finger upon, that made it impossible for
her to stop thinking about Nimrod. After agonizing about it all through
the day and into the night, the servant girl reluctantly decided that she
had no choice. She had to assist Nimrod any way she could- even at the
risk of her life.

As the servant girl was considering her options to help him, Nimrod
lay scrunched in his torturous prison, feeling his life slip away. Though
his will power was great, and his prayers to Yah were strong, the lack
of food and water had begun to affect him. As he slipped in and out
of consciousness, his mind began to show him forgotten images from
before the curtain of darkness had descended. People he could not name
and surroundings he could not place bombarded him with feelings both
familiar and strange.

Nimrod saw horrible images of himself and people he felt a strange attachment to, but had no memory of, being dragged away by cruel men.
He saw a brown skinned man and a woman, along with a young boy
and girl, having what looked like regal garb torn from them. Nimrod
could hear himself scream along with the rest of them, as they were all
subjected to unspeakable tortures. Finally a red-hot piece of metal filled
his vision, followed by pain beyond words as existence became a long,
anguished scream. Then he felt his mind slip away and he could see and
feel no more.

The images and feelings were so disturbing that Nimrod found himself struggling inside the box, banging his head, knees and backside against the tight wooden walls. The servant girl, who crouched nearby inside a stand of bushes, could actually hear the walls of the solidly built wooden cage straining, and marveled at the boy's strength. She carried a sack bearing food and a jug of water, having crept stealthily across the compound to the cage area. Avoiding the sleeping guards posted at intervals had actually been easy, and she was about to make her way across the open field to the cage when Nimrod began his quaking assault upon his prison. Finally his struggles subsided, and after checking to make sure no guards were alerted, she darted across the moonlit expanse to the box.

"Nimrod," she whispered as she crouched beside the cage.

He had heard her run across the field, had heard her speak his name, but thought it only another product of his fevered nightmares. Then he breathed deeply, catching her familiar scent and the smell of the food in her bag, and he knew she was real. Though he was very weak, Nimrod managed to click his tongue once, perceiving her crouching next to his cage.

"You," Nimrod croaked hoarsely, "you should not... have come here..."

"I...I had to come," the servant girl said, a tear running down from her one good eye. "I could not let you die for what you did for me... Take some water please, and I have some food."

Nimrod had to twist his head awkwardly as the water was poured through one of several holes in the top of his cage down into his parched lips. Then the servant girl dropped several chunks of bread and dried meat down to Nimrod's hungry mouth. As she fed him the girl looked around frequently, making sure none of the sleeping guards had awakened and detected them.

"What is your name?" Nimrod asked. "And why are you taking the risk to do this?"

"My name is Enana," the servant girl replied. "And I ask the same of you: why did you take the risk to help me?"

Nimrod contemplated for moment before he replied:

"Because that's what I was supposed to do..."

Enana smiled as she placed the empty bottle back into the sack.

"And I think this is what I am supposed to do," she shot back. "And tomorrow night I shall return with tools to get you out of there…"

Nimrod shook his head negatively.

"No! No you will not! If they catch you pounding away at this box trying to free me, they'll stuff you in here right along with me."

"But I have to get you out Nimrod," Enana exclaimed. "Don't you see they plan to kill you?"

Nimrod thought for moment, and then the possible answer came to him.

"Enana, you must listen to me carefully," he began. "You must seek out Princess Hamash."

Enana looked puzzled.

"The Princess? Shamshi's daughter? What do you have to do with the Princess, and how is she to help?"

"The Princess is my friend," Nimrod replied. "It's a long story. Seek her out. Princess Hamash can get me out of here and keep you from getting into trouble. "

"But how?" Enana asked, her voice filled with doubt.

"You go to the market each morning to get food for cooking, Enana. Is that correct?"

"Yes," Enana replied. "It takes a while to gather the supplies needed to feed all of you."

"Good," Nimrod said. "Tomorrow you will go to the stand of the man with the big voice who sells cow milk. Princess Hamash goes there each morning with a Kushite elder to get milk before her lessons. There is where you can find her and tell her of my plight."

"But Nimrod, it is a marketplace," Enana replied. "There are many people there with many big voices, all shouting to sell their wares."

Nimrod smiled bitterly, shaking his head.

"I am sure you have noticed, Sister Enana, I can't give you directions based on what I have seen. If I were free I could guide you there by following scents and sounds that I had become accustomed to when the Princess and I took lessons together. The man is a cowherd and has a voice that is stronger than the voices of other cow herders. That is all I can tell you. Will you please try?"

"Of course I will, Nimrod." Enana said with a determined smile. "I'm going to find your cowherd and your Princess. I am going to get you out of there!"

The next day Ulli approached Nimrod's cage as usual. But instead of walking right up to the box, the cruel mountain boy lingered a short distance away. He wanted to hear the groans of agony and discomfort that the starving boy would never utter when he knew that Ulli was near. He had heard such noises the day before and once again leaned against a tree, patiently waiting for the sounds of suffering he enjoyed.

But there were no sounds. No moans, no groans or sighs of discomfort emerged from the cage, even after Ulli waited a long time. Suddenly the thought that Nimrod may be dead occurred to him, and he rushed over to the cage feeling joyful, yet disappointed. Ulli wanted Nimrod dead, but he also wanted to see the Kushite boy suffer for as long as possible.

"Dung skin," Ulli whispered, "you dead?"

"No I am not dead Ulli," Nimrod replied, "but you are going to wish you were when I get out of here."

Ulli noticed the strength in Nimrod's voice. Eyebrows rising along with his curiosity, he peered into one of the holes of Nimrod's cage. There Ulli saw a boy that he thought was at death's door, now filled with new vigor and determination. Grinding his teeth in bitter frustration Ulli knew that there could only be one explanation: someone had been giving Nimrod food and water. Furious, the mountain boy began kicking and pounding at the cage, screaming at Nimrod to reveal who had been helping him. Nimrod merely smiled, enjoying the sounds of frustration coming from his enemy. As he flailed against the cage, the mountain boy kicked at the wrong angle, howling in pain as he nearly broke a toe. This amused Nimrod to no end, causing him to burst out in laughter, though it racked his contorted body with pain.

"Keep kicking fool! Ha ha! You'll break me out of here and cripple your own foot as well," taunted Nimrod. "I'm going to be free, and when I do you'll be howling about a lot more than just that toe!"

Ulli plopped down on top of the cage, nursing his foot and grinding his teeth in anger. Over and over again he mentally turned over information, trying to figure out who could have come and given Nimrod food. Then it dawned on Ulli. He suddenly realized who would've had access to food and who had the motivation. He leapt to his feet, wincing due to his nearly broken toe.

"It was that one-eyed cripple!" Ulli shouted. "She was the one, wasn't she dung skin?"

Suddenly fear gripped Nimrod's heart, but he said nothing. Ulli was smarter than Nimrod thought he was, but there was no way he could figure out their plans. Enana was surely seeking out the Princess at that very moment, which meant Nimrod needed to keep Ulli there with him for as long as possible. With that in mind, Nimrod tossed out another taunt.

"You have the mind of a crazed rat Ulli," Nimrod replied. "I don't know what you're talking about and I don't think you do either."

Ulli began pacing back and forth, favoring his aching foot with every step. Swinging back towards Nimrod's cage, he pointed accusingly.

"You and that one-eyed cripple are planning something, right?" Ulli roared. "Well, you are not going to get away with it! I'm going to report her to the battle master right now!"

"Wait!" Nimrod cried, as Ulli began running away as fast as his injured foot would carry him.

"I'm going to stop whatever it is that you two are up to," Ulli shouted back. "She'll get the black skin beaten off her. And you- I swear by all the gods- you're going to die in that cage!"

The sights and sounds of the market, along with colorful banners and equally colorful characters hawking their wares surrounded Enana as she shuffled back and forth among the surging crowd. She had been there since sunup, and spent the last 2 1/2 hours going from one side of the market to the other trying to keep an eye on two loud voiced cow herders. Altogether there were 10 cowherds plying their wares that day, and four were women. Enana cautiously ruled the women out, checking with each to make sure they were not standing in for a husband, brother or employer. Of the six remaining men, only two of them fit the description that Nimrod had given her, but unfortunately they were on opposite sides of the market. So she went back and forth until she was lucky enough to discover a vantage point where she could turn her head to observe both men in the distance. Unfortunately her vantage point left her more exposed than she would have liked to be, as it was right on the steps of the guard house for the warriors who policed the market, a place Enana would never think of coming near if not for the dire circumstances.

Perhaps half an hour had gone by before Enana swiveled her gaze to the left. There she spied a tall, fair-skinned young woman with regal clothing walking with a female Kushite elder. Flanked by two bodyguards bearing royal insignia, they were heading for a cowherd's stall and Enana knew she spotted the Princess. Her feeling of relief was short-lived though, because just then a runner bound up the stairs and began reporting to two guards near her. She could not hear everything they were saying, but they were getting a message from the runner which included the words "capture" and "crippled slave girl." She immediately knew that they were talking about her. Enana could see the Princess and the elder speaking to the cow herder as she slowly descended the stairs and began walking their way. Pacing her steps, she tried in vain not to look crippled as she made her way over.

Enana tried not to think of the danger she was facing and kept her eyes on her prize. Having settled on price and quantity, the princess and the elder handed the cowherd a palm sized payment slab, and he began filling up a small jug of milk from the contents of a larger one. Enana held her breath, praying she could get to Princess Hamash before the guards recognized her. Suddenly she noticed two men in the crowd whom she recognized. In the subtle Su hand language, she signaled her peril and that she may require help distracting the guards. Their arrival was indeed timely, because it was at just that moment the guards spotted her.

"You there," one the guards shouted, "girl with the limp, stop where you are!"

Realizing that time had run out, Enana began to run as fast as her crippled leg could carry her. The two guards, noting that she could not move fast, began sprinting towards her almost leisurely, when suddenly their path was blocked by a herd of bleating sheep.

"He's stealing my herd!" one of the men who had exchanged signals with Enana shouted.

The other man Enana had signed to lead a sheep on a rope, apparently trying to drag it away. The rest of the herd followed it, causing a jumble in the middle of the aisle and the slowdown of Enana's pursuers.

"I am not stealing," the other man shouted. "This one is mine! He just sold it to me. If he can't stop the others from following it, then they're supposed to belong to me also!"

One of the guards grabbed the rope holding the lead sheep from the man's hand and began shouting at him. Then he locked eyes with his companion and pointed at Enana. Nodding his understanding, the tasked guard pushed away from the herd and ran after the limping servant girl.

Princess Hamash and elder Eshri had heard and briefly glanced at the commotion, and then took the jug of milk and began to walk away. Enana approached to within several feet, causing one of her bodyguards to step forward, blocking access to the princess.

"Princess Hamash!" Enana cried. "Please hear me!"

The princess and Elder Eshri stopped and turned around just in time to see the guard catch up with Enana and strike her in the belly. It knocked the wind out of the servant girl, robbing her of her ability to speak. Then the guard began to drag her away as Princess Hamash and Elder Eshri looked on. With a shrug, the princess turned back around and began walking away, beckoning the elder to follow. Eshri hesitated though, sensing something was out of the ordinary.

"A moment, princess," she declared, "I think we should hear what the girl has to say…"

The guard dragging Enana away had been given orders not to let the prisoner speak to anyone, and clasped his hand over Enana's mouth while simultaneously choking her. Enana struggled with all her might, but the guard was too strong. A tear began to roll from her one good eye at the thought of failing Nimrod.

"She's just a crazed servant gone bad." The guard snarled at Elder Eshri. "She has nothing to say that a princess would want to hear."

Determined to do something, Enana stomped down on the guard's foot as hard as she could. He screamed out in pain, lifting his hand from her mouth to pull out a dagger. Looking down, the guard saw that his foot was bleeding, and then slammed Enana brutally to the ground, raising the dagger in fury.

"Stop!" the guard's companion near the sheep cried. "Bring the girl alive and unhurt fool!"

As Princess Hamash and her entourage looked on, the guard reluctantly sheathed the dagger, lifted the dazed Enana up by her throat again and began dragging her away. The slam to the ground had again knocked the air from her lungs, but she managed to choke out one word before she was almost out of earshot:

"N…Nimrod!"

Princess Hamash and Elder Eshri both stopped suddenly, their eyes widening. The princess then turned and walked toward the guard and struggling girl.

"Unhand her," she ordered. "Now!"

"But Princess, the man replied, "I have my orders."

The Princess gestured towards her bodyguards and the man holding Enana instantly found himself facing two spear tips, inches away from his throat. He released Enana and Elder Eshri hurried over to gather her up. Princess Hamash joined in and they sat Enana down on a nearby bench. The Princess handed her the jug of milk as Enana caught her breath and took a sip.

"Now my dear," said Elder Eshri in a firm, yet gentle manner. "What do you have to tell us about Nimrod?"

The horns and drums that signaled a royal inspection of the warrior training compound blared, causing Battle Master Kan to hurriedly gather his young trainees into formation. When the doors to the main hall flew open, the battle master was sure he would be praised and congratulated on the fine crop of warriors he had honed over the past two years. Instead, the king came in with 20 heavily armed military men, including the feared Tituma, whom he had recently promoted to Shabra to lead his army. Beside the king walked his daughter, the beautiful Princess Hamash and a strange little elderly Kushite woman. Lastly, to Kan's wide-eyed surprise, there was his very own servant girl. Instead of being returned to him rope-bound for helping Nimrod as he requested, she stood before him unafraid and in the company of the royal entourage. The battle master concluded right then and there that it was not going to be his day.

"Greetings my King," Kan said, falling to one knee and bowing his head low.

The King looked down and snarled at him.

"Where is the blind boy, Kan?"

"Er…what do you mean my King?" asked Kan nervously. "What boy?"

The Princess tried to rush forward but was held back by her father, crying:

"You know full well we are talking about Nimrod! Produce him now, or things will go badly for you."

"Things are about to go badly for dear cousin Kan as it is my sweet," replied the King with a harsh coldness.

"Attend me Shabra Tituma!"

"Yes my King," the dangerous looking warrior said, stepping forward.

"Your main reason for being here is to assess the training of the battle master's charges. If they pass your inspection, he may yet live. But right now, I would like you to teach Kan the folly of not answering his King's direct question."

"It will be my pleasure sire," replied Tituma.

The Shabra held forth his hand and nearby warrior slapped a spear into it. Flipping it over in one smooth motion, he whipped the butt around, cracking it on the side of the still kneeling Kan's head. The battle master fell back, screaming in pain and crying for mercy, which Tituma ignored as he beckoned five more warriors to join in. They proceeded to beat Kan to a pulp with spear butts for several moments, until the King held up his hand for them to cease.

"Now," the King asked again, nudging the quivering battle master with his foot, "where is the blind boy, Kan?"

His face bloody, body covered with welts and knots from head to toe, Kan managed to lift a shaky hand and point a finger toward the crowd of boys. They all stood in shock, having just witnessed their iron handed teacher get beaten like a rabid dog. Ulli was especially pale and nearly fainted from fright when the battle master's quivering finger pointed directly at him.

"That boy, the fat one, he will take you to him..."

"You have him in some sort of cage," the Princess growled, "where is the key?"

"It is in my chamber, hanging on the wall..." Kan replied weakly.

The King pointed at one of Kan's nearby guards and the man hustled away. All of the battle master's men feared that they would share his fate, which caused the key to be placed in the King's hand with great haste. Ulli was called forth and complied shakily to stand before the King and his entourage. Princess Hamash and Enana glared at him with profound fury and Ulli swallowed hard, his bladder a mere quiver away from a terrified, embarrassing release.

"I recognize you as one of my cousins," hissed Princess Hamash, "I recall playing with you when we were small, which is the only reason I don't ask father to hang you."

"Yes Princess…thank you Princess," Ulli croaked.

"But you will be punished, of that you can be sure," King Shamshi added in a dangerous tone. "How harsh the punishment shall be will be according to the state of her friend Nimrod. Now take us to him boy, and you had better pray he is alive."

Ulli did pray. He prayed long and strong to the mountain gods of his ancestors and even to a few demons as he led the royal entourage across the compound. It was an especially hot day, the hottest since Nimrod had been confined, and they all feared the worse. As they approached the box, Ulli pictured the battle master's fate, knowing that if they found Nimrod dead his end would be much, much worse. Finally the entourage circled the box and stood over it. For a moment there was only silence as everyone looked up at the hot sun, until Enana finally spoke:

"Nimrod…" she cried, her voice cracking, "Nimrod I did it. I brought the princess, just as you asked."

Her answer was only silence. Then King Shamshi himself opened the cage and peered inside. A blast of hot air assailed him and stepped back, shaking his head.

"It is so hot inside…and I do not think that he is breathing," the king announced sadly. "I believe we have come too late."

A cloud of despair descended over all those gathered around the cruel torture box, as each contemplated their relationship with Nimrod. Enana's guilt was overwhelming, especially when it came to mind that she had never really thanked him. Princess Hamas remembered Nimrod as she first saw him - the innocent blind boy that became her first true friend. Elder Eshri shook her head at the loss of a truly gifted child, potentially the greatest priest she would have ever known, and a great student who was a pure delight to teach. Shamshi lowered his head also. Though he cared nothing for Nimrod, his eyes were misty due to the destruction of his demonic overlord's plans to use the boy to get a phoenix egg. The wrath of the Fire Lord would be great, possibly resulting in the early collection of a chilling debt he made long ago. It was this debt, and the consequences of its early collection, which caused the sadness in the eyes of the cold hearted king.

Enana and Elder Eshri lowered their heads and began to weep. Tears streamed down Princess Hamash's face too, but her eyes also burned with fury. Looking around, she saw the pile of bones and bread crusts, obviously left by Ulli to taunt her starving friend, and she finally lost control.

Before anyone could stop her, she leaped forward. Seizing Ulli by the arm, she spun him around, kicking him in the groin so hard he was lifted off his feet. As King Shamshi and one of the guards grabbed her and pulled her back, Ulli doubled over in pain. Then a flood of yellow liquid gushed from between the mountain boy's legs and he fell down, curling up into a quivering ball of pain, shame and wetness.

"I changed my mind father," cried the Princess as she struggled to pull away and get back at Ulli, "blood or no blood, hang him! Hang him now!"

Just then a weak, yet familiar voice seized everyone's attention.

"Before you all hang the fat one…" the voice croaked, as everyone gasped and turned towards the torturous box from whence it came, "Can I please first have some water…"

Chapter 5: All Hail Nimrod And Enana!

A cool late fall breeze floated in from the window behind her, caressing Elder Eshri's shoulders as she leaned on her cane scanning the eyes of her attentive students. Princess Hamash sat before her along with her newest charge, the former servant girl Enana and the ever attentive Nimrod. Glancing across the room and through the open door, the elder noted her fourth, unofficial student. Ulli sat on a bench just outside the door, his lap piled high, as usual, with Nimrod's weapons, helmet, provisions and accoutrements. Ulli's head was hung low, his demeanor humble, as befitting someone recently sentenced to a lifetime of slavery. But Elder Eshri knew that he was paying attention. This was because they were going over a subject that always elicited wide-eyed wonder and many questions: The issue of Yah's Tree of Life and its Branches of Strength. And, as usual, it was Enana who had the most questions. Elder Eshri nodded towards her as she eagerly raised her hand.

"So, the Tree of Life represents the pathway that the Yah created for us to become one with Yah and all creation?"

"That is correct my dear," Elder Eshri replied.

"And its Branches of Strength serve as both map and ladder to get us there…"

"That too is correct," the elder nodded.

"But you said that the Branches of Strength where messengers - actual living beings," replied the former servant girl. "How can a map and a ladder be alive?"

The elder was about to open her mouth when Nimrod's hand shot up. Elder Eshri tapped the floor twice with her cane, the audible equivalent of a nod giving the blind young man permission to speak.

"I know how," Nimrod chimed in. "It is because the branches of strength are everywhere, even in a map or ladder."

"That's not the reason!" Princess Hamash interjected, causing Elder Eshri to frown at her for speaking without permission. "It's because the map and ladder are made from the branches…"

"That's nonsense!" Enana spouted, as all three students began to argue.

Even Ulli leaned in toward the doorway as the conversation got more and more heated about the nature of Yah's Tree of Life and its mysterious Branches of Strength. Elder Eshri let it go on for several moments before several sharp taps of her cane brought them all back to attention.

"You are all half right," the teacher declared, "but I suppose only experience will allow for more comprehension. I am a high priestess of Caanaan from the Temple of Yah Asherah, and I think that it is time for me to show you something…"

The students looked puzzled as the elder sat down cross legged in the middle of the floor before them. Setting her cane aside, she placed her hands on her knees, closed her eyes and began to breathe in a deep and rhythmic pattern. Clicking his tongue, Nimrod could feel her taking deep breaths as she pushed out her stomach, while the other students, including Ulli, looked on with awe and curiosity.

"Oh, no, here it comes," the Princess blurted out with a combination of awe and fear, "here comes the scary voice."

Everyone turned towards Princess Hamash with the intention of questioning her about what she meant when suddenly the strange voice she spoke of called out. It seemed to be coming from their teacher who still sat on the floor cross-legged, but also seemed to come from the air around them.

"We are here," declared the unearthly voice emerging from Elder Eshri's mouth. Sounding like a combination of roaring winds and raging waters, the voice bounced off the wall like an echo. "Wisdom will be given for those ready to receive it. Prophecy will be spoken for those who care to hear it."

"Don't ask it anything!" Princess Hamash cried out fearfully. "It will tell you something you don't want to hear!"

As Enana looked at the Princess with great curiosity, Nimrod clicked his tongue, directing his senses towards his teacher with greater scrutiny. And he was startled. The image that returned to him was not of Elder Eshri, but of a large, broad shouldered, human-like being with huge extra limbs protruding from its shoulders. Clicking his tongue again, Nimrod realized that these were not extra limbs, but overlapping wedges of light emanating from its upper spine that resembled wings.

"Who are you?" Nimrod half whispered.

"I am known by many names, in many lands, and across many ages. In the land along the Nile river I am Tehuti," the being said, flexing its wings of light. "In this land some call me Enki and in the land of this vessel's birth I am called Ratzi-El. I am one of the branches of the Tree of Life, a messenger of Yah. I see and salute you o shining one called, Nimrod. Do you wish to glean your fate?"

"Nooo!" screamed Princess Hamash.

"Yes," shouted Nimrod, ignoring her.

"Very well: You were born to rule and shall rise to the heights of glory as the savior of all the world- but only if you can survive even greater depths of tragedy and pain!"

Nimrod felt good about the first part, but fearful about the second half of his prophesy. As a person who had been cruelly blinded, violently enslaved, attacked by a demon and nearly killed in a torture box, he shuddered to think about what could be greater than the pain he had already suffered. Then Enana suddenly spoke up too, while Princess Hamash shook her head and waved her hands negatively.

"What of me, great branch spirit?" Enana asked

"You too shall rise to glory, but only after condemnation and salvation due to the ultimate sacrifice!"

Then the being that had taken over Elder Eshri turned towards Princess Hamash.

"And you. I have told you once of your fate. Hopefully you have begun to prepare yourself, for your suffering shall be great! But remember: if you can endure, the purest love of Yah, creator of all, shall set you free."

"I don't want to hear it again," moaned the Princess, covering up her ears. "Please don't make me hear it again...."

"Then I shall not Princess," the being replied as it scanned all the faces in the room. "Harken well the lessons from the spirit of this vessel, for she is a true servant of the Creator of us all. Farewell!"

The strange voice of the Tree of Life spirit continued to echo around the room for a moment. Then all was silent. Suddenly a loud gasp arose from Elder Eshri and they all rushed over to help her to her feet.

"So my children," Elder Eshri declared to the students around her. "I have given you a glimpse of one of the branches of the Tree of Life. You have much to think about, so your lessons for today have ended. You are dismissed."

As their teacher began to putter around the room stacking lesson plans and organizing scribal instruments, the students gathered their things and left the room. Obviously not wanting to speak to anyone, the Princess hurried away, shoving past Ulli with her usual disdain. Nimrod and Enana, both lost in their own thoughts, stopped just outside the door so that Nimrod's manservant could do his duty. Now enslaved to Nimrod for life by royal decree, Ulli had become resigned to his fate over the course of the last six moons. He said nothing as he pushed Nimrod's pointed, feather plumed warrior helm down over his master's thick, long locks. Then Ulli kneeled, reaching around Nimrod's waist to strap on his short sword and dagger. Finally Ulli offered Nimrod his spear, but he pushed it away, yanking the water flask from Ulli's waist instead.

After nearly draining the flask, Nimrod clicked his tongue. Directing his attention to Ulli, he nodded in satisfaction. It seemed the early morning runs, rigorous sparring in the evening and the stretching exercises taught to them by Elder Eshri had finally began to take their toll, because Nimrod perceived a flatter belly and much stronger muscles on Ulli than ever before. This was very important, because strength, even the strength of his manservant, had become Nimrod's main priority in life, even more so than upholding the righteousness of Yah. After barely surviving the ordeal of the torture box, Nimrod vowed no one would ever be able to do such a thing to him again.

Enana pushed her own long locks back from her one good eye, admiring Nimrod in his warrior's garb with a smile. During the months since the king released her from bondage and reassigned her, first to tend to Nimrod, then as Elder Eshri's assistant, she had vacillated between running off to join the rebellion proper and staying to find out more information. At least that is what she told herself at first. It had not taken her long to understand that her real reason for not leaving was Nimrod. Enana's gratefulness and admiration had blossomed into real and true love for her blind savior, which she did not know quite how to express to him. So she masked her emotions by engaging Nimrod in political discourse, finding him quite receptive to condemning the reign of Shamshi, but reluctant to go any further due to his relationship with Princess Hamash. She also thought that Nimrod hesitated because of the king's apparent kindness, which to Enana's keen sense of observation was dangerous and suspect.

"Is this the hour for your meeting with the king?" she asked.

"Indeed," Nimrod replied. "Are you going to give me another lecture about him?"

Enana saw Ulli's ears perk up after Nimrod's question. This was something she noticed every time they spoke of King Shamshi in his presence. Ulli pretended not to be listening, but Enana was sure he noted everything they said. Because of this, she kept her comments about the king to a minimum when he was near. Enana suspected the mountain boy's punishment was just a ploy to put him in place to spy for the king, and she had decided to express this to Nimrod at a time when Ulli was not around.

"No Nimrod, no lectures," she sighed. "Just be careful. The world of politics is dangerous."

"I am always careful, Enana," Nimrod replied. "I shall see you at dinner, as usual."

"Until then," Enana said as she walked back into the classroom to assist Elder Eshri.

As she turned to leave, Nimrod listened to her footsteps as she walked away. He was also enjoying the lingering smell of the sweet perfumes Enana had taken to wearing of late. Though he had no eyes, he was not blind to what was going on between them. Enana had tended to him after his ordeal in the box, hardly ever leaving his side for two months, and he had gotten to know her well.

As she nursed him back to health, Enana had confided that that she too was an orphan from a distant trading town called Imsu and felt as badly about her deformities as Nimrod did about his. With nothing else to do, she had read documents to Nimrod concerning spirituality, history and politics. And it was during one of their many political discourses that Enana revealed her affiliation with the rebels, laying out all the reasons why Nimrod should join also. It all made sense to him because Shamshi was an invader. But openly fighting against him would mean the end of his relationship with Princess Hamash, and this was something Nimrod was not sure he could do.

As time went on, Enana and Nimrod had grown closer, their hands often involuntarily enfolding during reading sessions. It was during these times that Nimrod detected a gradual shift in Enana's breathing and body odor, which he recognized from interactions he had noticed between courting or newly married couples. Though he said nothing, Nimrod understood these things and their implications. And he wondered what Enana would say if she knew he felt the same.

But even so, knowing how they both felt was not enough for Nimrod. Before he decided to go to Elder Eshri to arrange formal courtship and find a way to raise the bride price, he had to be sure that Enana's feelings were genuine - not just a sad combination of pity and gratitude. This was one of the other motivations for Nimrod seeking to be strong – to see to it that no one else ever looked at him with anything approaching pity, to command respect and be worthy of the love of someone like Enana, a true queen to Nimrod, who considered herself a cripple.

Because his quest for strength and power had instilled a hunger for the status that only royalty could confer, Nimrod was determined to take on any challenge offered by King Shamshi, even if he would likely turn against his benefactor later. With this in mind, Nimrod put aside affairs of the heart, turning his attention to his appointment with the king.

With Ulli in tow, Nimrod strolled through the palace halls toward the throne room. Halfway there Nimrod noticed a raspy sound coming from Ulli's breathing and stopped to face his servant.

"What is it Ulli?"

"Nothing master…"

Nimrod clicked his tongue, directing his attention towards Ulli's chest area. He could sense a swelling in the area of his left lung that intensified as Ulli breathed in and out.

"Don't lie to me, Ulli." Nimrod snapped back. "You think it is the sickness that runs in your bloodline?"

"I…I don't know," Ulli replied with fear in his voice. "Remember master, you promised not to tell. They would kill me for my weakness. Especially the king, who slew his own infant son for having this affliction…"

"The barbarity of you mountain people lies beyond my understanding," Nimrod growled. "Go. Rest and recover your strength. I will see the king alone."

Ulli nodded and began walking back the other way as Nimrod continued. Soon he found himself standing before the huge doors of the throne room. There an assistant rushed forward to confirm his appointment and confiscate his weapons. Then the huge doors opened and they walked through.

Clicking his tongue, Nimrod perceived the huge, cavernous room and the two dozen or so courtiers huddled together in small groups. No doubt they had come to beg their respective cases and troubles before the king. They had to wait, but Nimrod had been summoned, so he did not.

A long carpet of red dyed animal skins led to the throne, which the assistant directed Nimrod to walk upon it. On either side a dozen guards stood at attention in full battle armor, holding long spears. The men were stark still, with only their eyes following along as Nimrod approached the throne. As he stopped to drop down upon one knee and bow, King Shamshi spotted him, shooing away an assistant who was whispering in his ear.

"Ahh, Nimrod!" said the king as he leaned forward. "It is so good to see you! I have heard of your domination of the warrior's games of late. Few can throw a spear, shoot an arrow or spin a sword to match you, even outside your age range. It seems you are quite recovered from your tragic ordeal."

"Hail, King Shamshi! I have indeed recovered well. How may I be of service to you? Must the princess travel again? If so I shall protect her with my life…"

"No, no, that is not it, Nimrod." Shamshi replied. "I have a most important errand for you. One that I hope your race and your fame can help to accomplish."

"You have only to tell me, my king, and it shall be done."

The king leaned forward, calling in a low voice for Nimrod to approach the throne. Clicking his tongue to better sense his surroundings, Nimrod bound up the stairs to stand right in front of the king. Shamshi put his hand on Nimrod's shoulder, pulling him even closer.

"There is a rebel leader in the lands just to the south of here," the king began, "who has been causing me no end of headaches. He is called Ekur-Sin. He ambushes my men with tactics of stealth and guile, and then blends back into the wilderness to disappear. He also slaughters entire villages that he deems loyal to me. Most of the villages have been Kushites - his own people. Your people Nimrod…"

"You wish me to hunt this man down?" Nimrod asked. "But what can I do that your armies cannot?"

"Your fame is known and you are a Kushite Nimrod," Shamshi replied. "I wish you to parlay with him. Learn what you can and report back to me. It is rumored that this man is insane, due to the especially brutal nature of the killings. There have also been rumors that he may be related to those who once ruled this land, so I wish to know more of him…"

"And you wish me to find out for you," Nimrod said, finally understanding, "hoping my fame and my race with induce some feeling of trust…"

"Exactly," Shamshi replied.

"But if he kills whole villages he suspects of allying with you, he will consider me a traitor also…"

"That may be so, but I think your fame will make him curious enough to talk to you," Shamshi replied. "And fear not, I will not subject you to undue risk. The princess would never forgive me for that! You will have a contingent of warriors with you for your safety. Go south immediately and seek to arrange a meeting."

"What do I tell him, sire?"

"Tell Ekur-Sin that land and wealth will be his if he will cease his rebel activity. Take note of the way he answers as much as the words he speaks. Then return and report back to me."

"Your will be done" Nimrod said with a bow.

Nimrod pivoted, and then walked down the stairs, away from the throne and back across the long carpet towards the large doors. The courtiers watched him leave with great jealousy, and then they all rushed to line up before the throne to beg for audiences.

Later that evening, Nimrod strolled into the dining area of Elder Eshri's quarters. He was early as usual, greeting the elder with an affectionate hug and kiss upon the cheek. Then he sat down in his usual seat to await the rest of his adopted family. Soon Enana and princess Hamash arrived, arguing as they walked in.

"I will not tell you," princess Hamash growled at Enana. "It's not something I wish to discuss."

"But it came out when that "branch" spirit appeared," Enana shot back. "You can't expect us not to ask about it…"

"I know, but I keep telling you I don't want to discuss it," Princess Hamash stated again, gesturing at their teacher, who stood over a pot stirring the steaming contents. "Even Elder Eshri respects my wishes in this matter."

Enana looked to the elder, who was now filling their bowls with the contents of the pot. Elder Eshri raised an eyebrow and shook her head.

"Leave the princess be Enana," she said, "she will speak of it in time."

Enana sighed and looked to Nimrod, who sat listening intently.

"What do you say Nimrod?" Enana asked. "We shared our prophecies, why should we not know princess Hamash's too?"

"Because she did not volunteer it," Nimrod said flatly. "I would be first in line to draw swords against any who threaten the princess because I care for her just that greatly. But we can't force her to share in this matter."

"Thank you Nimrod," the princess said, then rapidly changed the subject. "I hear you have been given a mission by my father, to meet with this rebel Ekur-Sin."

A look of grave concern flashed across Enana's face, which she quickly replaced with a look of curiosity.

"I have heard of Ekur-Sin," Enana said. "He is a very dangerous man by anyone's standards. Why are you being sent to speak to him?"

"To offer him a peace arrangement," replied Nimrod, before plunging a spoonful of stew into his mouth. He chewed the lamb chunks combined with savory gravy created by Elder Eshri and swallowed, then continued. "The king would know the man's mind, regardless of his answer. And I must admit being interested in meeting him myself."

"Why are you interested in meeting this terrible man," Elder Eshri asked as she sat down before her own bowl.

"Because he is strong," replied Nimrod. "I am interested in strength – how to get it, maintain it and keep it. King Shamshi has not been able to crush him, and that interests me."

Ekur-Sin and his chief lieutenant Mardruk watched from their place of concealment atop the hill overlooking the small village spread out before them. They were once again observing the curious Kushite youth who led a party of 30 or so mountain invaders to one village after another. For nearly an entire moon rumors had trickled in about someone seeking to meet him, prompting the rebel leader himself to finally come forth. He was told they sought parlay for peace, but Ekur-Sin was sly enough to know they were really sent to spy upon him.

This was the second village that he had followed them to, and the rebel leader had just about made up his mind to signal his hidden archers, along with his contingent of 120 men awaiting on the other side of the hill, to descend upon the men and destroy them.

The only thing that had kept him from doing it so far had been his curiosity about the young Kushite. What was he called? – Nimrod, a unique and powerful name which meant "subduer of panthers" in their ancient tongue. Ekur-Sin had indeed heard of the strange blind warrior who could best older, more experienced and sighted men in the war games, but that was not the only reason he had spared him. Due to the council of wise old Mardruk, his confidant and the former leader of the rebellion, he had decided to observe Nimrod, finding similarities between the youth and himself that he thought went far beyond coincidence.

They both had achieved fame at a young age; Nimrod was 18 and Ekur-Sin, now nearly 28, had begun his career in the rebellion at 19. They both had tall, bulky builds, dark brown skin and gaits that were almost identical. Though he could not see the youth's face due to the cloth tied around his head and sightless eyes, these similarities elicited a thirst in Ekur-Sin to find out if they shared kinship. With that in mind, rebel leader had decided to capture Nimrod and slay the invaders accompanying him. Just as he was about to give the order, a runner trotted over from the other side of the hill.

"Ekur-Sin," the runner huffed as he halted before the rebel leader, "there is a strange woman, really just a girl, who is demanding to meet you."

"Most likely another spy," Ekur-Sin replied, rubbing his short, scruffy beard, "kill her before she alerts Shamshi's men."

The man nodded, and then turned to do as his leader bid him. As he was walking away he said under his breath:

"Too bad, even crippled as she is, she is still most desirable."

Ekur-Sin, whose hearing was quite good due to years of stealth warfare, leapt over, spun the runner around, and seized him by the shoulders.

"Does she have an injured face? Ekur-Sin asked forcefully.

"Yes, great one!"

"And a crippled leg?

"That too…"

"Bring her before me immediately," Ekur-Sin ordered. "And do not harm her!"

The runner hustled away, returning moments later leading a young Kushite woman wearing a sheepskin cloak pulled tight against the chill of the fall evening. Her long thick locks covered the left side of her face, but anyone looking closely could still see a horrible scar where her left eye should have been. They both looked at each, nodding in a mutual silent greeting, and then Ekur-Sin rushed over and embraced her.

"Ahh, my future queen, Enana!" the rebel leader exclaimed. "What brings you here today? You cannot await our next meeting in the market?

You must see your beloved Ekur-Sin now?"

Enana gave Ekur-Sin an uncomfortable smile.

"You presume much Ekur-Sin," Enana replied. "Don't announce our wedding just yet…"

"But my dear," Ekur-Sin declared, clutching his heart with both hands as if he had been stabbed, "since our work in the rebellion brought us together, I have told you that there can be no other for me. Say yes now, so that I can secure the bride-price and we can set the date…"

"I did not come here to discuss this." Enana replied, pointing down the hill towards the village. "I came here to discuss…him."

Ekur-Sin looked down at the village. Nimrod was now speaking forcefully with the village elders, no doubt trying to glean information about him. But the rebel leader knew they would tell Nimrod nothing. All in the region were loyal to Ekur-Sin, because Ekur-Sin was the rebellion. After looking back and forth between Nimrod and Enana, the canny rebel leader noticed a look on her face that revealed something to him: Enana's concern for Nimrod was more than friendly and far beyond mere rebel business.

"You care for him don't you? Ekur-Sin asked, his eyes narrowing.

Enana ignored the question.

"He is a great warrior and symbol for our people. I have him nearly ready to join the rebellion."

"And you love him too," Ekur-Sin stated flatly. "I have archers at the ready, you know. With a wave of my hand, I could have him cut down…"

"But you won't!" Enana shot back. "Like you, Nimrod is a born leader who would be a boon to our cause. I know you can see it even from here…"

Ekur-Sin looked back down at the village, focusing on the youth who was leading the discussion with the elders. He indeed looked like a natural leader, which Ekur-Sin admired. He even considered what a great benefit the youth could be in their struggle. But cold tendrils of jealousy had tightened around his heart, and the rebel leader was incensed that someone else had the love he would claim for his own. Grinding his teeth in anger, he seized Enana's arm forcefully.

"Say you will be mine, or he dies!"

"Ekur-Sin, please don't to this!" Enana implored, trying to twist away from his steely grip. "You are a better man than this, I know you are..."

"I am a great leader and soon will reclaim my heritage!" Ekur-Sin growled. "I am a warrior! Through strength of hand I take what rightfully belongs to me! Agree to marry me or he dies!"

"Please Ekur-Sin..." Enana tearfully implored.

"Signal the archers, Mardruk." Ekur-Sin barked to his second in command, who stood a short distance away with a concerned look upon his face. "Tell them to kill them all..."

Mardruk shook his head.

"But, wait, my lord...we cannot!"

"You will do as I say, Mardruk!" Ekur-Sin hissed angrily. "The council voted me battle leader and your day is done. This Nimrod is an agent of the enemy and should perish along with them!"

"Nooo!" Enana cried. "Please don't hurt him... I...I will do as you ask."

"Very good, Enana, very good indeed" the rebel leader said, releasing her arm with a triumphant smile. "We shall discuss the date later. Now go down and bring him to me. I would very much like to meet this Nimrod."

As Nimrod and his entourage emerged from the village, he thought he heard a familiar voice calling out his name. Clicking his tongue, he perceived a person coming down the side of the nearby hill he had only casually noticed before. Another outcall, coupled with the familiar scent of her perfume, let Nimrod know exactly who was approaching him.

"Enana!" Nimrod cried as he trotted forward and crushed her in his arms. "What are you doing here?"

Enana hesitated before she answered, trying to push aside the trauma of her forced betrothal. She knew Nimrod had the ability to sense when something was wrong.

"Where is Ulli?" she asked.

"I left him behind. He had taken ill." Nimrod answered. Sensing the strain in her voice, he clicked his tongue to perceive her breathing and heartbeat. "Something is wrong Enana...what is it?"

"Ulli's illness has likely saved his life..." Enana answered, ignoring Nimrod's question.

"What are you talking about?" Nimrod replied with concern.

"Nimrod you have no idea what is really going on out here. I have quit the castle and joined the active rebellion. Follow me and I shall take you to see Ekur-Sin."

"You know him?" Nimrod asked. "You know where to find him?"

"He found you Nimrod, as soon as you set foot in these lands. Come, he is up the hill…"

"But he is dangerous, Enana. Have you not heard he killed entire villages of our people?"

"Ekur-Sin killed a few people, in one village, one time," Enana corrected him. "Those other villages were the work of King Shamshi. As I said you don't know what is going on out here…"

Nimrod took a step back. "Shamshi killed all those villagers?"

"Not all, but most. It is common knowledge among those of us in the rebellion," Enana stated. "Shamshi took advantage of a mistake Ekur-Sin made to defame him. But the rebellion will not be stopped and Ekur-Sin is our greatest weapon. Come now."

Nimrod beckoned to his men, but Enana shook her head negatively.

"Only you Nimrod, they cannot go. Ekur-Sin has true hatred for the mountain people and would slay them if you brought them near."

Nimrod considered for a moment, and then waved the men back.

"Stay here until I return," Nimrod directed them.

The men settled down to make camp just outside the village as Enana and Nimrod made their way up the hill. As they wound their way up the steep trail obscured by thick trees and shrubbery, Nimrod clicked his tongue to perceive his surroundings. He realized then that half an army could have been concealed there and they would not have even known it. Finally they reached the top, where Ekur-Sin awaited with the elder Mardruk standing nearby, leaning on his cane. The rebel leader had pulled out a dagger and was running a stone across the blade. As Nimrod and Enana came to a stop before him, Ekur-Sin continued sharpening without looking up.

"Nimrod, meet Ekur-Sin, battle leader of the rebellion," Enana said, "Ekur-Sin, this is Nimrod."

"I have heard tales of the wondrous blind warrior," said Ekur-Sin, still sharpening his dagger. "I wonder just how good you really are…"

Nimrod noted a challenge in Ekur-Sin's voice and began clicking his tongue rapidly. Sensing a change in Ekur-Sin's breathing and posture, he snatched his short sword out and spun it before him, just-in-time to block a lightning fast dagger throw from the rebel leader. But Nimrod not only blocked the thrown blade. His senses were so acute that he angled his sword against the dagger in such a way that it spun over his right shoulder - away from Enana who stood to his left. Plucking the dagger from midair as it spun, Nimrod threw it back to Ekur-Sin, sinking the blade halfway to the hilt near the rebel leader's big toe.

"I am that good," Nimrod said coolly, "and if you try such a thing again with Enana nearby it will be the last thing that you ever do - rebel leader or not."

Mardruk's eyeballs fairly popped out of the sockets as he observed what Nimrod had done. Then the old warrior looked over with sadness at his young protégé. Shaking his head at Ekur-Sin's callousness, he wondered where he had gone wrong. Ekur-Sin's eyes widened also at Nimrod's feat, before narrowing in anger at his threatening words. An angry retort formed in his mind, but he repressed it in favor of a chance to gloat about his latest conquest and taunt his rival.

"It was just a test mighty Nimrod," the rebel leader said slyly. "I never intended for my betrothed to be put in danger."

"Betrothed?" Nimrod gasped, turning to Enana. "What is he speaking about Enana?"

Enana could feel a deadly tension growing between the two men. Her mind raced as she contemplated how she might defuse it.

"Please Nimrod, you have to let me explain," cried Enana.

"There is nothing for my queen to explain," declared Ekur-Sin haughtily. "We shall be united before the rising of the next moon. But we are not here to discuss nuptials, Nimrod. I called you before me to administer a test…"

"What sort of test," Nimrod asked suspiciously.

"Why, a test of your loyalty, Nimrod." replied Ekur-Sin. "You come here with a contingent of hated enemies, yet Enana claims that you have an interest in joining our rebellion."

"I do have an interest in freeing our people Ekur-Sin," Nimrod replied. "But for reasons of my own, joining the rebellion at this time would be quite difficult."

"Let me stop you right there Nimrod," shot back Ekur-Sin. "There can be no middle ground in this struggle. You either stand with us or die with them. Just as those mountain dogs that you came here with are dying now."

"What are you saying?" Nimrod asked. "Those men and I came on a mission of peace. Stay your hand Ekur-Sin!"

"It is too late," the rebel leader declared as he pointed down the hill.

Suddenly sounds of battle and cries of pain could be heard from the field below, as archers hidden in the village opened fire, peppering Nimrod's entourage with barrage after barrage of deadly arrows. Those left standing were quickly overwhelmed by dozens of Kushite warriors who streamed from around the hill, pouncing upon the mountain invaders as they faced towards the archers. In a matter of minutes it was all over.

Four warriors were spared, only to be bound, dragged up the hill and tossed down before Ekur-Sin, who had by this time lit a fire. With a look of maniacal hatred in his eyes, the rebel leader sat on his haunches, heating up the point of his dagger in the flickering red and blue flames.

"Do you know what happened to the family who once ruled these lands?" he asked Nimrod.

"I have heard rumors Ekur-Sin," answered Nimrod. "Rumors of monstrous cruelty, but that does not mean that we should be like them. Please, I implore you - be a wise and just leader."

"They put out their eyes with hot metal!" Ekur-Sin screamed as he seized one of the bound prisoners by his reddish brown hair. "I saw it all Nimrod! I was hidden, I could do nothing and I saw it! My entire family, cousins, uncles, young and old! Anyone who was known to carry our royal blood was cruelly blinded. And then they cut their throats!"

Nimrod, lifting his hands palm out in a peaceful gesture, dropped to his knees before Ekur-Sin and his intended victim.

"I implore you Ekur-Sin to stop this. As a victim of such horror, I beg you not to subject another to it!"

Enana came close also. Peering into the rebel leaders eyes, she could perceive the deep pain behind his drive for torturous revenge. The horror Ekur-Sin had witnessed did something terrible to him, something that had stripped all compassion away, leaving only a hunger for violent, bloody vengeance.

"You remind me of them Nimrod!" declared Ekur-Sin, tears now streaming from his hate-filled narrowed eyes. "That is why I did not kill you outright! Someone did to you what they did to my family, and I'll wager it was these mountain dwelling curs! Take out your dagger Nimrod! Heat it in the flames and join me! Join me in our just and righteous revenge!"

Shuffling forward on his cane, Mardruk spoke up also.

"Ekur-Sin, you must listen to them!" The old warrior declared. "Our warriors will follow you anywhere, but they have begun to doubt you ever since these tortures began...and since the incident... in the village."

"They were traitors and they had to be slain!" Ekur-Sin screamed, his heated blade poised to plunge into the eye of the whimpering prisoner.

"But there was no proof, Ekur-Sin!" Mardruk replied.

"The proof was their failure to obey me!" The rebel leader snarled. "I gave them the same choice that I give Nimrod now, to slay the mountain invaders or face being slain!"

"Ekur-Sin, please you must stop," cried Enana.

"Are you turning against me also my beloved?" Ekur-Sin hissed dangerously. "Beware! Even you must be careful not to incur my wrath. No more promises from you can shield Nimrod now! Make him to do as I say if you would see him live to witness our nuptials!"

"Promises," Nimrod repeated mentally. Then suddenly it dawned upon him what had taken place. Enana had secured his safety with a promise to marry Ekur-Sin, a man who was clearly insane. Even if they resolved this current situation, there was no guarantee of her safety with such a man. And there was something else, something that had been building up inside of Nimrod since the ordeal in the torturous box. Nimrod had fought long and hard during his warrior training and in the brutal warrior games to ensure that no one would ever be able to threaten him and get away with it again. Now a mad man stood before him, threatening to take both his life and the woman he loved. These factors, along with the bitter sting of jealousy Nimrod felt when he heard of their impending marriage, caused white hot anger to overcome him. Taking no time for further contemplation, Nimrod came to a grim conclusion, and immediately decided to act upon it.

Enana saw Nimrod's hand reaching to his side, towards his dagger, and she screamed out:

"Nimrod, nooo!"

But it was too late. In a move Nimrod had practiced countless times, he pulled the dagger forth, twirling it's blade into his fingers in one smooth motion. Then, clicking his tongue rapidly to pinpoint his target, he threw the blade straight into Ekur-Sin's heart. With a look of total surprise, the rebel leader looked down at the hilt of the dagger sticking out of his chest. Then, with a deep sigh that sounded more like resignation than pain, let go of the prisoner and fell to the ground.

Several warriors started forward but Mardruk waved them back as Nimrod kneeled over Ekur-Sin, respectfully clutching the dying man's hand in a warrior's clasp.

"I am sorry it had to be this way," Nimrod said sadly.

"Let me see," Ekur-Sin said, gasping for breath. "Let me see you…underneath that thing…"

Not wishing to deny a dying man his last wish, Nimrod pulled the cloth down that covered his empty sockets. Ekur-Sin's eyes grew wide as a weak smile spread across his face.

"Nami!" Ekur-Sin gasped. "Oh, Nami it's you! You survived!"

Then he grasped Nimrod's hand even tighter, lifting his head slightly from the ground.

"It's up to you now. It is you who must lead…lead our people…to freedom."

Nimrod had no idea why the dying rebel leader was calling him someone else's name, nor why he felt compelled to pass his position on to him. He just knew that, for some strange reason, he could not let go of Ekur-Sin's hand. For some reason he could not understand, Nimrod just did not want to let his hand go.

As he stared up at Nimrod intensely, tears of happiness rolled from Ekur-Sin's face. Then a deep sigh emerged from his mouth, his eyes went glassy and the rebel leader drew breath no more. Clicking his tongue, Nimrod perceived the warriors standing nearby and thought them likely to attack. But they did nothing but look on in sad astonishment.

'Nami', Ekur-Sin had called him. The name sounded strangely familiar, but he had no recollection of it. Finally pulling his hand free of the steely death grip, Nimrod stood up, feeling a profound sense of sadness that he could not understand. Enana leaned down and closed the rebel leader's eyes, then flung herself on Nimrod's shoulder to weep.

Mardruk, leaning on his cane, simply stared at them, shaking his grey head sadly. Then, after a few moments of contemplation, summoned one of the nearby warriors to stand before him.

"Spread the word to the others," Mardruk announced, gripping the nodding warrior by the shoulders and looking into his eyes. "We have new leadership potential for the rebellion! All hail Nimrod and Enana!

Chapter 6: He Is Worthy!

The long halls of the palace seemed much longer for Nimrod as he struggled to put one foot in front of the other. It had taken the entire day to figure out how to say goodbye without saying it outright, and most of the evening to muster up the courage to do so. But it could be put off no longer. When the sun rose on the morrow, Nimrod knew his time walking these grand halls would be done until the reign of Shamshi was over. The responsibility that Enana always mentioned had caught up to him, Mardruk and the rebel council had confirmed it and the words of a dying man had demanded it: Under the tutelage of Mardruk, and with the assistance of Enana, Nimrod was to be molded into the sword of the rebellion. But this required doing the hardest thing he had ever done: saying goodbye to his first and dearest friend without even the benefit of honesty.

Though Nimrod hated lying, some personal and tactical deceit had come into play in the days since he had returned from seeking out Ekur Sin. First he told king Shamshi that the other warriors had been killed and he himself spared to deliver a warning that the rebels would never give up. Feigning loyalty, Nimrod spent several evenings pouring over maps with Shamshi's military leaders, supplying false information about the group he was secretly about to lead. Giving false information to Shamshi was easy though, compared to lying to Princess Hamash. Faking concern about the disappearance of Ennana when he knew she resided with the rebels and making false plans with the princess for their future as friends had emotionally drained Nimrod, and he was relieved that this day it would come to an end.

He had spent the earlier part of this final evening with Elder Eshri, speaking about spiritual matters and dodging questions about the whereabouts of Enana. It had been easier with the elder because Nimrod took comfort in knowing that when the rebellion succeeded he and his teacher could possibly be reunited. But when the dethroned Shamshi was run out of the country, Princess Hamash was sure to flee with him. And if he were killed, the fiery princess would likely despise his killers, which meant she would despise him. And so, it was with heavy heart that Nimrod left Elder Eshri, remembering her parting words as he strolled towards Princess Hamash's chambers for the final time:

"Yah loves you young man, no matter what happens or wherever you go. As long as you breath and you live in the love of the creator, nothing is beyond or above you."

NIMROD THE HUNTER

Walking past the cruel tapestries depicting the conquests of Shamshi's vicious family, Nimrod thought he caught the faint, familiar scent of sulfur.

It was a fragrance he had not smelled since the incident with the demonoid, Squeekil, but one he would never forget. Then he heard a blood curdling scream in a voice he knew all too well.

"Aaaaaaaah!" the young female voice screamed.

"Princess!" Nimrod cried as he dashed towards her chambers.

Rounding the corner, Nimrod clicked his tongue rapidly, perceiving the body of one of her guards crumpled against the wall in front of her doorway. As he got closer, he found that the guard had actually been thrown right through the Princess's heavy wooden door, killing him instantly and bursting a large hole through it.

Nimrod pulled his sword and leapt through the gaping hole. Clicking his tongue rapidly, he took note of the ghastly tableau before him. The other guard stationed near the Princess had been literally torn apart, his body strewn all over the room. Against the far wall there was a huge hideous demon, scaly, with jagged horns protruding all over a bulky body that shimmered a sickly red and purple. Nearly half its bulk had disappeared into a void similar to the one that Nimrod had called forth to dismiss the demonoid, Squeekil. The other half of its body was still within this realm, and in its large scaly claw it clasped the unconscious body of Princess Hamash.

Remembering the further conversations he had with Elder Eshri about dealing with the ghastly denizens of the infernal planes, Nimrod tossed his sword down and ran forward, calling upon Yah through the power of his silver medallion. The demon simply laughed at him and shifted to continue stepping through the portal, until the light of the eight pointed star blasted forth from Nimrod's chest. The creature's eyes grew wide as the light wrapped protectively around the body of the Princess, searing the creature's hand and arm like meat cooked over a fire. The demon screamed in mortal agony and let go of the Princess's body, which remained floating in the air wrapped in the light of the eight pointed star. Then it looked at Nimrod with piercing hate filled eyes.

"I have been instructed not to harm you," the beast grumbled in a rumbling voice. "Else I would crush you where you stand. But know favored one - I am of a much higher order than the puny little imp you faced as a child. The soul of the Princess was bequeathed to us! We shall not be denied!"

With that, the demon raised his large claw and spoke a strange word in its own language. Suddenly a ghostly apparition, the exact duplicate of the form of Princess Hamash rose from her body. But unlike her body which was asleep, the spirit of Princess Hamash screamed in mortal terror.

"Help me Nimrod!" She cried. "Don't let them take me! Save you me Nimrod! Help me pleeese!"

Nimrod found he was totally confused. He could perceive the Princess's body wrapped in the protective light, but her voice coming from somewhere else indicated that she was still in danger. Then Nimrod realized: The creature had snatched her living essence, her soul!

"Leave her alone creature," Nimrod cried. "She is under the protection of the creator! Let her be!"

Clutching the struggling spirit of the Princess to its chest, the demon tossed its horned head back and laughed heartily.

"Haaa ha, ha, ha ha! Ahh, but this is rich," the demon chuckled as it walked through the portal carrying the struggling spirit of Nimrod's friend. "Perhaps one day you shall learn how to protect the real prize little priest, but that day is not today."

As the portal closed behind the demon, Nimrod could hear the final horrified screams coming from the spirit of Princess Hamash. And the sound pierced his heart like a sword. Though he ran forward and caught her body when the sacred light dissipated, though he could feel her heartbeat and perceive that she was still breathing, Nimrod knew that he had failed. Moments later when the king, Elder Eshri and other guards arrived, they found him sitting on the floor hunched over, her limp body in his lap. Wailing to the creator, he was shaking uncontrollably and his nose ran profusely. As he rocked back and forth holding the spiritless shell of his first true friend, Nimrod cried for the first time he could remember. His grief was boundless, his despair too large to measure. He cried endless dry tears through the night.

Ginbrak, the Meshkem assassin, sat beneath a starry sky before an open fire behind a hill near a small human settlement. He was grasping a sharpened stick that was getting too hot for a normal human to keep holding, but he barely noticed the sizzling temperature. He was a Meshkem, once a willing human who volunteered to be infused with demonic strength and skin like armor. It was hard to cut a Meshkem, even harder to kill a Meshkem due to their strength and hide, so the heat meant nothing to him.

Tossing the stick so that it spun around, he caught it to rotate the leg of the man he had just caught and killed over the fire. Though he had been turned nearly 3 decades ago, after making a pact with demonic forces to achieve victory over an enemy and gain hundreds of years of life, he still had not acquired a taste for raw meat. Human meat was good, as any of his Meshkem brethren would attest to, but raw human could not beat the smoky flavor of roasted, at least not to Ginbrak. The other Meshkem who dwelled along with him in their dark underground holes had teased him about cooking his meat, until he killed one of the taunting fools and ate him. As was their way, everyone joined in on the feast. The Meshkem never let meat go to waste, even if it came from another Meshkem.

Ginbrak grasped the stick in his clawed, lizard like hand and flipped it again. Though the promise of especially succulent meat from a sacredly gifted youth was enticing, he hoped this latest assignment given to him by his master, the demonic Flame Lord, would finally bring him more of a challenge. Ginbrak was a feared warrior before he was turned, with few who could stand against him. And as a Meshkem no opponent had lasted for more than a few seconds, which quickly became boring for one who lived for battle. This was why he gladly accepted the boon of fetching the phoenix egg. Ginbrak was convinced that the Flame Lord could turn the infant phoenix bird into a monstrous minion for their cause. He just hoped this Nimrod youth proved as challenging as they said he might be. Ginbrak loved a bit of sport before a meal.

Nimrod and his servant Ulli walked the red carpet leading to the throne once again. But this time there was no whispering, no murmuring from the courtiers. In the days since Princess Hamash's demonic abduction, a somber mood, like a dark cloud that threatened never to dissipate, had fallen over the entire castle, especially the throne room. And especially over King Shamshi, who sat upon his throne this day as if it were made of thorns. As Nimrod and Ulli bowed before him, he shoved a cloth he had been crying into behind him and straightened in his seat of power. His eyes were red from days of grieving over the spiritless shell of his beloved little girl.

"Nimrod step forward," the king ordered.

"Yes sire," Nimrod replied, rising and approaching the throne.

"No one loves my daughter more than I do, but you come close in your devotion to her," Shamshi said.

"You speak the truth my king," replied Nimrod, stifling a sniffle of sadness.

"Because of this I shall ask of you a task most dangerous. I have discovered a way to return my daughter's spirit to her body..."

"Truly?" Nimrod asked excitedly. "Can such a thing be done?"

"It can Nimrod. And it will, when you bring me a phoenix egg from the hidden Valley of the Sun!"

Both Nimrod and Ulli gasped. What the king spoke of was considered a mere legend. King Shamshi beckoned a scribe to come forth and took an inscribed tablet from him. Turning it over in his hands, he looked at it, then beckoned Ulli forward and gave it to him.

"This map cost me a fortune to acquire," the king declared. "But acquire it I did for the sake of my poor daughter. Follow the directions and at the rise of the next full moon the path to the hidden valley will be revealed. Only one of pure heart can get the phoenix egg, and you, Nimrod, are the only such person I know. I shall send a small contingent of warriors with you. Bring back the egg Nimrod. Save my daughter."

Nimrod took the map from Ulli and ran his hands over it. One side carried written instructions, while on the other side a map was carved into the baked clay.

"For your daughter and my friend, King Shamshi," Nimrod replied with conviction. "It shall be done. I shall come back with the egg or I shall not return alive."

With a final bow, Nimrod and Ulli turned and strolled from the throne room, down the long halls and out of the castle. Outside a contingent of 15 warriors awaited and they began their march to the east, towards the mountains that were said to surround a legendary hidden valley. In stories told since the beginning of Haltamti, the Valley of the Sun was said to be the source of immense power and spiritual awakening. It was a place where holy men and women were said to be drawn to by the creator to be given gifts and prepared for quests of glory. It was said that no man could find the valley, but must be spiritually drawn to it by the creator. How King Shamshi acquired a map to it was a mystery, but Nimrod was not concerned with that. Getting the phoenix egg was the only thing he cared about.

After several days march, they found themselves where the map had ultimately guided them, standing before a steep cliff that went up to the clouds. A beautiful, sparkling lake lapped at the bottom of the cliff and they seemed to be at a dead end. But the cryptic instructions on the map told them to wait for the rise of the full moon. So they made camp, set a watch detail and settled down to rest. Nimrod, who had set the pace for the march, was especially tired, and laid down for a much needed rest. Hours later, he was shaken awake in the light of the full orb they had awaited.

"Master," Ulli cried. "Wake up! You have to see this!"

Nimrod leapt to his feet clicking his tongue to perceive what was happening. Ulli was pointing to the area where the lake met the cliff, along with several other warriors who were awake. Nimrod had to concentrate hard and click several times to convince himself that what he perceived was indeed real. Somehow the water was dammed off, as if an invisible wall held it back for several feet away from the cliff. Just off the shore there was a set of stairs and a stone carved pathway leading from the shore, across the bottom of the lake and to a large cave below the water line. This cave apparently would lead them through the mountain and, according to the instructions on the map, to the hidden Valley of the Sun.

"We have our pathway!" Nimrod shouted to the warriors around him. "Let us get through it!"

Though they all found it strange and disconcerting, the warriors lit torches and followed Ulli and Nimrod onto the lake bottom, staring at the shimmering wall of water that threatened to come crashing down upon them at any second. Walking up another set of stone stairs leading into the cave, they came to a strange tunnel that had apparently been carved many ages ago, perhaps before the lake was even formed.

After the last of the warriors filed through, a bulky dark figure with catlike eyes detached itself from the shadows near the trees along the shore and silently followed them. Careful to keep his distance, Ginbrak blended into the darkness as he stalked the warriors through the mountain.

Large spike-like formations hung from the ceiling of the cave, which gave off a strange green glow that everyone could see but Nimrod. As for the blind young man, his perceptions ranged far beyond the abilities of his fellow warriors. Clicking his tongue with great concentration revealed many creatures lurking in the side tunnels and hiding behind rocks. Most of them were small, about the size of rats, but some were larger, around the size of dogs. Nimrod sensed hunger coming from the creatures, but much fear also, which is what held them at bay and kept them from attacking. He saw no need to frighten his men, so he did not warn them specifically of the animals as they spent the next several hours trudging through the tunnel. Instead Nimrod simply instructed them to stay ready and alert.

Ginbrak, pacing the warrior party in the darkness, was a single target walking alone, and thus incurred the wrath of an especially bold, large creature from the shadows. With the face of a bat and a body similar to a panther, it leapt at the Meshkem out of the darkness. Ginbrak, with his Meshkem eyes especially formed for seeing in the dark, saw it coming and offered the creature his forearm to sink its teeth into. Snarling and shaking it head, it tried to grind through his scaly, thick hide to get at some meat. But its teeth could not break the Meshkem's skin.

"My turn," Ginbrak said in a growling whisper.

Drawing the stubborn creature towards his own sharply fanged maw, he seized its muzzle to silence it with his other hand and tore through the beast's throat with one bite. Ginbrak liked the flavor, finding that it almost tasted roasted, and pulled the creature in tight to feast. Tearing through the leathery hide, the Meshkem chomped with relish. After eating through the neck and part of its shoulder, Ginbrak tossed down the remains of his lunch and kept going. The other creatures that would have followed the hapless beast to join in on the kill faded back into the shadows. It was clear that a superior predator had come among them, so they watched Ginbrak leave with fear and respect. Then they crept out to eat the rest of what he left behind.

The torches had begun to burn down after several hours of tromping through the tunnel, when suddenly light appeared. Hustling forward with happiness to be out of the dank interior of the mountain, they emerged into the light of day. Nimrod was the first to perceive what the rest of them saw after their eyes adjusted: They had come into a valley of immense beauty. Vast greenery speckled with colorful flowers and giant majestic trees were everywhere. The air they breathed was the most wonderfully fragrant and fresh any of them had ever experienced, and colorful birds and insects flitted through the air. After taking in this breathtaking sight, the sound of water cascading over rocks lured them around the corner of the rock face they emerged from and they found themselves on the bank of a sparkling river.

In the distance they could see the beautiful snow-capped mountain from which the river sprang. Nimrod checked the map, which explained where they had emerged and where to go next, and they began to follow the water to its source. According to the notes on map, this mountain rose up from the very head of the valley and was one of the most sacred places known -- the Mountain of the Phoenix. Just then, as if on cue, they all heard a tremendous, beautiful and very melodious cry from the sky. Looking up, they saw a huge bird. It swooped down from on high and circled above them, revealing its shocking beauty and immense power for all to see.

The bird's body was perhaps the length of a large man's leg, and its wingspan wider than a man was tall. That alone was impressive, but it was the birds shining yellow-gold and silver-gold feathers that stole away the breath. Even Nimrod could perceive the stunning hues, not as the colors that everyone else saw, but as pulses of spiritual light similar to the light he could perceive coming from the eight pointed medallion when he employed it against demons. The bird dipped its wings and came in for a closer look at them, causing them all to feel a wave of sacred power rush over them like a waterfall. Everyone, including Nimrod, suddenly felt unworthy to be in the presence of the majestic creature, and fell to their knees. Some of the warriors began to cry and cover their heads, while Nimrod's medallion began to glow and rise from his chest.

As the phoenix bird made a final circular pass above them, the medallion jerked tight upon its chain and spun around Nimrod's neck, hovering in the air and pacing the bird above. Then, just as suddenly as it came, the astonishing bird flapped its wings, let out another soul shaking cry, and shot straight into the glowing light of the sun to disappear. Nimrod's medallion dropped back onto his chest and everyone slowly began to get to their feet. Ulli got up from the ground wiping tears from his eyes. Shaking his head, he looked at Nimrod doubtfully.

"How, master," the stupefied young mountain man asked, "do you intend to take an egg from such a creature?"

"Yah will provide," Nimrod replied, his hand resting on the medallion.

As the party began walking along the bank of the river once again, Ginbrak cowered in a dark crevasse near the tunnel that led them though the mountain. Covering his bleeding ear holes due to the sacred cry of the phoenix bird, he realized that he had narrowly escaped with his life. Had the wretched bird detected him sneaking across the field to follow Nimrod and his party, he would have no doubt been torn apart. The Fire-Lord had warned him to beware the flying protectors of the Valley of the Sun, about how they lived to destroy creatures such as the Meshkem, and he had secretly scoffed. But now, after experiencing the cry of the phoenix and feeling a mere brush of its sacred power, he was convinced.

Ginbrak decided he would stay in the tunnels. There, safely hidden in the darkness, he would lay in wait for Nimrod's party, amusing himself with hunting more of those tasty tunnel creatures, perhaps even influencing them with his Meshkem abilities to attack Nimrod's men. Then, after the spy accompanying Nimrod handed over the egg, he would kill them all and take his leave from this terrible sacred place.

After many hours Nimrod and his party came to the foot of the mountain, where a moderate sized village had sprung up. There was no mention of this on the map, but when they saw the waving banners depicting a phoenix bird carrying a spear, they all knew who lived there. It was another of the legends about the enchanted valley come to life. They would soon meet the famed Protectors of the Phoenix.

As they approached the village, a large contingent of Kushite warriors, perhaps 100 or more, emerged in formation and marched towards them. The warriors with Nimrod grew tense and placed their hands upon their weapons, until Nimrod shouted:

"Stand down all of you!"

Nimrod's men stood at ease, observing the strangely clad warriors arrayed before them. They all wore skirts and sashes made of an unfamiliar cloth that matched the colors of the phoenix bird. All carried spears that seemed to be tipped with gold, along with golden edged short swords and daggers. Several of them carried the phoenix banners and they all stood silently, seemingly waiting for something. Just as Nimrod was about to step forward, the warriors parted and a tall, white haired priest strode towards them.

The man's pitch dark skin was lined with age and he wore a long robe glittering in the colors of the phoenix bird. A brilliant silver-gold feather stuck up from the back of his head, shoved into a cloth that was tied around his eyes like Nimrod's. As he walked closer, Nimrod and everyone in their party gasped. The priest was apparently like Nimrod, physically blind, but with apparent gifts of extraordinary perception.

"Greetings visitors," the priest declared.

"Greetings great priest," Nimrod replied. Bowing low, he signaled to Ulli and the rest of his party and they did the same. "We have come to see the Mountain of the Phoenix, so that we may assure those back home that the world still has sacred places."

"Ha!" the priest snorted. "You are here to steal a sacred phoenix egg, as so many have tried to do before you."

Nimrod tried to hide the panic he was feeling at how easily the priest saw through him. He did not know what to say and started to stammer.

"But, I, but…"

"No need to insult me with lies Nimrod," the priest went on. "The phoenix you saw looked into your souls and told us of you. All save you, Nimrod, cannot pass."

"Good priest, how do you know my name?"

"When one with your potential is born anywhere in the world we know of it," the blind priest replied. "And so do the earthly emissaries of the creator, the great phoenix birds."

Suddenly Nimrod dropped down to one knee.

"If you know what is in my heart, then you know that my purpose for wanting an egg is pure…please help me."

"Indeed your purpose is pure," the priest said, turning to Ulli. "But the purposes of others are not."

Nimrod turned towards Ulli.

"What is he speaking of servant?"

Ulli gulped as his eyes shifted back and forth.

"I, uh, don't know what he is speaking of…"

"We care nothing about the deceits that led you here Nimrod," the priest said, waving his hand dismissively. "We only care about your test of destiny."

Nimrod took a step back.

"Test?" he asked. "What test?"

"Go up the mountain," the priest replied. "Seek the great grandmother bird and ask her for her egg. But be warned: If you are found wanting she will kill you instantly, and even if you acquire the egg, your initiation afterwards may make you wish you had not."

Nimrod bowed his head in thought for a moment.

"Since you know what is in my heart, if I do survive the initiation, will I be given the power to save my friend?"

"Perhaps," the priest replied. "But know that whatever happens, the gifts you will receive are not for personal gain, personal glory, or even personal love. They will be for the greater good of mankind and for the work of Yah, the name you call the creator."

"I understand," replied Nimrod thoughtfully. "And I am ready."

"Then step forward Nimrod!" the priest cried. "You must appear before the great bird naked, just as the creator made you, to ensure you carry no other influences."

Nimrod stepped in front of the priest, who then took his weapons and his medallion. Then the priest removed his clothing and handed them to an assistant. A large cup of milk was passed to Nimrod by a nearby assistant. He gulped it down heartily, finding it sweeter than any he had ever tasted. Then the priest stepped close to him.

"The milk from our sacred cow is like no other. It will help raise your spirit, giving true declarations power and instantly revealing all lies." the elder declared. "Now, prepare to receive the feather!"

The priest then reached up and plucked the feather from his headband. Holding it before Nimrod's face, it began to glow. Clicking his tongue, Nimrod perceived it as a hand sized bolt of golden light, with waves of power radiating from it.

"This feather shall be your totem as you make your way up to the nest. It shall serve as your protection against the fearsome guardians of the mountain. But since you are not yet totally pure, it shall burn. You will not be harmed, though the pain may be too much. Are you ready?"

Nimrod bowed and held out his hand.

"I understand. I am ready!"

The priest put the feather in his hand and it felt like fire. Everyone nearby saw a blue flame flare up in his palm as Nimrod winced and groaned. When the flame died down Nimrod's hand seemed untouched, though it was clear he was in terrible pain.

"Embrace the pain! The sacredness burns through your sins! Do not let go!"

"I won't!" Nimrod cried, leaping to his feet, grasping the feather tight. His hand was shaking and sweat poured from his naked body.

The crowd of Phoenix warriors parted, revealing a path that went straight through the village and up the mountain. Nimrod began to run as fast as his legs would carry him up the path leading to the nest of the great mother bird. As he ran, he could hear the spears of the Protectors tamping rhythmically as the voice of the priest cried out:

"You will see many creatures set to protect the nest Nimrod. Hold the feather forth without fear and they will let you pass. May the creator grant that we see you alive once again!"

Naked as the day he was born, holding the feather like a torch in the night; Nimrod slapped his feet upon the earthen pathway up the mountain at a steady pace. The mountain was heavily wooded near the bottom, and it was here that he encountered the wolves. There were many of them, silver in color, with red glowing eyes and snapping jaws. But as fearsome as they were, the wolves cowered before the light of the feather and Nimrod continued.

On and on he trotted. About halfway of the mountain, he encountered the Bashmu, horned dragon-like beasts he had heard of in the ancient myths and legends of the region. They bellowed and snorted, scratched at the dirt and snarled, but back peddled when the light of the feather shined before their yellow eyes.

Hours went by, as Nimrod encountered one creature after another from the sacred lore of the ancients. Some were giant versions of creatures like scorpions and spiders; others were giant, strange and humanlike. Still others were composite creatures, like the flying goats and long necked, serpentine felines. All respected the feather and gave way. At last near the top of the mountain, he encountered a creature nearly as legendary and sacred as the phoenix itself - the great white gryphon.

A pack of the huge, milk-colored mighty beasts, with the body of a lion, face and wings of a great eagle, stood before him. There were six of them, and they blocked the path to the summit steadfastly. At first Nimrod held up the feather as he had when dealing with the lower beasts, but to no avail. The gryphons were not cowed. After standing before them, enduring their roars and snapping beaks for several minutes, Nimrod finally simply asked:

"Great gryphons, I beseech you in the name of the creator. Allow me to pass for an audience with the great grandmother phoenix! Do this, and I shall grant you a boon someday!"

The gryphons looked at each other, growled several times, then dipped their heads and stepped back. As Nimrod walked past, one of them nudged him with its feathery head. This sent an image to Nimrod of the gryphon giving him a ride in flight to the bottom of the mountain. Nimrod nodded at the creature and smiled. If he survived his encounter with the mother phoenix, he knew he had a fast way back down the mountain.

On he went, at last rounding a bend onto a rocky plateau. There Nimrod clicked his tongue and perceived a most awe inspiring scene. Dozens of large t-shaped rocks stood before him, stretched out like a small forest. And upon each rock perched a mighty phoenix bird. As he approached they all reared up, extending their wings as if to take off. But instead, each emitted a musical cry. Different notes from different birds blended harmoniously, becoming a sort of song – a symphony of the phoenix birds. At first Nimrod was knocked to his knees as every fiber of his being became infused with the power of the notes. The burning pain from the feather dissipated and Nimrod clasped his hands together, thanking Yah for the privilege of hearing something so beautiful, so healing, and so sacred.

Suddenly the feather in Nimrod's hand began to vibrate, shaking loose from his fingers. Slowly it rose, dancing before him, darting back and forth. Nimrod rose and the feather began to lead him through the forest of singing phoenix birds. Up the feather guided him to the very summit of the mountain, and there she was.

Perched upon a huge nest made from what looked like spun gold, sat the great, grandmother phoenix bird. Nimrod clicked his tongue repeatedly, to perceive her in all of her majesty. She was much bigger, nearly three times the size as all the other birds in her flock, and flared with a light of such brilliance that it would have blinded a person with sight. The edges of her wing feathers looked as sharp as arrowheads and there was an aura about her that seemed very, very ancient. The feather guiding Nimrod flitted up to her, inserting itself among the others that were shining upon her silver-gold breast. Nimrod got down upon on one knee, crying:

"In the name of Yah, I have come to beseech you, the mother/father creator's most sacred earthly emissary. Bequeath me an egg so that I can save my friend."

The mother phoenix bird screeched, and the force of it knocked Nimrod over onto his back. Suddenly he felt a great wind, and then huge claws clamped down upon both of his upper arms. With a mighty leap, the great mother bird beat her wings and they were aloft. Soaring directly into the sun, they flew higher and higher until a blazing white light appeared. Nimrod recognized it as the same sacred light that Elder Eshri took him to so many years ago. Suddenly he found himself floating before the same sacred presence, which he now knew to be the essence of the almighty creator. Once again in this sacred light filled space, he perceived his own spirit as a tiny dot, the spirit of the phoenix bird as a larger dot, and the light of the creator as infinite. For long moments they hovered, until a great voice boomed out. It was the same voice that had spoken his name those years ago.

"He is worthy!" the voice boomed.

Suddenly Nimrod found he was back standing before the great phoenix bird's nest. The great mother herself stood before him, holding a glowing silver-gold egg in her beak. Nimrod extended his hands and she gave it to him. Then she and all the other singing phoenix birds on the plateau below took off into the sky. There they swooped in intricate, overlapping patterns as they engaged in their symphony of song. Nimrod thanked the mother phoenix and her flock. Then, with great reverence, began walking back down the path towards the gryphons, holding the strangely warm and exquisitely hued silver-gold phoenix egg.

Chapter 7: Tool Of The Flame Lord

The children playing outside were the first to notice the great white gryphon swooping down towards their village. Unaccustomed to seeing the mighty beasts come near except in times of trouble or for rare sacred rituals, the children ran to tell adults. The adults ran to the large building situated in the middle of the village that served as their main gathering place. From here the great priest emerged, along with Ulli, the rest of Nimrod men and some warriors of the village.

They all ran to the village square, just-in-time to cheer Nimrod as he descended to the ground, riding between the creature's huge, white, feathery wings. Nimrod leapt from the gryphon's back and bowed to thank it. The feathery head dipped in salute, and then it flapped its mighty wings and took off back to the mountain. Nimrod then lifted the beautiful Phoenix egg above his head, waving it back and forth in triumph, as the multitude cheered for him even louder. The entire village closed in, bathing Nimrod in their admiration, as the Phoenix priest put his hand upon the blind youth's shoulder.

"You accomplished a great deed indeed today young one," said the priest with a smile. "But I am afraid your greatest test is to come."

"Thank you great priest," replied Nimrod. "I do not know what form the test you speak of will take, but I do know that I must get this egg back home to save my friend."

"I understand Nimrod," said the priest. "But, before you do, let us speak privately. I would prepare you in some small way for what may lie before you."

Only Nimrod and the priest went into the great hall, shutting the door on the cheering crowd so that they could be alone. They sat down in chairs facing each other, and the priest poured them both a glass of wine. Waiting respectfully for the elder to begin the conversation, Nimrod sipped with one hand, while caressing the warm Phoenix egg with the other. The two sightless men sat silently for several moments until a sigh from the older priest began the conversation.

"I am called Amin-Sur," the priest began. "I am a Phoenix priest, from a long line stretching back to the time of creation. You too are Phoenix priest Nimrod, if you choose to accept it, and if you survive your initiation."

"Great Amin-Sur," Nimrod began, "if facing a mountain full of fearsome creatures is not an initiation, then what is?"

"Nimrod, Nimrod," Amin-Sur said, shaking his head. "There is no initiation more fearsome than facing the truth within."

"What do you mean good priest?"

"I was once normally sighted," Amin-Sur answered. "I knew that acquiring a feather from the great Queen would entail plucking it from her very breast. I also knew that in doing so the eyesight I was born with would be forever taken from me. I thought this was my initiation, but alas, it was not."

The priest leaned over and tapped Nimrod's chest.

"The initiation was what I faced inside, like yours will be. I prevailed, and was granted the gift of sight beyond sight. You will get such gifts also, provided you survive what is coming."

"So much as happened in my life already," Nimrod replied. "Can you tell me, Amin-Sur, what will happen?"

The priest shook his head.

"Alas, that I cannot say Nimrod," he replied. "For each man and woman is different. I can only say that you will probably face a combination of truth and whatever happens to be your worst nightmare or failure in life."

Nimrod contemplated for a moment, turning the beautiful egg in his hand over and over. Amin-Sur nodded.

"As you suspect Nimrod," the priest said, tapping upon the egg, "it is the egg, or rather the bird inside of it that initiates you. It already knows you and shall bond with you in stages, but the uniting will not be complete until it sees that you care for others more than yourself. Be prepared, be strong and remember: Only one in a generation is chosen by the creator to be a Phoenix priest. It is an honor beyond compare."

"Can you at least tell me what gifts I will be granted?" Nimrod asked.

"Besides the gift of seeing beyond sight, which you have some form of already," replied the priest, "your ability to focus and express your will shall greatly increase. You should manifest the ability to commune with the spirits of the natural world called the "Alu." You will be able to perceive "Anyunwu," the life force of all living things, and commune with "Okonku," the spirits of those who have passed on to be with the creator."

"Do you have all of these things as a Phoenix priest?" Nimrod asked.

Amin-Sur nodded.

"Indeed, and you will also. Provided you survive and do not go mad. In order to insure you have the greatest chance, I ask that you stay here until the phoenix bird inside your egg decides to initiate you. It would go easier if I assist you."

Nimrod shook his head.

"I thank you great priest, but I need to return home as soon as possible."

"Somehow I knew you would say that," Amin-Sur replied. "Just remember: when the initiation happens, hold onto something that keeps you strong."

"I shall remember, great Amin-Sur," replied Nimrod reverently. "But now I think we must be off."

As they prepared to leave, Ulli showed uncommon initiative, suggesting that the phoenix egg be transported in a thick, protective bag of some sort. Taking his servant's advice, Nimrod and his entourage then left the Defenders of the Phoenix, with the egg safely stashed in a sack tied around his waist. Having rested and enjoyed good hospitality, they made good time back to the tunnel leading out of the valley. Indeed there was a kind of jaunty energy in their stride from accomplishing their goal that even the looming dark pathway could not dampen. Everyone was happy, except Ulli, whom Nimrod perceived to be in some sort of distress.

"Is there something you want to tell me Ulli" Nimrod asked about an hour into the tunnel.

Ulli shifted uncomfortably, peering into the darkness of the long cave much more fearfully than before.

"It is just..." Ulli began nervously, "the valley, the Defenders and the phoenix birds. It was all so sacred, so good. I realize now how I have wasted my life... made wrong decisions."

"You can change Ulli," Nimrod replied. "No one is far from Yah's love, if you reach out for it."

"Is that true master? Is it really true that forgiveness can be earned, no matter what a person does?"

"Ulli," Nimrod asked again, "what is it?"

"Let me think master," Ulli replied. "Please, just let me think."

Nimrod wanted to press Ulli, but decided to let the matter rest for the time being. For several hours they trudged through the tunnel before finally nearing the light of day at the end. The warriors cheered at the nearing rays of the sun, and that was when the creatures of the cave struck.

Coming from everywhere at once, the cave beasts Nimrod had perceived earlier suddenly rushed them. Swarming in from the ceiling and side tunnels, they leapt upon Nimrod's men furiously, in a coordinated manner that seemed uncustomary for such primitive beasts. Nimrod and Ulli were surrounded, but not harmed, as the rest of the warriors were torn apart, their screams and cries terrible. As he clicked his tongue to survey the carnage that surrounded them, Nimrod knew that there must be something else going on, some unseen intelligence behind the attack. Just then that unseen intelligence emerged from the shadows to stand right in front of them.

Nimrod clicked his tongue, perceiving a being unlike anything he had ever encountered. It was the size of a man, but had grayish-green skin like a combination of reptile and elephant. It had no ears, with only holes where they should have been. A crudely formed, overhanging brow jutted out over piercing eyes with irises similar to those of a cat. And rippling arm and leg muscles led to dangerously clawed hands and feet. The beast carried a short sword, dagger and spear like a seasoned warrior and spoke with voice of a man, though the tone was that of a beast.

"At last we meet chosen one," Ginbrak growled. "You know what I am here for. Give me the egg."

"This egg goes back with me," Nimrod retorted, pulling forth his short sword. "Call off your cave beasts and face me sword to sword creature, if you dare!"

Ginbrak grinned. With a grunt and a wave of his clawed hand, the cave beasts turned and ran back into the darkness.

"I was hoping you would say that," the Meshkem replied. "Follow me."

The creature led them out of the cave, back across the floor of the lake and to the shore. There it began practicing with its various weapons to warm up. Nimrod handed the sack containing the phoenix egg to Ulli and did the same. Clicking his tongue, Nimrod noted the smooth form and seasoned moves of his monstrous opponent. He realized then that he was dealing with something that had once been a person. It was a man that had become some sort of beast, and that gave Nimrod an idea about how he might defeat it.

"Are you ready chosen one," Ginbrak asked.

"I am," replied Nimrod. "But why do you call me 'chosen one'?"

"Because you were chosen a long time ago to retrieve the egg," the creature replied. "You have been Shamshi's pawn and a tool of the Flame Lord, my master from the infernal planes."

"You lie!" Nimrod cried. "Shamshi sent me here to help save Princess Hamash!"

Ginbrak chuckled.

"You really have no idea do you, young fool? Shamshi pledged his own daughter to the Flame Lord. It is how his family has risen to power for ages. One each generation must be sacrificed. The more good and holy they are, the better and the tastier. Thanks to you, they cannot enjoy her flesh, but I am sure her terrified soul gives them much entertainment."

Ginbrak's words hit Nimrod like a war-hammer. Suddenly many things started to make sense. Shamshi allowing the princess to be trained in sacred spirituality, the tree of life being's dread prophecy, Shamshi's kindness towards him - everything. A rage unlike any he had ever felt before threatened to overcome him, but he knew he had to keep his head. So Nimrod fought the emotion back with the breathing techniques taught to him by Elder Eshri. Then he spoke a vow from the core of his very being:

"I will stop you creature. I will stop Shamshi and this Flame Lord demon also. This I swear by Yah and on the blood of my people!"

Ginbrak threw back his head and bellowed out his laughter.

"Haa, haa, haa, ahh! You, boy, shall be eaten shortly, by me," he guffawed. "And consider it a mercy compared to what the Flame Lord would do to you!"

"I am going to destroy you all," Nimrod shouted, "the whole vile lot of you!"

"Then call out your weapon of choice, young warrior!" the Meshkem shouted.

Nimrod whipped his blade in a defensive pattern before him.

"Short sword!"

Ginbrak charged, letting his spear fall to the ground, simultaneously pulling his own blade. The creature was unbelievably fast, giving Nimrod barely enough time to put up his defenses. Ginbrak pressed him, unleashing a barrage of thrusts and strikes unlike anything Nimrod had encountered before. Making matters worse, this close up Nimrod was able to perceive Ginbrak's armor-like skin much better, and he realized that his blade would not penetrate it. Nimrod's defenses were strong, and he deflected most of the barrage, but found himself cut in several places when the creature stepped back.

"Aaah, but this is disappointing chosen one," Ginbrak said with a grim smile. "It looks as though I will be eating you much sooner than I wanted to. Are you prepared to die Nimrod? Are you prepared to be Ginbrak's meal?"

Nimrod ignored the creature's taunting, instead calling upon the faculties within him that allowed him to communicate with animals. Probing into Ginbrak's blasphemous and vile spiritual aura, Nimrod perceived that Ginbrak's kind was obsessed with meat. Specifically the meat of the goodly priesthood folk they enjoyed preying upon most, whose flesh had a most intoxicating effect upon them. Searching Ginbrak's animal mind closer, he pulled forth a fond memory of a most foul sort: Ginbrak's blissful recollection of eating a high priest from a sacred order several years ago.

As Ginbrak came in for another attack, Nimrod pulled this memory from the back of his mind, slapping it atop the Meshkem's current intentions. Just as Nimrod had experienced with the rats and other creatures, Ginbrak hesitated as his animalistic traits overtook his higher, manlike mind.

His eyes rolling up towards the back of his head, Ginbrak moaned in pleasure, smacking his lips at the memory of eating the priest. With his concentration greatly diminished, the Meshkem's grip upon his sword loosened, and Nimrod stepped forward and seized it. Reversing the blade, Nimrod forsook all mercy, thrusting it to the hilt through the middle of the beast's chest. As he suspected, the weapon was specially crafted for these ferocious creatures to fight each other, so it was far more effective than his own blade would have been. Ginbrak fell to the ground, moaning and shaking in pain.

Just as Nimrod was about to turn and beckon Ulli to hand him the egg, he felt a tremendous blow to his head and found himself crumbling to the ground. Barely conscious, he perceived Ulli running past him, right over to the creature he had just defeated. To his horror the beast was getting up, pulling the sword from its chest, with Ulli helping it to its clawed feet. Nimrod's pain shaken mind swam with confusion at the scene before him: Ulli was handing the sack containing the phoenix egg to the horrible creature!

"Thank you," the Meshkem said. "You have done well for us Ulli, so Shamshi and the Flame Lord instructed me to reward you."

"Truly?" Ulli said smiling, "is the gold nearby?"

Ginbrak grinned evilly, pulling his arm back as if reaching for something behind him. Then, in a lightning fast and brutal move, the Meshkem thrust his claw forward into Ulli's chest. The sound of claws penetrating cloth and flesh, and then breaking through bone was sickening. Ulli screamed in blood curdling, terrified pain, and then went limp and silent. After a moment of rummaging around, the Meshkem at last pulled forth Ulli's heart, letting his body drop to the ground. Then Ginbrak dipped to pick up his spear using the clawed hand that held the sack, and began walking towards the barely conscious Nimrod. He strode over casually, biting into Ulli's\ heart like a ripe apple.

"You know Nimrod," the Meshkem began, chewing thoughtfully and swallowing, "no one has ever hurt me before. Not since I became a Meshkem. If I still had a heart, I would indeed be dead, instead of enjoying this fools heart as an appetizer. You were a worthy challenge chosen one, and I shall salute you as I feast on your roasted flesh."

Though Nimrod's head throbbed badly, he ground his teeth and struggled to get up. But Ginbrak slammed his foot down on his chest, pinning him to the ground. Finishing Ulli's heart with a final bite, chew and swallow, the Meshkem plucked the spear from his other claw. Twirling it around to point the blade at Nimrod's chest, he reared back for the thrust. But suddenly the sack in his other hand shook violently and a blinding golden light exploded from it.

Ginbrak's head flew back, the spear falling from his quivering grasp, as he screamed so loudly it hurt Nimrod's ears. Then, his face contorted in shock, the Meshkem lifted his other arm, only to find a charred, smoking nub burned to the elbow. His catlike eyes grew even larger when he saw what rose before him.

There, hovering in the fading light between Ginbrak and his intended prey flapped a tiny phoenix bird. Opening its golden beak, it let forth a melodious cry, causing the Meshkem to scream once again. Then, with an anguished moan, the monstrous being turned tail and ran. His legs a blur, Ginbrak dashed away as fast as he could through the nearby forest, howling in pain and clutching his burned up stump.

The tiny phoenix bird, about the size of a sparrow, flapped slowly over to Nimrod, finally landing upon his chest. Then it leaned over and a tiny tear dripped from one golden eye, splashing onto the area above Nimrod's heart. This sent waves of ecstasy coursing through his body, and Nimrod's throbbing head and cuts healed instantly. Even his empty eye sockets felt as though they were being filled again, while one word shouted in his mind:

"Allalu!"

The bird told Nimrod its name, and for a moment, caused him to experience pure, unbridled joy. But then the dark images that had flashed through Nimrod's mind many times came back again. Much stronger and clearer, this time they were accompanied by the meaning that had eluded the blind youth for most of his life. As the little phoenix bird flitted away and took off for the setting sun, Nimrod's blocked memories came rushing back to him. Thus began Nimrod's descent into the lowest depths of loss and pain. Thus began the horror of Nimrod's initiation.

3-year-old Nami-Tu-Tu was puzzled by the urgency and nervousness of his parents. All the servants had fled the palace for some reason, leaving the king and royal family to fend for themselves. But instead of doing the normal things he had seen the servants doing, like cooking or cleaning, or getting him food, Nami's parents seemed to be preoccupied with packing bags with belongings. He had tried to get their attention several times, but they kept telling Ekur-Sin, his 12-year-old brother, to pull him out of their way. Ekur dragged his little brother into the room they shared and instructed Nami to gather his belongings. Finally the child put his foot down, refusing to budge.

"Ekur, why aren't we getting food?" the little brown skinned, bright eyed child asked his older brother.

Ekur-Sin was bent over the side of his bed, gathering items that belonged to him and his brother and stuffing them into a medium sized sack. He finally looked up at Nami with a sigh, trying to decide how to explain things to him.

"Nami, we'll eat later, after we get safely away from the palace," he told his little brother.

"But I'm hungry now!" the little boy pouted. "Why do we have to leave anyway?"

"Because, it is not safe for us here anymore."

"But why?"

Ekur put the sack down and stooped down to get eye to eye with Nami. He was nearly 10 years his brother's senior and much bigger than Nami, but always tried to reach him on his level. He placed his hands on his little brother's shoulders.

"Look Nami. We lost the war. Remember the bad people that father spoke about who wanted to take our land?"

"Yes. But father said he would chase them away. Father said..."

"I know what he said, Nami." Ekur interrupted. "But he could not chase them away. The mountain people were too strong. And some of our people helped them. They are coming to hurt us now, so we have to get away."

"But why?"

Ekur-Sin rose and cuffed Nami on the side of his head sharply. Nami's eyes filled with tears and he turned to run from the room. But Ekur grabbed him forcefully.

"I'm telling!" Nami cried, sniveling.

"Look Nami, I don't have time to…"

Just then they both heard a loud crash, followed by the sounds of many men fighting.

"We are out of time!" Ekur cried, seizing Nami by the hand.

Pulling his little brother along, Ekur-Sin ran down a long hallway, and into a room near the rear of the castle. The sounds of the battle were getting closer and closer as he looked down from a window at the vacant rear court near the stables. Swords clashed around the corner in the very hallway they just came from.

"I want mother and father!" cried little Nami.

"Forget about them for now," Ekur said, shaking his brother's shoulders. "They told me to get you away from here no matter what. And that is exactly what I intend to do!"

"But we can't leave without them!" Nami sobbed.

"We'll come back for them later, I promise," Ekur lied.

Looking down from the window again, Ekur gauged the distance to the ground to be about two stories, much too far to risk jumping under normal circumstances. But this was not a normal circumstance. The sound of the fighting had ended, followed by the screams of dying people. Ekur knew he had to make a decision then and there.

"Look Nami," he began, "I am going to jump down from this window, then I want you to jump and I will catch you. Remember how we play 'warriors brave'?"

"Yes," replied Nami tearfully.

"Well now we have to do it again, this time for real. Alright?"

"Alright…"

Ekur-Sin could hear footsteps coming their way as he climbed upon the windowsill. He leapt to the ground and rolled, just as his father had taught him during battle training. One of his ankles was hurt, but he could stand upon it. Limping over, he placed himself under the window.

"Jump Nami!" he cried.

Nami was still very small, and pulling himself up to the windowsill was harder than he thought it would be. He heard footsteps just outside the door when he finally threw his legs over. Looking over his shoulder, he spied mean looking, white skinned men bursting into the room and he hesitated for a moment. Glancing down, he spied Ekur below waiting with open arms, but just as he kicked off into the open air, a strong hand seized his shirt, snatching him back into the room.

"Nami! Noooo!" cried Ekur from below.

Nami struggled hard, as hard as a little 3-year-old boy could against the strong arms of a full grown warrior. He bit, scratched and kicked, only to find himself held at arms-length by a laughing, mean looking, yellow-haired warrior in battle armor. The mean warrior's companions looked out the window, spotted Ekur, and began notching arrows to their bows. Nami screamed out to his brother.

"Run Ekur, run! They are trying to shoot you!"

Ekur-Sin darted away from the window with a limping run, diving behind a wagon, then a water trough and a pile of hay as arrows flew past him. Finally he dove into the nearby creek. Tears filled his eyes, blending with the water he swam through, as he cursed himself for a failure. Knowing the fate in store for Nami and any other members of his family that the evil mountain people managed to catch, he vowed to avenge them. As Ekur-Sin swam away towards the river, he vowed to kill every mountain invader he could find. From that day forth, hatred would became his only emotion.

Nimrod was tied up, dragged through the castle, and was soon tossed down on the floor of the throne room with his parents and two cousins. As they huddled together in fear, an evil man they called Shamshi sat upon his father's throne, shouting and pointing at them. Finally he waved his hand and they were taken away to the lower levels of the castle. As they were dragged along, the bad white skinned men kept hitting and kicking them, before finally tossing them into the dark room where the king's wine was kept. There they stayed for many hours. Nami's parents tried to console them with lies about everything being alright, even though they pulled aside to engage in a strange, ominous argument:

"You have to do it, my love," Nami's mother cried tearfully.

"But I can't! I cannot bring myself to hurt my own children..." Nami's father answered, looking at his young son and cousins.

"We cannot let them suffer what is coming. You know what Shamshi does to those who refuse surrender..."

Just then the door burst open and they were all dragged out. The whole family was kicked and shoved towards the room where they stored the wood and created the big fire that heated the castle in the winter time. There they were greeted by more guards and two grim looking men holding sharp instruments. Nami's father was shoved to the floor and stabbed many times, and then one of the men pulled a hot piece of metal from the fire and shoved it into his eyes. Then the king died, screaming as the other man cut his throat.

One by one, Nami's two teenaged cousins and mother were subjected to the same torturous deaths. But when they seized Nami a strange thing occurred. A great terror overcame the men and they could not bring themselves at first to harm him. After an argument, one of the men shoved the heated metal toward Nami's eye and that was when his little mind shut down. Somehow Nami felt detached from his body, as his mind settled in a place where he could feel no pain, experience no misery. Nami simply slipped away, leaving a flesh and blood body housing a person that ceased to be. His body could feel his eyes being burned out, but the personage called Nami could feel nothing at all, could remember nothing at all, could care about nothing at all.

NIMROD THE HUNTER

This place of safety saved the 3-year-old Nami, but could no longer be a refuge for the 19 year-old warrior named Nimrod. All the torturous pain, the burning agony and the images of his family killed before his eyes came back due to the tears of the phoenix bird.

And the horrible emotional agony was unrelenting.

Again and again he heard the screams of his family and witnessed the anguished looks upon the faces of parents who could no longer protect him. Then the images shifted and Nimrod's chest felt as though it would burst with grief as he relived the death of Ekur-Sin, his only living relative to survive the torturous tragedy. From the earliest time he could remember, his big brother had been there to protect, to teach and look after him. On that dark day of death and torture, the sole comfort his 3-year-old mind held on to before it shut down was the thought that Ekur had escaped. Ekur had survived! Ekur would live! Now he had repaid his brother's love by killing him! If only he had revealed himself earlier in their encounter! He was sure now that their love could have overcome Ekur's insanity! If only he had not let his pride and jealousy guide him, then he would have been reunited with his only living relative, instead of becoming his executioner.

Then the memory of Princess Hamash came roaring into his mind, her spirit in the clutches of that foul demon. She had screamed out to Nimrod to save her, and Nimrod had tried. He had tried as hard as he could to save his friend, but he was not strong enough. Her final screams as the demon stole away her immortal spirit pierced his ears even now. Nimrod then cried out, shouting and groaning his anguish to the sky.

Finding the grief and sadness too much, Nimrod reached over and snatched up the sword left behind by the flown Meshkem. As he put the blade to his stomach, he thought of his beloved Enana. Nimrod wanted her to be the last thought he had before he fell on the blade to put an end to all the pain. But just as he was about to lean over and end it, the medallion on his chest vibrated and he heard the words of Elder Eshri:

"Yah loves you little one, no matter what happens or wherever you go. As long as you breath and you live in the love of the creator, nothing is beyond or above you."

Nimrod could hear the words so clearly in his head, it was as if his beloved teacher stood there speaking to him. Tossing down the sword, he got up and started walking. He could not take his own life, which was explicitly against Elder Eshri's teachings, but he did not know what to do. So he trudged through the forest, walking and walking and walking. The moon was high and a strong breeze blew all through the night, which dried up the sweat that Nimrod produced from the hours and hours of plodding. He hoped, as he walked long and far, that he could somehow walk away from his grief, somehow out distance his pain.

As the sun rose Nimrod found himself in a beautiful field of wild blue flowers. The fragrance was intoxicating, the setting alluring. Accepting that his pain was inescapable, he decided that this lovely field would be his final resting place. Instead of violently taking his own life, Nimrod decided to end it by simply doing nothing at all. He would not seek out food, nor would he seek out water. He would simply lie down. Lie down and rest until the end.

 And so Nimrod collapsed amongst the colorful flowers, secure in his mind that he would soon be with the creator. For three days and three nights Nimrod lay there, wracked with hunger and thirst beyond reason. But the emotional pain was still even stronger, so he remained where he lay in the field. As the sun rose on the fourth day no moisture was left to coat his parched throat, his lungs expanded in weak rasps and Nimrod knew his suffering would soon come to an end. Pulling flower stalks down, he wrapped them around himself as a shroud for his both his body and his relentless grief. Then Nimrod breathed deeply, inhaling the sweet essence of the budding flowers as he felt his life starting to slip away.

'I shall die in my nest, and I shall multiply my days like the phoenix.'
Job 29:18

Chapter 8: The Wonders Of The Natural World

As his breath came in shorter and shorter gasps, Nimrod saw a glimpse of the sacred white light that he had stood before with Elder Eshri and the mother phoenix bird. Smiling, he expected to find himself drawn into the light, where he could finally lay his burdens down. But instead of being drawn in, Nimrod saw his family emerge from it. His mother flashed him the smile he thought he had forgotten, while his father looked at him with the stern, yet caring demeanor Nimrod knew and loved. His two teenaged cousins, chubby Adad and his pretty sister Shar looked at him with a familiar, playful twinkle in their eyes, while dear Ekur-Sin stood in the middle of them all with a concerned, yet happy smile.

"Mother, father," Nimrod cried. "I am coming to join you now!"

"No, you are not son," his father stated. "You are going to stay right there!"

"We love you cousin," Shar said.

"But we want you to live out your time on Earth," added Adad.

"Young man, you have a job to do," his mother stated, shaking her finger at him. "There are a lot of people depending on you becoming who you are supposed to be."

"But...but," Nimrod said sadly, "I don't want to stay here. I want to be with you."

"We are with the creator, son," his father declared. "That means we are with you, in your heart, wherever you go."

Nimrod looked at Ekur. His brother's smile only made him feel guiltier, so he swung his gaze back to his mother and father.

"But I killed Ekur," Nimrod said with deep anguish. "I don't deserve to live anymore."

Then Ekur-Sin spoke up, speaking slowly and gently.

"Little brother, it is alright. I was sick. I let the illness of others seep into my heart. But you are different, stronger. You can fight the evil without it destroying you. That is why the world needs you now."

"But I killed you Ekur," Nimrod replied with boundless grief. "You were the last of the family alive besides me and I killed you out of stupidity and jealousy..."

"It was the will of the creator that you kill me little brother. I was too far gone. I would have kept hurting people, killing innocents out of blind rage and hatred. I forgive you little brother. You must stay there!"

"You…" Nimrod stammered, "You forgive me Ekur? You don't hate me?"

"I forgive you little brother, now and forever!"

Guilt like the weight of a mountain lifted off Nimrod's spirit, but the trauma caused by the murder of his family was still there.

"It means the world to me to hear you say that big brother, Nimrod replied. "But what I saw… the pain is too much. The loss is too much to bear…"

Nimrod's father took a step closer, looming over him authoritatively.

"Son, you will endure! Your mother and I did not raise a coward! Get through this and become Nimrod in truth! Become what your real name means: Subduer of tigers! A man of great strength!"

"We want you to live cousin, and free our people," said Adad. "Just say you want to live and the creator will help you."

"How do you know?" Nimrod asked.

"The creator told us," Nimrod's mother said. "Just say you want to live son! Say it!"

Then the entire family began shouting it:

"Say you want to live! Say you want to live! Say you want to live!" Say you want to live!"

Nimrod sighed deeply as his will strengthened.

"I want to live!" he shouted along with his family. "I want to live! I….want… to live!"

Suddenly his family disappeared and Nimrod found his consciousness back in his weak, starving body. He felt a tickling, scratchy feeling where his eyes used to be and heard a hum that grew louder and louder. He also felt thousands of little winds flitting along his body, tickling and caressing his skin.

Reaching up with a shaky, weak hand to inspect the itchy sockets where his eyes had been, he pulled the cloth off his face and was startled by a rainbow of colors. Then he blinked – blinked! - for the first time since he was three-years-old. And, to his astonishment, could feel eyeballs brushing against his eyelids! But as he looked around, he found he did not have the sight that he used to have before the torturous tragedy. As he blinked again to further clear his vision, he realized his new eyesight was different.

As the source of the humming slowly came into focus Nimrod found himself surrounded by thousands of beautiful, multicolored tiny birds. They were humming birds, hovering all around him, their wings flapping so fast they seemed to be floating. Nimrod could see their brilliant colors, though not as he remembered seeing. Now he perceived all living things near him as patterns of throbbing spiritual light, similar to the way he saw the phoenix birds, but not as powerful. As he marveled at the majesty of it all, a rainbow colored bird came close, poking its long curved beak between his lips. There it squirted sweet nectar that tasted the way the flowers smelled. It was delicious, and Nimrod found his mouth opening up for more. The humming birds then zipped back and forth around his face, flitting in one at a time to feed him more of the nourishing flower nectar.

Within moments, Nimrod felt strength returning to his chest and found that something about their humming also soothed his emotional pain. Then suddenly he realized that this was what Elder Eshri had so often spoken of, what his family had just mentioned. It was the love of Yah in action! It was the healing power of the creator, coming not from words or teachings, but from the blessings built into the wonders of the natural world.

Then sounds of little feet coming near made him swivel his head and look towards the ground. There Nimrod saw dozens of woodland creatures - squirrels, rabbits and other small furry beasts, each with its own glowing aura of spiritual energy. The creatures carried nuts and berries in their little paws and brought them close, offering the food to the starving human. Nimrod opened up his mouth and the little paws began stuffing his face with nourishment.

For long moments Nimrod drank and drank. And, opening his mouth for more of the nuts and berries, he chewed and chewed. As the woodland creatures cared for him in the emerging light of the new day, Nimrod felt a sense that life, like Elder Eshri taught him, could indeed be renewed. With that realization, even more of the pain he felt melted away and Nimrod found himself crying, truly crying for the first time in many years. He cried because his heart felt light again knowing that his family loved him and Ekur forgave him. He also cried because he knew, somehow he just knew, that the creator would give him what was required to save Princess

Hamash. He also cried because he realized what was happening was a sign from the creator; that Yah did not wish him to leave the earth at this time and that he had much more to learn. And, as a group of small creatures with stripped fur wiped his weeping eyes with flower petals, Nimrod sensed that it was the animals that could show him the way.

And so he rose.

Surrounded by woodland creatures, Nimrod strode shakily, yet boldly forward, finally leaving the emotional pain of young Nami behind. And sitting on his shoulders, perched atop his head and even riding atop his feet, the animals chattered, each trying to tell Nimrod what it knew of rebirth and renewal. Nimrod decided he would eventually listen to them all, and was about to step into the deep woods with his new friends, when he heard a familiar cry from on high. Looking up, he saw a streak of silver gold flash overhead as Allalu came around for another pass. Tilting his wings with a melodious cry, the phoenix bird looped once through the air, then took off again into the light of the rising sun. Nimrod took this as a great honor, a congratulations from a creature known as the ultimate symbol of rebirth and renewal. So he dipped his head with a smile, accepting Allalu's salute for surviving his initiation.

The animals took him to a huge, partially hollowed out tree next to a babbling brook, and there he made his home. After resting for a week or so, his lessons began. The first thing Nimrod found out about the hidden world of animals is that they interacted with the spirit world constantly. Indeed, animals had trained the world's first priests, which is why so many spiritual orders utilize animal masks and totems. Elder Eshri had described Nimrod as a natural priest, which was why the woodland creatures recognized him as candidate for teaching the secrets of their hidden world. He was a rare human whose ego and intellect did not get in the way, especially in the area of the first secret they conveyed to him about the true nature of food.

The animals taught Nimrod that food should suit the makeup of the consumer and was not for eating simply because one happened to be hungry. The plant eating animals told Nimrod that humans were similar to them in this regard and were not natural consumers of meat. Most humans they tried to communicate with failed at this level, as the animals would try to point out good food for the humans while the humans would constantly attempt to eat them.

So they taught Nimrod more great knowledge, including the fact that most plants want to be eaten, particularly by humans, in order to become one with the spark of the creator inside them. They taught Nimrod to commune with the plant world the way they did, letting the plants themselves speak to him. To his amazement, Nimrod found his food reaching out to him, drawing him to the proper grass, root, nut or berry at the proper time of day, week or month, resulting in a robustness of health Nimrod never achieved while eating meat. Because he turned away from eating flesh forever, the animals revealed even higher teachings.

Confirmation that he was doing the right thing came in many forms, not the least of which was a string of salutes from Allalu. Many times after Nimrod would master one of the animal teachings, the phoenix bird would swoop by at dawn of the next day, tipping his golden wings and emitting his musical cry. Though he never landed during his sojourn with the animals, Nimrod knew the phoenix bird was often close by, encouraging him in his studies with the forest creatures. And this encouragement was often needed, because all Nimrod learned about was not of a goodly nature. One of those things was the disturbing phenomena of the "dark mist."

Concentrating with his new spiritual eyesight, Nimrod noticed that streaks of negative life energy, the lingering effect of animals being violently killed or terrified, gathered like storm clouds in the night air. These streaks of negativity would form dark mists, which could over time transform into whirlwinds of evil disruption, were if not for the simple singing of song birds in the morning.

When the sun rose, it was the melodies coming from the birds that dissipated these dark mists, causing a lightness of spirit to once again descend upon the forest. This interaction made it so that even animals who knew that they were food for predators could live happily, enjoying the moment without worry about the inevitable. Many a morning at the rising of the sun, Nimrod would watch this spectacle of the natural order which was so necessary, yet invisible to most of mankind. To join in Nimrod crafted several wooden flutes, graduating from being a spectator to actively engaging in this mystical morning renewal. Nimrod learned many, many tunes, his pipes mimicking the songs the birds taught him.

Nimrod also found out that the forest predators were the unacknowledged spiritual protectors of the natural world. Despite being depicted in fables as evil creatures, meat eaters like wolves, tigers, lions and bears stood guard against the unseen dark forces of the natural and supernatural world. When negative amalgamations of emotion and disruptive life energy combine with insane spirits of deceased animals or humans, they could eventually take on near solid form and terrify the forest. These evil entities, from creeping wormlike things to hulking, bear-sized apparitions, would haunt the forest, especially at night, in search of weak animals to leach life energy. It was the howl of the wolf, the screech of the owl or the growl of the hunting cat that would chase these beings away, causing them to starve and dissolve into nothingness.

Nimrod was introduced to and taught by each class of animal in the forest, who showed him how to interact with the natural world in a way unknown to most. Nimrod received these teachings for many months as he lived in the forest among its creatures. After 14 moons had gone by though, he realized that the only class of creature he had not learned from was the class of large cats, which in this region of the world meant the tigers.

Nimrod had spotted a few of the elusive felines, but had to beware, because tigers were notoriously capricious creatures. Knowing that they ruled the forest, the huge striped beasts would just as soon eat other creatures as look at them. Even so, Nimrod was determined to get to know one, because the other animals told him large cats possessed the ultimate powers of spiritual protection. And Nimrod wanted to know how that power operated. He did not get to learn from a tiger though, until many months had passed by, after a situation that nearly cost him his life.

One day while meditating near the banks of a river, Nimrod heard a vicious roar and a tiger burst forth from the brush near him. Its eyes were fiery and glazed, and Nimrod could tell it was in great emotional pain. Nimrod remained in the meditation position, his legs folded; hands peacefully placed upon his knees, and tried to communicate with it.

But the creature roared and charged. With no time to get up, let alone run, Nimrod picked up a handful of sand and dashed it into the feline's eyes, simultaneously rolling out of the way. Knowing that peaceful communion with the beast was now out of the question; Nimrod knew he had to find some means of escape. Since the river at this point was filled with sharp rocks and churning white water, diving in was out of the question. So Nimrod ran to a nearby tree and started climbing.

As the tiger shook its head, growling and blinking, Nimrod climbed to the thinner, upper branches, just in case it decided to climb after him. After the huge cat blinked its eyes clear, it sniffed the air, looked right up at Nimrod, and with a roar, bound over to the tree and climbed up after him.

Nimrod knew he was in trouble. Desperately trying to think of something, he reached into the tiger's mind. There he saw the source of its anger. It was a female tiger, whose cub had just been swept away into the river as they fled from hunters. Nimrod despised those who hunted innocent animals, and had, during the course of his stay in the forest, helped creatures to escape death and capture quite a few times. But he was still a human, and the mother tiger did not know that he was any different. She simply wanted revenge against humans for the loss of her cub.

With no other options before him, Nimrod opened up his mind, calling for help from his animal friends nearby. But none of them wanted to get involved due to their fear of the enraged feline. Then Nimrod decided to take a different tact. Reaching out again, he asked his woodland friends to inquire around about the whereabouts of a cub tiger in or near the river. As the tiger inched closer and closer, images came to him of various tigers and cubs, until finally they communicated the image of a scared, wet, shivering ball of fur on a big rock surrounded by water. Nimrod recognized the area he was being shown and immediately transferred the image to the threatening cat. She slowed down, stopped growling, and then looked up at him curiously.

It took Nimrod several more minutes to communicate to the now calm and curious she-tiger that he could help. Then she finally climbed down, bound over to the river back and looked over her shoulder at him. Cautiously, Nimrod descended from the tree and joined her. They looked in each other's eyes, and then the big cat stepped aside and let Nimrod take the lead. Over an hour later they rounded a bend in the river and there, amidst the flowing current, was the large rock, upon which sat a shivering, howling tiger cub. The water was much calmer here, so Nimrod dove in and swam over. Careful not to scare the cub, Nimrod sent images of its mother into its mind. This, accompanied by a roar to get its attention from its mother on shore, calmed it down. Nimrod gathered up the cub and moments later deposited the soaking fur ball right down in front of its parent.

Licking and snuggling her cub happily, the mother tiger looked up at Nimrod, sending an image of a large animal being eaten. This, Nimrod later learned, was a thank you from the perspective of a tiger, meaning good hunting to you. The cub and mother then trotted off into the woods and Nimrod doubted he would ever see them again. But the next day, as he sat meditating in the same spot along the river, the tigers came back. The cub leapt up and began playfully licking his face, while its mother groomed herself and watched casually, letting Nimrod know he had made new friends. It was then he began to witness the mysteries of these feline guardians of the natural world. It was then Nimrod began to learn the spiritual protection abilities of big cats.

The first thing the tiger taught Nimrod was how to move through the forest the way they do, silently, softly and swiftly. It turns out that all cats, but particularly large hunters, had a profound communion with the plant world, with the ability to enlist growing things in their quests to hunt and protect. Nimrod found, to his amazement, that big cats are so silent during the hunt because grasses will bow, a noisy bush will twist and tree boughs will even rise to let them pass. This was because the entire natural world, the plants included, acknowledged them as protectors against beings they called "twisted ones."

The she-tiger trained Nimrod for nearly 6 months before revealing the nature of these twisted ones, both to prepare him and to get her cub ready for battle. As Nimrod learned to cultivate the special feline aura required to enlist the plant world in their stalking sessions, he tried to prod his teacher to reveal more information. He later learned why she wanted him to be prepared well first, due to the danger of confronting the twisted ones.

One day when her cub had attained a size nearly matching her own, and after Nimrod had learned to maneuver like a big cat through the forest, she came for him. Scratching on his hollowed tree one early morning, she woke Nimrod up at the crack of dawn. Then they began a journey through the forest that took most of the day, until they at last arrived at a ravine that wound among some steep, rocky hills. Looking at him with the expression for stealth, she leapt down into the ravine, followed by her cub and Nimrod.

The long gouge in the earth seemed to be a dry creek and it wound like a snake through the hills. Finally they came to what Nimrod at first thought was a small cave. But it was not. Clicking his tongue and observing with his new spiritual sight revealed it to be a portal to another world. But unlike the other portals, Nimrod had witnessed to another plane of existence, this one did not emit a sulfurous odor, indicating that it probably was not a demonic realm. Both cats sat before the portal and began to emit a rumbling sort of purring sound. Just then, a brownish mist swirling around a set of eyes began to emerge from the portal and the tigers roared with great force, but in a different tone than he had ever heard.

Suddenly, the mist-like being seemed to hit an invisible wall that kept it from coming through. The mist swirled and the floating eyes seemed to squint in anger and confusion, as the tigers kept roaring. Finally, frowning down at the roaring felines keeping it from emerging, the invader faded away, retreating back into its own world. But the tigers did not stop. They slowly approached the portal, continuing to roar, causing it to shake and flicker. Looking over her shoulder, the mother tiger sent an image to Nimrod, and he produced a flute from his waistband. Piping with great vigor, in a tune he often used to assist the birds in their morning spiritual cleanse of the forest, Nimrod joined in the assault on the doorway to another world. After several moments more of the roaring and flute playing, the portal dissipated, leaving an ordinary dirt wall.

The mother tiger blinked at Nimrod and nudged her cub, thanking them for a job well done. But then she put her nose to the ground, sniffed around and growled dangerously. Nimrod took this to mean that they had come too late, that something had gotten through, and that now the time had come to hunt. Both cats took off down the ravine, top speed at first, until they realized Nimrod could not keep up. Then they slowed down and he caught up, perceiving both cats glancing at the ground, sniffing the air and growling dangerously.

Clicking his tongue to perceive with more detail, Nimrod realized they were following tracks. But they were indeed strange tracks. Having stalked all manner of creatures at the behest of the mother tiger, Nimrod had never noticed prints such as these. The tracks seemed similar to a small woodland creature he knew, but they were many times the size they should be, capped off by claws more than twice the size of a tiger's. After a while, they followed the tracks up out of the ravine to a nearby cave. Here the tigers stopped to sniff the air while Nimrod clicked his tongue, then concentrated to turn on his spiritual eyesight. Then a most strange thing occurred.

Suddenly a shadowy figure of a pale-skinned man appeared near the mouth of the cave. The tigers saw him and stepped back fearfully. After trying, Nimrod found he could not perceive the man by clicking his tongue. Only his spiritual sight would allow him to be seen, so Nimrod knew he was dealing with a deceased person. His face mournful, the dead man floated closer.

"It took my children," the man said in an anguished, eerily raspy voice.

"What?" Nimrod asked, "What took your children?"

"The thing inside," the spirit replied. "It attacked our caravan in the night. It dragged away many."

"What is the nature of this beast?" Nimrod pressed.

"The fangs and claws render you immobile," the spirit replied. "It looks like a monstrous weasel, but with the hide and teeth of a snake. It is bigger than both your tiger companions put together. It ate all the rest of us. Please save my children."

"Are you saying that your children are still alive inside?"

"Yes, but it will feed again come morning. I can see your spirit warrior and you are strong. Please save my children."

Looking closely at the floating apparition, Nimrod noted that the dead man was of the race of mountain invaders. This was the first time in many months that he had given any thought to the world of men and he hesitated. Then, deciding that politics had no place in the current situation, he nodded.

"I will save your children." Nimrod replied.

The spirit smiled, and then disappeared.

Nimrod found the tigers simply wanted to charge in and attack, but he convinced them to let him sneak inside for a look first. Utilizing the stealth techniques the big cats taught him, Nimrod crept into the cave, which was large and ran back a considerable way into the hill. Nimrod kept going, coming to an area that was pitch-black and imperceptible for any ordinary man. But he had no problem perceiving a huge animal, just as the spirit had described it, lying atop a pile of bones and human offal. It was sleeping soundly, so Nimrod risked going around it to an area deeper inside the cave. There he perceived two children, around 9 and 10 years old, sprawled next to each other. From how they were positioned among dried bones and slippery entrails, Nimrod knew that trying to carrying them out would be too noisy. They would have to draw the twisted one out and destroy it first.

After creeping back out of the cave, Nimrod communicated what he had found to the big cats. Then he cast about, trying to devise some sort of plan. The tigers informed him that the common way to deal with such a situation was to go and recruit other tigers to come and join in the battle, but Nimrod knew that would be too late for the captive children. Clicking his tongue at the nearby hills, he noted how rocky they were and suddenly a plan started to form. Sending the appropriate images to his feline companions, he led them up a hill and they got to work.

Hours later, the snoring monster felt a tremendous set of teeth clamp down upon its leg, crunching down to the bone. Waking up with a tremendous howl, it bolted upright. Peering ahead, it spotted the stripped culprit running from the cave and gave pursuit. The tiger cub raced from the cave mouth and headed for a trail between two nearby hills. The monstrous beast came bursting forth from the cave, roared and gave chase. The bite upon its leg had been a mighty one, as the cub had been instructed to do. But the bleeding limb did not slow it down much as it raced to destroy the creature who dared to attack it.

Suddenly the cub turned a corner, and just as the monster came close to the bend, a tremendous avalanche of stones rained down upon it. Above the beast on the summit of the hill, the she-tiger shoved the last stones down, battering the creature and blocking its way through the ravine. Snapping and growling, the dazed monster turned back around in an attempt to get back to its cave, but another deluge of stones rained down upon it from the opposite hill, burying the monster as it howled in pain. As the dust cleared, the creature could be heard whimpering for several moments, then it went silent.

Nimrod made his way down the hill from which the last deluge of stones originated. Slowly he and his tiger companions approached the stone mound under which the man-eating beast lay. Deciding that if it was not dead, it soon would be, they made their way to the cave. Here Nimrod said goodbye to his feline companions so that they would not scare an already horrified pair of children. With a nod, his tiger friends trotted off as Nimrod entered the cave. First he brought out the girl, laying her on the ground at the mouth of dark cavern, and then he brought out the boy.

For several hours they did not stir, even after splashing water onto them from a nearby spring. Finally near nightfall they began to wake up and the first thing they did was start screaming. Nimrod had to shake them as he tried to get them to understand they were safe. At last they came around, and began asking about their father. Regrettably Nimrod had to tell them the truth. Just as they began to cry about it and Nimrod began to console them, he thought he heard rocks moving. Then he heard a roar coming from the direction of the fallen monster. More rocks clashing and more roaring told Nimrod that the beast had not been killed.

The children heard also and began crying again, until Nimrod shushed them to silence. Casting about for a place of refuge, he noticed a rocky ledge halfway up one of the hills. The sides were too steep and the holds too small for the creature to reach them and it seemed an ideal place to run to. Leading the children over to the rock face, he spoke gently, but forcefully.

"Can you climb?" he asked.

"I can," said the boy.

"I can't climb," said the girl tearfully. "Does this mean you are going to leave me?"

Clicking his tongue to perceive the boy closely, he pointed up the steep wall of the hill.

"Get going," he ordered. Then he turned towards the girl.

"Get on my back," he said.

The handholds were plentiful and they made their way up to the ledge easily. Just as they reached it, a limping, bleeding, but still deadly looking beast came charging towards them. Getting up on its hind legs brought the huge monster only a third of the way to the ledge, where it proceeded to roar, growl and snap. Nimrod took the opportunity to pay closer attention to the creature, noting that it did indeed resemble the small crafty weasels he played games with in the forest, combined with some sort of monstrous reptile.

As he observed the thing, it suddenly dawned upon him why the tigers call the beings they confronted "twisted ones." Somehow the beings that came through the portals combined with Earthly animals and changed them, twisting them into something else. Such creatures would transform the natural order, so the creator gave the role of protectors against them to the greatest beasts of the land, the big cats or "rods" as they were called in the local language. This also gave him further insight into the name bestowed upon him by the creator: "Nim," meaning power or force in the old language, and "rod," which together meant power of the big cat. As the beast below snapped and hissed, Nimrod's respect for the large felines increased, along with his own sense of responsibility. Realizing now why the creator had named him Nimrod, he understood that it would be his job to stand with the natural world against the threat of these unnatural beasts just as the tigers did.

Looking down with his spiritual sight, Nimrod noticed a strange shifting in the aura of the monster, confirming that it was two beings joined as one. He also noticed that the creature was bleeding and hoped it would die before too long, leaving him and the children to go their own way. As the beast finally curled up at the base of the hill and went to sleep, Nimrod and the children did the same, waiting for the next day when the monster, hopefully, would no longer be a threat.

But when the sun rose the creature awoke and began what would become an entire day of menacing roars and hisses. It was a quite a task, but Nimrod managed to keep the two children calm by assuring them that the injured creature below would soon die. They just had to wait it out. And so they did. For three days and nights they waited, and though it was clear the stubborn beast was weakening, they were also. After draining Nimrod's small water flask on the second day, it became clear that the beast could hold out until they died on the ledge. Wracked with thirst, it was then that they began to think desperate thoughts.

After a brief search, Nimrod found two long rocks that fit his hands comfortably. He then began scraping them against other rocks to sharpen them. Many hours went by as he ground them down to sharp points. Then he turned to the children under the light of the full moon.

"We cannot stay here any longer," he flatly stated, looking into their fearful eyes.

"But you cannot go down there," the boy cried weakly. "That thing will kill you."

The girl, whom Nimrod found was much more pragmatic, looked at her brother and shook her head.

"We won't last another day up here with no water," she croaked with a dry throat. "We all die anyway if we just do nothing."

Nimrod nodded.

"That is correct," he said, hefting the sharpened stones. "When the sun rises, I am going to leap down upon that thing and plunge these into its eyes. Then I want you two to run, as far and as fast as you can."

"But it is too strong, even if you stab it in the eyes, it will probably kill you," cried the boy.

Settling down and curling up to sleep, Nimrod closed his eyes to rest.

"I know that," Nimrod replied to the boy. "You two just get yourselves away from here."

NIMROD THE HUNTER

When the sun came up the creature rose. Just as it did each morning, it began a litany of threatening roars and hisses. But this time, it was a little less robust, its tone a little more tired. Nimrod knew what it would do next, as it had done the mornings before. The beast would turn around and drag itself to the nearby spring, water itself and come back to roar again. But this time when the beast turned its head, Nimrod dropped down upon its back, plunging one of the stones right through its eye. The other stone missed and slammed into its nose, cutting a red horrific gash through the flesh and down to the cartilage below.

The creature reared up, bellowing its pain to the world as Nimrod locked his legs around its neck and held on to the stones lodged in its face. As it bucked and shook, the two children climbed down the rock face and took off running, just as Nimrod instructed them to do. But the boy, after running a short distance stopped to turn around.

"Let go Nimrod!" he cried. "Let go and run!"

The creature heard him and swung its good eye towards the sound of the boy's voice. As if strengthened by the thought of prey escaping, it reared up mightily and shook Nimrod off, throwing him against the rock face. The boy screamed, causing the creature to swivel back and forth, looking from the fleeing children to the prey before him. Then, with a swat of its huge claw, it gashed Nimrod's head to the bone, then turned and took off after the fleeing youths.

His head bleeding profusely, Nimrod could feel the paralyzing effects of the creature's claws as his body turned numb. With his back against the rocky wall of the hill and consciousness fading, Nimrod prayed to Yah. Not for himself, but for the two children running for their lives. The children were slow and weak from days of thirst on the ledge, and though the monster was grievously injured, it was faster. The boy stumbled and fell, his sister ran back to get him, and then they realized it was too late. Hugging each other tightly, they watched their doom bearing down upon them. Nimrod perceived it all, his heart about to break, when suddenly he thought he heard a familiar sound. Lifting his face to the clouds, he managed to cry out, though he did not know if what he heard was real or a delusional result of his head injury.

"Allalu!" Nimrod shouted in desperation, "Allalu… if that's really you…please help now! Save those children if you can!"

His answer was a loud melodious cry, accompanied by a silver and gold flash of feathered ferocity streaking down from above. As the monster loomed over the whimpering children, large silver talons tore through its neck, stopping it in its tracks and causing blood to spurt high in the air. Now many times the size he was when first hatched, Allalu banked in a tight circle, swooping around for another pass at the agonized howling creature. This time the phoenix bird's talons, blazing with blue and red flame, raked across its scaly face from side to side. Then, as Nimrod and the children witnessed in utter astonishment, the monster's head burst into flames and quickly burned to ashes. The leviathan's body collapsed like a fallen tree as Allalu wheeled a tight, protective circle around the amazed children. Then the phoenix bird flapped its mighty wings and shot across the field towards Nimrod.

Allalu swooped down, landing on Nimrod's upper leg. Then, emitting another melodious cry, he leapt atop Nimrod's shoulder. With a tilt of his feathered head, Allalu dropped a tear upon Nimrod's injured skull, causing the feeling in his body to return and the gash in his head to heal instantly. Gazing with his spiritual sight into the golden eyes of this sacred bird, Nimrod sensed boundless power, answers to untold mysteries and a profound feeling of friendship. Slowly Nimrod pushed forth his hand as Allalu thrust forth his talons. Then human fingers and silver claws intertwined, sealing their bond as Phoenix priest and Phoenix bird brother. From that moment forth Nimrod and Allalu would always hunt together.

Chapter 9: The Ritual of Empowerment

As the children ran over to Nimrod, Allalu took off into the air. But this time instead of disappearing into the sun, he circled the area and landed atop a nearby hill. The children rushed into Nimrod's arms and he hugged them. Then they stumbled over themselves asking questions:

"Where did that bird come from?"

"Is that a phoenix bird?"

"Why did it help us?"

"How do you know that bird?"

"Does your head still hurt?"

"Can we meet your bird?"

Nimrod grinned and was about to address their questions, when Allalu emitted a sharp sound of warning. Turning that way to perceive what the cry was about, Nimrod heard the sound of many feet approaching from the other side of the hill upon which Allalu perched. Seconds later several warriors appeared.

The men, 10 strong-looking Kushites, were all well-armed, but approached respectfully, their swords sheathed and spears held casually. Stopping a few feet away from Nimrod and the children, they looked over at the dead monster, and then glanced up at Allalu atop the hill. Suddenly they all formed a semi-circle and got down upon one knee.

"We salute you," the man who seemed to be their leader said reverently. "For you are indeed a mighty Shedu, phoenix priest."

Nimrod stepped in front of the children, clicking his tongue to get a better perception of the warriors before him. Each was heavily muscled and carried a bow, a serrated spear, a sword, a coiled rope and a strange curved instrument that Nimrod had never encountered. For further insight he turned on his spiritual vision and was stunned. The warriors had auras similar to that of the big cats, indicating that they were masters of stealth and tracking.

"Who are you?" Nimrod asked. "And where do you come from?"

"May we rise good phoenix priest?" the warrior asked.

"You may," replied Nimrod, "though I did not ask you to bow in the first place."

"We are known by many names in many nations," the warrior said as they all rose to stand proudly. "We are the Capturers, and no one who is not one of us can know where we reside."

"What do you capture," Nimrod asked, realizing the answer as soon as it slipped from his mouth.

"We capture monsters like the one you and the phoenix just killed," the man replied as the rest of his companions grunted in agreement. "We are tasked to defend against leviathans and defeat those who would rouse them."

"Well you are too late." Nimrod replied with a grin. "The, what did you call it...leviathan...is already dead."

"I think we are not late, good Shedu," the warrior said. "We were coming to rid the world of that beast and came over a hill just yonder in time to see you and the phoenix kill it. We have never seen anyone not trained by us do such a thing. Your tactics were sound, and given the right weapons, you could have slain the beast by yourself. We think we were meant to meet you."

"Meet me?" Nimrod asked suspiciously. "Meet me for what?"

The warrior stepped forward and placed his spear at Nimrod's feet.

"To ask you to become one of us, great warrior!"

Nimrod stepped back and concentrated, looking the men up and down with his spiritual eyesight. Never before had he encountered men with spirits as close to the purity he saw in animals like the men who stood before him. Though he did not know them or the group they claimed to be from, he and the men obviously shared a profound connection with the natural world.

"I will follow you good warriors," Nimrod replied, "to see if you are worth joining. But I must first attend to these children."

It took nearly a week to get to the stronghold of the Capturers. During this time they delivered the two orphans to their village and kept going into deep uncharted forests to the east. Allalu followed along in flight, though at times the trees were so dense they could not see him. Nimrod could hear his flying friend's frequent cries though, as he paced them from above. When they finally entered a part of the forest that contained especially huge ancient trees, the leader of the band, whose name was Uparmu, declared that they had arrived.

Nimrod clicked his tongue in all directions, perceiving nothing but forest. Uparmu grinned, tapping his spear three times on the trunk of a nearby tree. Suddenly from somewhere above a large basket descended via a braided vine rope. It was big enough to fit them all and Uparmu and his men leapt into it, beckoning Nimrod to join them. Nimrod did so, noting the sturdy construction of the basket, which was made of vines and interwoven tree branches. The basket rose, higher and yet higher, until it finally stopped moments later. Uparmu and the rest leapt out, onto a floor made of the same material. Clicking his tongue to perceive this strange habitat, Nimrod was astounded to find himself inside an entire village situated in the tree tops. Stepping out, he found the floor, made of crisscrossed vines, to be sturdier than he thought it would be.

This system of vines, blending with the tree branches and trunks, created avenues where children played and people walked to and fro as if they were on solid ground. Their houses, conical structures of woven bark stretched around the tree trunks, were interwoven with the branches and vines also. As they walked along Nimrod also noticed a system of pulleys and vine ropes that delivered water and food. Dozens of small baskets moved above their heads, whizzing along on this amazing system. As the baskets went by sloshing with water, vegetables or fruit, women would unhook them, dip small vases in to draw out what they needed, and replace them to let the baskets move on.

"There is a similar system below our feet for handling social waste and refuse my friend," Uparmu said as he saw the look of wonder on Nimrod's face. "It is all given back to the forest, which then remakes it and sends it back to us."

Nimrod marveled at it all, wondering why this activity could neither be seen nor heard from the bottom of the forest. Uparmu and the rest of the warriors with them grinned knowingly at the look of confusion on Nimrod's face.

"Ahh Nimrod," said Uparmu. "I know what you are thinking. What you are seeing is the result of a sacred pact, similar to the one that you know of between tigers and plants sanctioned by the creator. We protect the forest and it keeps us shielded. No one can see or hear us from the ground, because the forest will not let them."

"This is like nothing I have ever known," Nimrod gasped, "like nothing

I have ever heard of. But Uparmu, why? Why do you live up here?"

"Because often the things that we hunt, also hunt us," replied Uparmu. "We need a place of refuge, where none can find our loved ones. We need a strong society to support us and that society must be kept secret. Welcome to the village of the mighty Capturers, Nimrod."

They walked for a few more moments, then stopped before a large building wrapped around the largest tree in the vicinity. The tree was very huge, seemed very old, as did the building wrapped around it. Uparmu and another warrior opened up a large flap that served as the doorway and gestured for Nimrod to enter. Clicking his tongue, he did so, finding himself in a long hallway leading to a large room. In a moment he emerged into a huge meeting hall, where four men sat cross legged upon mats. The men were very old Kushites, heavily bearded, their white hair cascading over their shoulders in long locks. Each elder held a weapon in his lap. A rope, a spear, a bow and quiver of arrows and one of the strange crooked sticks Nimrod had observed before. There was a mat in the center before them. They bid Nimrod to have a seat and he did so.

"I am Elder Sudruk," the most ancient man near the center said. "And this is the council of the Capturers."

Nimrod dipped his head respectfully.

"Thank you for welcoming me to your wondrous home."

"There is no time for pleasantries, young warrior," Elder Sudruk replied forcefully. "We have heard of your exploits Nimrod, and our friends the phoenix folk told us more while you made your way to us."

"You know my brothers, the Phoenix priests?"

"We do indeed, for we have worked with them during past times of crisis," one of the other elders replied. "We have asked them and they have granted us a boon. We need you, a phoenix priest and phoenix bird, to become permanent members of the Capturers. The need is dire because the activities of those who rouse leviathans have increased."

"Leviathans," Nimrod replied curiously, "this is what you call the "twisted ones, am I correct? The monsters formed from the unholy unions of our animals and invaders from other worlds?"

"Correct," Sudruk said.

"But who would want to rouse them!" Nimrod cried, shuddering at the thought of the beast he recently encountered. "They are too dangerous to control!"

"It is not about control, young man," the third elder chimed in. "It is about chaos and terror."

"Who would want to do such a thing?"

"King Shamshi would, for one," the fourth elder replied. "He and his sorcerers are responsible for opening up portals around the entire region, causing fell beasts to emerge all over the land. We need you and the phoenix to help put down these beasts. We need you to become a Capturer!"

Nimrod stood up. Examining the elders with his spiritual sight revealed noble, shining spirits that matched the atmosphere he had sensed as soon as he set foot in the village of the Capturers. It then became clear to him that the path the creator had sent him down included the responsibility he was being offered.

"I agree to join you," he said. "What must I do?"

"Come forward Shedu," elder Sudruk said. "And receive the tools of a Capturer!"

Nimrod walked over to each of the elders. Each handed him the weapon in his lap and announced its purpose:

"The rope, to bind and control!"

"The spear, to defend and destroy!"

"The bow and arrow, to dissolve and dissipate!"

"The throw stick, to banish and return!"

Nimrod attached the rope to his belt, tucked the throw stick next to it, tossed the quiver of arrows and bow over his shoulder and stood with the spear held before him. He was now armed just as Uparmu and the rest of the Capturers were, with the exception of a sword.

"The tools you carry have the spiritual capacities to enable you to defeat leviathans," said elder Sudruk. "As you train with them you shall become acquainted with the powers they employ. At that time you will truly be a Capturer."

Then all the elders stood up. Touching their chests with their palms and then pushing them towards Nimrod, they saluted him.

"We welcome you Shedu," they all said in unison, "go now and learn to be a Capturer."

Nimrod bowed and left the meeting hall. Outside he was greeted by

Uparmu, who grinned when he saw all the weapons.

"I am to train you Shedu," Uparmu said. "Rest well tonight, for tomorrow begins your life as a Capturer."

Nimrod was taken to another large building wrapped around a tree. It was the warrior training facility and he was put in a room with several boys aged 14 or 15. This, he found out later, was the usual age when men are plucked from their mother's bosoms to be trained to rid the world of leviathans. The boys were very curious, having heard rumors of a phoenix priest coming to train. So Nimrod spoke to the youths for a while, regaling them with stories of his life, and then they all turned to their beddings to rest for the events of the next day.

The next morning they were awakened by the sound of much activity in the village. Nimrod noticed that the commotion was dominated by the voices of women, who seemed to be issuing commands and calling out to men who answered them respectfully. This seemed very strange to Nimrod, who had never heard authoritative female voices being taken seriously in such a way. Emerging from the building along with the boys, Nimrod perceived many people coming and in and out of the meeting hall where he had met the elders. Turning to the boys, he asked them what was happening.

"You don't know?" one of them said.

"He is not from here," chimed in another, "he knows nothing of our ways."

"The women are preparing for the Ritual of Empowerment," the first boy said.

"What is the Ritual of Empowerment? Nimrod asked.

The boys looked at each other and laughed.

"You will see tonight!"

The boys led him to one of several communal eating halls. There they were served a delicious stew made of milk, vegetables, nuts and roots. Nimrod ate heartily, noticing how the young men and women attacked their meals. Looking at the group with his spiritual sight, he noticed how healthy, how strong and pulsing with life they seemed. This reminded him of his own development after he listened to the animals and turned to a life of only eating vegetables. Nimrod noticed a comely, dark skinned young woman with short hair across the table observing him.

"Do any of you eat meat?" Nimrod asked her.

"Meat?" she replied curiously, "you mean the flesh of animals?"

"Why, yes," Nimrod returned.

"Why would we do that? Then we would lose our connection with the forest. The plants and trees accept us as family because we are one with them through consumption. The animals help us because we don't eat them. None of us would ever destroy that bond. It is unheard of."

"The bond is indeed a blessing," replied Nimrod, delighted to be among people like him.

"Truly!" replied the young woman. "You are the phoenix priest named Nimrod?"

"Yes, I am Nimrod."

"I can tell that you hail from the land of the city dwellers Shedu Nimrod. By the way, I am called Lamashi."

"It is good to know you Lamashi," Nimrod replied.

"Have you been paired for the Ritual of Empowerment tonight?" Lamashi asked.

"What do you mean paired?" Nimrod asked.

"I can see that no one has spoken to you about it. Each Capturer warrior is paired with a Capturer woman in order to empower the weapons the warriors use."

"How is this done?" Nimrod asked, now extremely curious.

"Have you ever felt desire for a woman Nimrod?"

"Why, yes," Nimrod replied. Feeling a bit embarrassed, he thought about Enana, remembering how much he missed her.

"That desire is power. When paired with the desire from a woman, it draws the essence of the creator to earth," Lamashi went on. "We know how to direct the essence that comes from the unity of men and women and utilize it for many purposes. One of the most important is the empowerment of the four weapons."

Nimrod's mind was racing. If the night's events involved what he thought it might, it would indeed be an interesting ritual. Finally, he simply decided to ask Lamashi out right.

"Does this ritual involve intimacy between men and women?"

Lamashi giggled, surprised at how uncomfortable Nimrod seemed to be discussing the issue.

"For some, yes, especially older, married people," she replied. "But the power generated by the young is so strong that pairing can be done without consummation, through the dance. Do you find me attractive Nimrod?"

Clicking his tongue, Nimrod perceived Lamashi from head to toe, sensing a comely face with neatly trimmed, low cut hair, thick lips and large eyes with long lashes. And, like many other Capturer women he noticed, a fine curvaceous female form. Then he turned on his spiritual sight and looked again, seeing a thin sheen of beautiful light radiating from her dark skin and a shining, healthy spirit. She was indeed attractive to him and desire for her rose as he answered her.

"You are very beautiful Lamashi." Nimrod said with a smile.

"And you are quite fetching yourself Nimrod," she replied. "Though they are strange with no irises, I find your golden eyes quite... alluring..."

"My eyes are golden colored?" Nimrod asked.

Lamashi looked at Nimrod curiously, and then a light of understanding appeared in her own eyes.

"Ahh, you are a phoenix priest. You cannot see yourself, because to reach for the feather means you must lose your normal eyesight," Lamashi replied. "But I hear instead of a mere phoenix feather, you received an entire bird Nimrod."

"Allalu. He is my phoenix brother, yes," Nimrod replied. "And I would be delighted and honored to be paired with you tonight."

Lamashi looked again at Nimrod's handsome face, rippling muscles and solid golden eyes.

"I would be honored also Shedu," she said.

The boys sitting next to Nimrod, who observed the entire exchange with Lamashi, poked him with their elbows and began making lustful body movements, but ceased their teasing when Uparmu strolled over. The warrior grinned at Nimrod, frowned at the boys and dipped his head in greeting to Lamashi.

"I see you have found your pairing for the ritual tonight Nimrod," said Uparmu. "This is good, but first you must see the four weapons in action. If you have completed your meal, please come with me."

NIMROD THE HUNTER

Nimrod got up, nodded at Lamashi, poked at one of the boys, and followed Uparmu. First they went back to the warrior's house where he had spent the night and picked up his weapons, and then they headed towards the basket that brought them up. Seizing the side ropes, they jumped back in and it took them back to the floor of the forest. Once there they took a short journey through more thickly wooded areas, finally coming to a large clearing with no trees. Instead, there were a series of fenced in corrals being guarded by sturdy looking Capturers. The men wore white, priestly garb and bore whips and long crooks used for herding animals. Inside one corral roamed a dozen beautiful, milky white cows. Nimrod got close to pet a few of them and looked upon the heard with his spirit sight. Gasping in astonishment, he saw they all carried wing like structures attached to the spines like the tree of life being he had encountered with Elder Eshri.

"They are indeed special Nimrod," Uparmu said, noting the expression on Nimrod's face. "We got them from the phoenix priests. This is our allotment from the sacred herd they guard in their secret valley. The milk they produce is the very foundation of our abilities as Capturers."

Nimrod smiled.

"I have tasted their milk, he replied. "I know of its power…"

Moving on, they came to a group of corrals in which roamed a variety of strange beasts, a veritable menagerie of leviathan creatures.

"This," announced Uparmu, "is the Leviathan Keep. Run by carefully trained keepers, it is where we bring captured leviathans for examination, extraction and the training of our warriors. For you to understand, you will need to observe these things for yourself."

Nimrod clicked his tongue to perceive in detail what was going on. In a nearby corral a large flying goat tied to a stake in the ground was braying loudly as it flapped in the air. It kept yanking the rope, threatening to pull the stake from the ground and fly off. Two keepers spoke to it soothingly for a few moments in an attempt to calm it down. Finally one of the men thrust the loop of his crook around the beast's neck and pulled it to the ground. The other priest seized a hold of it and held it tight, whispering in its ear. Then the beast stopped struggling, drew in its wings and began eating grass like a normal goat.

"We found out ages ago that there are 2 or 3 dozen realms from which these creatures normally cross over," Uparmu said. "Over time we have learned the nature of these places and what sort of creatures come forth. Leviathans, with one exception, are always spirits of dead animals from another world that somehow find a portal to our own, where they possess the bodies of our animals and change them. It is the responsibility of a Capturer as a warrior to catch or kill them and as a priest to send these spirits back and ritualize to undo the damage they leave behind."

Nimrod nodded, beginning to understand.

"And the four weapons, they are not simply tools of violence, are they?" he asked.

"Indeed they are not," replied Uparmu. "Observe!"

They walked over towards another corral. This one contained a heard of bellowing creatures with the forelegs, heads and upper bodies of bulls, whose rear sections were the sinewy bodies of very large snakes. The creatures were very aggressive. Charging towards each other, they slammed their heads together loudly, and then their snakelike tails intertwined as each tried to overpower the other. They were awesome and formidable creatures indeed. Several well-armed keepers stood near watching over them and Uparmu approached the keeper standing nearest.

"Please bring one to the training corral," Uparmu told him.

The man nodded, waving his hand to signal the other keepers, and then walked over to one of the strange bull-snakes near the fence and grabbed it around the neck with his long crook. The beast bellowed once, and then calmed down as the keeper pulled it over to the gate of the corral. There another keeper the gate open and the beast was pulled through. Nimrod and Uparmu followed along, as the now strangely calm bull-snake was guided to another empty corral. Another keeper opened this gate and the bull-snake was led inside. Then Uparmu led Nimrod inside the corral and the keepers slammed it shut.

"Ready your spear and prepare to fend off the beast," Uparmu said, "but try not to stab it!"

Nimrod whipped his spear in a defensive pattern.

"Ready!" he cried.

"Keeper let go!" shouted Uparmu.

The keeper removed the crook from the strange creature's neck and pulled it back across the gate. It bellowed loudly as it recovered its senses. Huffing loudly, the angry beast looked around and saw Nimrod and Uparmu. Rearing up on its tail, it bellowed again, and then came stamping down on its forelegs and charged.

Leaping out of its way, Nimrod whipped and spun the spear before him. Meanwhile, Uparmu had taken out his rope, tied part of it into a loop and begun to spin it rapidly. As the circle of rope whirled above his head, Uparmu shouted.

"Keep him occupied Nimrod!"

Nimrod, clicking his tongue rapidly, poked at the creature's nose with the spear butt and retreated several times, causing it to roar in anger. Backing up, he continued taunting the bull-snake relentlessly, drawing its attention away from Uparmu. Then suddenly the circle of rope flew from Uparmu's hand and settled around the beast's neck. With a flick of his wrist, the rope snapped tight and the beast instantly became docile. Its eyes glazed over, it simply stopped and grew quiet. Uparmu, pulling himself close to the beast hand over hand via the rope, looked over at Nimrod and smiled.

"Very good Shedu!" cried Uparmu. "Now notch an arrow and shoot the beast!"

Nimrod did as he was told, but hesitated when he drew back on the bow.

"But it is subdued! Must we kill it?"

Uparmu laughed.

"Fear not Nimrod. It is the spear that kills! The bow and arrow will cause the dissolution! Shoot the beast!"

Not entirely understanding, Nimrod drew back on the bow and fired. Not wanting the bull-snake to suffer in case there was some mistake, he shot it directly in the heart. But when the arrow thudded into the flesh of the beast, no blood appeared. Instead, a light mist emerged from the wound. The mist got heavier and thicker and the creature's body shook violently. Suddenly a burst of light appeared in the mist and the snake portion of its body disappeared, leaving a common bull standing before them with a shifting, smoky being with disembodied eyes floating above it.

Uparmu took out the bent return stick and drew it near his mouth, uttering a prayer. Then he hurled it at the two floating eyes of the leviathan now looking scornfully at him. The stick flew directly between the leviathan's eyes, causing it to screech and howl, and kept spinning on as a small portal appeared around the invading spirit. As the portal sucked the creature in and dissipated, the throw stick turned in midair and began its way back. Uparmu then removed the rope from the bull's neck and it started grazing.

When the return stick spun back to him, Uparmu reached out, plucked it from the air, and poked it back into his belt casually. Then he picked up the arrow that Nimrod had fired and handed it to him. There was no blood on the arrow-head and it looked as if it had never been fired.

"Now you see what it means to be a Capturer," Uparmu declared as he grinned and clapped Nimrod on the shoulder.

"I do indeed," Nimrod replied, as they both heard a melodic cry from the sky.

Allalu circled overhead, observing Nimrod's progress as usual. He and Uparmu looked up and smiled, and for hours that day he was taught to throw the return stick and wield the lasso. They even practiced a few more times in the corral, releasing a few more animals from the possession of leviathans.

Uparmu found that Nimrod took to the lasso quickly, but mastering the throw stick would take some time. Overall though, he was very pleased and judged Nimrod nearly ready to go out on his first capture already. But first there was something else to show him.

Uparmu led Nimrod towards a small corral guarded by 4 keepers that was far away from the other corrals. From a distance Nimrod could tell there was a man-like creature being held and thought it must be some sort of ape leviathan. Hunched over, it sat on the ground with its feet and hands bound. Its eyes were blindfolded and four ropes tied to four stakes were tied around its neck, giving Nimrod some indication of how dangerous the creature had to be. As they got closer Nimrod clicked his tongue to examine the thing in detail and found himself gasping. The creature was almost identical to the beast-man Ginbrak! Uparmu noticed and placed his hand upon Nimrod's shoulder.

"You know of these creatures, my friend?"

"I have fought one before," Nimrod replied.

"The phoenix bird helped you?" Uparmu asked.

"Yes," Nimrod replied. "But not at first. I put it down before Allalu came along, but something happened…"

"You mean you fought a Meshkem alone," Uparmu asked incredulously, "with no assistance?"

"Is that what you call these beasts," Nimrod replied, "Meshkem?"

"Yes Nimrod," Uparmu replied, his respect for Nimrod growing in leaps and bounds. "They are our worse enemies and the foulest sort of leviathan that exist. Unlike the animals, they are men who make a pact with other-worldly forces, mostly from the demonic realms, in a bid for power and long life."

"Yes, the one I fought spoke of alliances with demonic forces. The creature's name was Ginbrak."

Uparmu's eyes grew very large.

"Ginbrak!" he cried. "He is one of their most renowned warriors Nimrod! It takes several Capturers to defeat one normal Meshkem. How did you survive?"

"It is a long story," Nimrod replied. "What do you intend to do with this one?"

"The same thing we do with all the Meshkem we catch. We have offered it the chance to be rid of the demonic influence and become a man again by drinking sacred milk, but, as usual, it refused. We have asked it to reveal the location of its lair in exchange for a quick, painless death, but it also refused. So now it will stay here until it slowly starves, for we shall not feed it the meat they always beg for."

"What will you do if it tells you the location of its lair? Nimrod asked.

"Why, we shall descend upon it in force, make them emerge and catch them, Uparmu declared. "We have developed special ways to flush them out."

Nimrod thought for a moment.

"I think I know a way to make it talk. Take off the blindfold and let me speak to it."

"Nimrod, we cannot remove the blindfold!" Uparmu replied. "Anyone who looks into a Meshkem's gaze can become helpless!"

Nimrod smiled and pointed at his solid golden eyes.

"I do not think this will happen to me Uparmu. I don't see the world the way most do…"

"Ahh!" Uparmu cried. "I see what you are getting at Shedu. But how are you going to get it to talk?"

"Take off the blindfold my friend and you will see!"

Uparmu signaled one of the keepers and he opened up the corral. Then he and Nimrod entered and approached the bound Meshkem. Nimrod got directly in front of it as Uparmu came close to its back and untied the blindfold. The creature blinked several times, and then focused in on Nimrod. Uparmu pointed his spear at its back, ready to dispatch the beast in the event Nimrod's idea did not work. The creature growled and spit, then addressed the golden eyed warrior standing before it.

"You are different from the others," the Meshkem said. "Why must you tempt me with your deliciously sacred presence? Why don't you just let me starve in peace?"

Ignoring the creature's words, Nimrod looked into the creature's mind the way he had with Ginbrak. There he found a multitude of abominable images and became nauseated. Concentrating, he found a memory of it brutally raping a priestess and then eating her flesh. Then he found the memory of the Meshkem being captured and placed in captivity. Concentrating his recently enhanced will, he made the memories so strong that the creature would virtually relive them. Then Nimrod pulled forth the fond memory and slapped it atop the creature's consciousness, causing its eyes to glaze over and it mouth to drool with pleasure. As soon as Nimrod was certain it was deeply engaged by the memory of its foul deeds with the priestess, he ripped the memory away and shoved in the despairing recollection of its capture and current state of starvation.

"No!!!" cried the Meshkem.

Looking into Nimrod's eyes, the creature tried to mesmerize him. Its cat-like irises pulsating, it tried to do to Nimrod what it had done to countless others before they became its meal.

"Give it back!" the Meshkem ordered. "Give it back human!"

Nimrod's golden eyes gleamed with the power of a Phoenix priest, deflecting the creature's abilities.

"You have no hold over me, foul beast! The creator protects me, now and forever!" Nimrod declared. "Tell me the location of your lair and I will give you what you want."

"Never!" the Meshkem screamed, struggling against his bonds. "I'll kill you! I will eat you raw!"

Nimrod gave it back a brief flash of the memory it asked for, and then snatched it away again.

Then he did it again and again and again. Finally the Meshkem's will broke and it moaned in despair.

"Like this creature," Nimrod taunted, teasing him with the memory again, "you want this?"

"Yes! Yes, please," the creature begged. "Let me have my fondest memory back! Let me spend my final moments there! Please!"

"The location, Meshkem!" Nimrod shouted. "Then you can have it!"

Howling in tortured anguish, the creature finally screamed out:

"West! At the meeting point of the two rivers, near the village of Imsu!"

Uparmu prodded the creature in the back with his spear.

"Where exactly creature!"

"There is a graveyard. The entrance is a stone crypt over a grave at the rear. No one suspects…"

Uparmu looked puzzled.

"You lie! Meshkem cannot nest on hallowed ground!"

"It once was hallowed," the Meshkem replied. "But we convinced a priest to curse it, in exchange for not eating his family. We ate them all anyway. No one suspects."

"Uparmu looked stunned and angered.

"This is new Nimrod. If what the beast says is true, the Meshkem have adopted new tactics," he said, shaking his head. "How many are there creature?"

"Nearly 3 score!" the Meshkem cried. "They are powerful! And they have harnessed leviathan the likes of which you have never seen! You cannot defeat them!"

"We shall see about that!" replied Uparmu. "Is it speaking truth Nimrod?"

Focusing on images now given context in the Meshkem's mind, Nimrod nodded.

"The beast speaks the truth," declared Nimrod. "Now I shall give it what it wants!"

With that, Nimrod let the Meshkem relive its foul memory, but only for a moment. Then he snatched it away from him for good.

"Nooo!" the creature howled. "You promised!"

As Nimrod and Uparmu looked at each other nodding in unspoken agreement, the phoenix priest said:

"I did indeed promise, but I did not say for how long, foul creature!"

"May the creator have mercy upon you." Uparmu added, rearing back with his spear.

The Meshkem's answer was a tremendous cry of bitter despair as Uparmu stabbed it. Then they walked away as the creature's body petrified and crumbled to dust.

When they arrived back at the village of the Capturers, Nimrod and Uparmu went straight to home of Elder Sudruk. The rest of the council was soon summoned and all were informed of what they learned from the Meshkem. The elders listened with grim silence, and then dismissed the messengers to discuss amongst themselves and meditate. As they made their way over to the meeting hall, Nimrod asked:

"What happens now?

"It shall take some time, several weeks at least. Scouts will be sent out to confirm, and then the elders shall pray and consult with the creator. They will then strategize with the warriors on how best to destroy the nest," Uparmu replied. "But we don't need to worry about that until the time comes. The moon is now full, so let us go and participate in the Ritual of Empowerment."

Long before they got to the main hall, Nimrod could smell the sweet fragrance of sandalwood. As they got closer, Nimrod perceived a line of women standing on both sides of a pathway festooned with sweet honeysuckle blossoms leading to the hall entrance. The women all wore close fitting green dresses and handed yellow roses to the warriors as they walked in. Nimrod and Uparmu took a rose and strolled inside. As they made their way down the long hallway, Nimrod turned to Uparmu, shook the rose and tilted his head questioningly.

"You give it to your intended for the ritual, Shedu," Uparmu said, smiling. "For me that is my wife Azali and for you it would be Lashami. Now observe closely and do what I do."

When they got inside the meeting hall they joined the men already there, who stood in a circle facing outward and away from a large purple table where they had deposited their weapons. Nimrod and Uparmu joined them, placing their weapons on the pile and turning outward like the others. Outside the men's circle the meeting hall teemed with women, who were all breathing in a strange pattern and swaying rhythmically. All the women wore dresses similar to those of the women outside, only theirs were provocatively shorter and each wore a green sash. The entire place teemed with sensual energy and Nimrod felt it rising inside himself.

Then the women formed a tight circle around all the men. Swaying close to the warriors, they walked by in a clockwise direction, caressing bare chests and faces as they glided by. When their intended came near the men would hand over their rose, causing their chosen partner to stop and sway before them. Uparmu's wife, a beautiful, tall woman with reddish brown skin and long braided hair, swayed near and he handed his rose to her. Then Lashami appeared; her swaying, glistening, coal black body an alluring contrast with her yellow dress. Nimrod smiled, gladly pressing his flower into her slim, delicate hand.

Suddenly flutes and harps started playing, and the women who had not been chosen as intended partners pulled back. These women joined hands as drums thumped out a lively beat. Lashami pulled off the green sash, draping it over Nimrod's shoulder as the other woman did the same with their intended partners. Then the drumming intensified, catching up to the flutes and harps in a harmonious blend, as everyone in the hall began the dance.

Nimrod clicked his tongue rapidly, observing the moves. Each dancer reached into the air, palms out, then pulled their hands down as if washing themselves under cascading water. Simultaneously, the couples wound their hips and thrust them as they approached each other, then the man would reach out, draw the woman in and they would turn sideways to bump their thighs together. The woman would then push the man away, seize his hand before he stepped too far and yank him back close to bump thighs again. Then the couple would turn, bumping their middle sections to the rhythm in a circular pattern, from thigh to crotch, from crotch to buttocks.

The dance was a sensual tease, apparently designed to provoke the highest level of passion without actual consummation between participants. It took a few minutes, but Nimrod finally got the moves of the dance and joined in, bumping against Lamashi's ample curves with passion. Then everyone began a powerful chant as they moved to the music, causing waves of tingling power to rise and wash over them. Uparmu and his wife danced next to Nimrod and Lashami, but after a while Uparmu seized his woman, picked her up and ran from the hall. Nimrod noticed many more couples leaving the same way and it was not hard to figure out how they intended to complete the ritual. After perhaps an hour of frenzied dancing, the hall was powerfully energized, and with his spiritual sight Nimrod could see a cloud of yellowish green force gathering over the weapons.

As the music and dancing intensified even more, Nimrod concentrated harder and witnessed a truly astonishing thing. Inside the cloud of power there were two spectral figures dancing! Each looked similar to the Tree of Life being he had perceived speaking through Elder Eshri, including the wing-like protuberances sticking out of their backs and glowing circles above their heads. One of them, male in form, gave off a purple hue identical to the table upon which the weapons were piled. The other being, a very curvy female, seemed to be absorbing the waves of yellow power in the room. They danced along with everyone else in the hall for a short while, before finally tumbling together in a blatantly sexual embrace.

Rolling around in the cloud of yellowish power, the glowing messengers of the creator humped and twirled, uniting to the beat of the music. Finally the female being opened her mouth in a silent scream of passion, the male being raised his arms in triumph, and they disappeared. Then a flash of light pulsed and quickly faded, leaving behind a swirling funnel of yellow and purple power. Descending upon the tools of capturing piled on the table, the swirling force was absorbed into each and every weapon. Then everyone in the hall hugged their partners and slid down to the floor, totally drained by the Ritual of Empowerment.

"Mightiest of the mighty, hero in battle, let me sing his song!" Sumerian text, 2,000 B.C.

Chapter 10: Mighty Kushite With The Phoenix Bird

Over the next three months as Nimrod became acclimated to his new life as a Capturer; he became immersed in the ways of his new people. One of the most crucial activities was the astonishing warrior training conducted by the Capturer battle masters. Unlike the training he received among the mountain people, the Capturers used extraordinary spiritual means to learn martial practices on levels unknown to most people in the world. After consuming copious amounts of the sacred milk, guided meditational techniques culled from the best of the Kushite lands they recruited from were used to shake the spirits of the warriors loose from their bodies. Then they were trained to leave their bodies to engage and practice fighting skills spiritually. This meant that many more hours of practice could be done than would ordinarily be possible, and with far more comprehension and recollection. It also left their bodies safe as they learned techniques so effective and deadly they could not be practiced in the flesh.

Each morning would begin with milk consumption, prayers to the creator, and then the trainees gathered into a circle for stretching and strength training. Special breathing in a seated meditational pose, accompanied by music and chanting, would prepare the warriors spirits to emerge from their bodies. Two battle masters would then douse a special liquid concoction onto two combatants, who would then leap from their fleshly shells to engage. Ethereal weapons would appear at the commands of the teachers and then the session would begin. As the teachers and other warrior-priest trainees would watch with their minds eye, the most lethal fighting styles Nimrod had ever perceived would be practiced to perfection.

Sword fighting techniques designed to draw an opponent in, expose their weaknesses and dispatch them quickly were taught, with emphasis on what the battle masters called "nicking." This was a concentration on slicing into knuckles, toes, hands, feet and the outside edges of an opponent's body during battle. Most combatants, like Nimrod had been, were trained to protect their chest, neck and other vitals, leaving it fairly easy to nick these outside areas. The brilliant stratagems of the Capturer sword masters revealed that continuous nicking during a conflict aggravated the opponent and could quickly cause a heavy loss of blood, both of which would lead to the enemy's fast demise.

Close contact practices included locks, holds and head butting. They also taught brutally effective throws followed up by groin smashes or eye gouges. Neck, arm and leg snapping techniques were also encouraged because no harm would come to the spirit bodies of the students. It was explained to Nimrod that these vicious combat techniques became necessary over the years due to the deadly encounters with the Meshkem and their enthralled human minions. It seems the abilities of the Meshkem could do much more than overpower a normal human. Over time victims could be transformed into mindless thralls with no concern for their own lives and an obscene obliviousness to pain. In the heat of a serious battle, these Meshkem thralls had to be put down effectively, thus the deadly techniques adopted by the Capturers.

There were exceptions to the rule of immediate, ruthless dispatching of an opponent and these exceptions mostly centered on weapons the Capturers called "mercy sticks." These specially carved, short wooden weapons, about the length of a man's elbow to his fingertips, were used in combat when deadly force was deemed inappropriate. Though they were mostly for non-lethal combat, the mercy stick techniques were perfected in spirit sessions first, in order to observe and strike the power points of the human aura. Because of this, a special sensitivity to the nature of the human aura was best coupled with this weapon, which was an area where Nimrod excelled due to his phoenix given spirit sight.

The mercy sticks were designed to strike at several power points of man's spiritual makeup, resulting in different effects that would not only stop an opponent, but make them face personal truths that they would be forced to contemplate. Striking at the point of foundation near the top of an opponent's groin would leave them temporarily paralyzed and acutely aware of every weak area on their body. The higher point above the belly would leave them entranced and stuck in a flashback of their entire lives, the next point higher and to the right of the belly struck by the stick would leave them in a confused state as words from every conversation they ever had bounced around inside their minds. Striking the point directly on the other side would leave them giddy with happiness and enraptured in joy, while jabbing the mercy sticks to the point on the right side of their chest would cause terrible pain and contemplation of all their sins. But it was the point right near the heart that was the most revealing, uplifting and potentially debilitating. This area, when tapped with the right amount of skill, would open up the capacity in an opponent for love of his fellow man and profound regret for harming others. But this flowering, if an enemy failed to embrace it by clinging to anger and hatred, could lead to instant death or total madness.

Nimrod excelled at the martial teachings of the Capturers, especially at combat with the mercy sticks. Many a time he would leave his opponents laughing, paralyzed or confused due to his innate skills and a special trait from his phoenix priesthood that his teachers quickly recognized. The savvy Capturer battle masters explained that one of the things that made the phoenix birds so formidable was their ability to look directly at the aura of any living being, instantly perceiving its nature and how it would fight or flee. They had this ability because everything in flesh happened first in the spirit, and the phoenix birds, as the creator's most important animal protector, living simultaneously in the spiritual and material worlds. As a phoenix priest, Nimrod shared in this ability; as a Capturer, his teachers taught him how to perfect it in battle.

After three months of intense spirit training with the Capturers, Nimrod and his classmates acquired the equivalent of years of learning via normal teaching methods. The entire class was formidable, but his classmates and teachers alike knew as they watched Nimrod's battle flow, stamina and technical innovation, that they had among them a warrior with no known peer. Because of this Nimrod was chosen to lead a scouting party into the town of Imsu near the lair of the Meshkem. Their mission was to scout out the level of influence the creatures had on the town before the assault on the nest began; to help any thralls who were not too far gone and to dispatch any who were beyond help.

Nimrod chose a team of five Capturers, three of his young classmates and two seasoned warriors, including Uparmu. Paced by Allalu in the air, it took them nearly two days to get there on foot. When they arrived in the town of Imsu, they saw nothing out of the ordinary; nothing indeed that would indicate Meshkem infestation. It seemed a typical riverside settlement, where goods came from upriver and down to be distributed in all directions via land. Thus it had a bustling business district with wagons and caravans containing goods and people rumbling though the street. Sales people at their stands also hawked their wares. Their trip had been fairly long, so they decided to visit the local drinking hall for a stout beer and a good look at the local population.

As they approached the doors of the drinking hall, they noticed a group of Kushite men, mostly older and grey headed, sitting on the steps leading to the door. They all looked up as Nimrod and his men approached and when it became apparent that the Capturers intended to go in, one elderly man grabbed Nimrod's hand.

"What are you doing young man?" he asked apprehensively.

"Why I am getting myself a tall, cool drink grandfather," Nimrod replied with a smile, "would you like one?"

"If you go in there it will cause trouble," the old man whispered fearfully. "The mountain men run this town now. Stay out here with us and drink."

Nimrod looked at Uparmu and they both shrugged. Then they sat down next to the elder as the rest of the warriors took up defensive positions around them.

"So they won't let you into your own drinking house now?" Nimrod asked.

"Oh we can go in, but only to deliver or pick up goods," a tattered looking elder who seemed slightly inebriated stated. "Would you really buy us a drink young man?"

Uparmu grinned.

"We will get you all the drinks you want grandfather," he said. "First tell us of this town."

"Alright," the first elder said. "What do you want to know?"

"Has there been any word of people mysteriously disappearing," Nimrod asked. "Anything out of the ordinary?"

"Oh you speak of the Meshkem," the tattered elder stated.

Nimrod nodded as the rest of the Capturers looked at the elder with wide eyes.

"What do you know, grandfather? Uparmu asked.

"I know that there used to be disappearances and random killings, but the priestess put a stop to it a short while ago. She used her sacred powers to save our town."

"Where is this priestess," Nimrod replied. "We would very much like to speak to her."

"She dwells at the temple of Yah," the old man replied. "Over near the docks. Biggest building in town. You can't miss it."

"Thank you elder, we shall go there immediately," Nimrod replied. "But first, do you wish to drink in this establishment again?"

"We can't drink inside anymore, I told you," the first elder said sadly. "The mountain men won't let us."

"Who owns this place?" Uparmu asked.

"I do," the first elder stated sadly. "At least I used to. But you don't own what you can't protect."

Uparmu and Nimrod looked at each other, and then they signaled for two of the younger warriors to go into the drinking house. Shortly after they went in loud shouting could be heard, then fighting and the sound of items breaking. All the elders on the steps looked at the Capturers as if they had gone mad, and then twisted their necks to stare at the door of the drinking house.

"It's a nice place grandfather," Nimrod said with a grin. "We are going to give it back to you."

A jug flew forth from a window. Clicking his tongue, Nimrod deftly caught it before it hit the ground. Uncorking the vessel, he sniffed it, and then took a long draught. Then he tapped the establishment's owner on the shoulder to get his attention and shoved the jug toward him. The old man smiled, seized the vessel and took a drink.

"Aren't you going to help them?" he asked wiping off his mouth. "There are several guards inside, all big mountain men."

"If they need our help they'll ask for it," Uparmu said, reaching out his hand and wiggling his fingers. "Please pass the brew."

Sounds of more fighting, accompanied by loud groans could be heard coming from the building. Then a large, yellow haired man ran out crying. His eyes were very red as he looked down at the other Capturers, then he bound down the stairs and took off down the street, bawling like a baby. Nimrod and all the Capturers grinned.

"Second point mercy stick strike," remarked the remaining younger warrior.

"Yes, definitely," Uparmu agreed.

Finally the two younger Capturers emerged. One had a man twice his size in a thumb lock that had the large mountain invader walking on his tip toes. Releasing the man's hand, the young Capturer wagged his stick at him, causing the mountain man to hustle down the stairs and run away. The other young Capturer dragged a man over by his leg, dropping him right in front of the elder who was the rightful owner of the bar.

"I think this man has something to say to you grandfather," the young warrior said as Nimrod handed him the jug.

The man, a silver haired, red faced mountain invader, propped himself up on his elbows and looked at the elder. There was a blissful smile on his face as he spoke.

"The bar is yours again grandfather," he replied. "I don't know what came over me to take something that was not mine. My apologies, please."

The elder stood up and looked at the man incredulously. Then he looked at the Capturers.

"What did you do to him?"

"We gave him a heart," Nimrod said. "Or rather, awakened the one he has in him. Good day elder."

As the Capturers walked away they could hear the conversation between the owner and the thief and it made them all laugh.

"Come on in grandfather," the mountain man cried. "Let me help clean up this place for you. And I will bring you all the profits I have made by morning."

"What?" the elder replied. "How much is it?"

The Capturers could indeed see the large temple on the shore of the river ahead. It was a wooden structure, painted white, with the sign of the eight pointed star adorning it. As they got closer they noticed a large garden surrounding the temple, filled with individual flowers and fragrant flowering bushes. As they approached the large front door, a young man in a white robe came toward them.

"Welcome to the house of Yah!" he cried, "I am Kuhunte, all are invited inside for fellowship with man and creator."

"Thank you," replied Nimrod as they all bowed respectfully. "We have heard of a great priestess."

"There are several here my friend," Kuhunte replied. "You wish a funeral priestess, a wedding priestess or perhaps a spiritual cleansing?"

"We seek the priestess who stopped the Meshkem," stated Uparmu, getting right to the point.

"Oh," replied Kuhunte, "you seek Enana!"

Nimrod perked up at the sound of a familiar name.

"What did you say?" he cried. "What is her name?"

"Her name is Enana. Follow me and I shall take you to her."

Nimrod did not dare hope it was his beloved friend. It had been nearly three years since he had been with Enana and he missed her every day. Often he thought of seeking her out, but the events in his life had not allowed it. As Kuhunte opened the large double doors and led them inside, he could hardly breath at the thought that it may be his Enana living at this temple. Kahunte led them down a long hall, through two massive rooms and into another long hall. Presently they found themselves before an elaborately carved door which apparently led to an inner sanctum. Here Kahunte knocked and called out the name of the priestess and Nimrod almost fainted when he heard her familiar limping footsteps.

When the door swung open Nimrod was clicking his tongue rapidly. Then they both howled each other's name.

"Nimrod!!!"

"Enana!!!!"

Kahunte and the Capturers looked on in astonishment, as Enana ran into his arms. Nimrod picked up his long lost friend and hugged her like he had never hugged anyone before. When he put her down she stepped back and looked at him.

"By the creator!" she cried. "You have changed Nimrod! You look…incredible! And your eyes!"

"It's a long story Enana," Nimrod replied, clicking his tongue to perceive her closely. Enana had changed also, becoming even more voluptuous and strong than before. Turning on his spiritual sight, he sensed the shining spirit he would expect to see in his beloved Enana, but there was something else. Somewhere deep inside her, there was something hardly perceptible. It was a kernel of darkness that seemed to be trying to get out, to spread. Nimrod decided that something had happened to his friend. Something tragic, which he was determined to discuss later. Now though, he embraced her again in absolute joy. Finally remembering his manners, Nimrod introduced the rest of the Capturers.

"Capturers!" she cried. "The Meshkem hunters!"

"Indeed good priestess," replied Uparmu. "But we have heard that you rid your town of the beasts. We are here to ask how you accomplished such a thing."

"That is a long story for another time great Capturer," she replied. "In the morning we will discuss it. Right now I must engage in a crucial ritual. Kahunte, are you ready?"

NIMROD THE HUNTER

As Kahunte approached the door from which Enana emerged holding a key, Nimrod clicked his tongue rapidly.

"Enana, what is going on?" he cried.

"We need to close this door my friends," Kahunte declared. "The priestess must be locked in for the night."

"Enana!" shouted Nimrod.

"I shall explain everything in the morning my beloved," Enana said as Kahute slammed the door shut and locked it.

Kahunte slipped the key into his pocket, and then beckoned for the Capturers to follow him. A few minutes later he showed them to a guest room, promised to bring food and then went away.

"You obviously know this priestess Nimrod," Uparmu said. "What do you think is going on?"

"I do not know, but I sense something is wrong. I must go to her!"

"Wait Nimrod," Uparmu said, grasping him by the shoulder. "She is a priestess and this is her temple. We have women in our village who do overnight rituals also. Let us respect her wishes and leave it for the morning."

Reluctantly, Nimrod agreed and settled down with rest of the Capturers to rest. After a while Kahunte came back with trays of food and jugs of wine. They ate all the vegetables and left the baked mutton alone. After disrobing, they took out their beddings and rolled them out on the floor, ignoring the soft beds provided. After a brief conversation, they all went to sleep. But Nimrod woke up in the middle of the night with a nagging feeling of dread about Enana.

Not wanting to wake the others, Nimrod put on his clothes, strapped his mercy sticks to his back, and crept out into the hallway. Clicking his tongue, he stealthily made his way back the way they had come. After ducking behind walls and curtains several times to avoid detection by priests, he found himself back in front of the door behind which Enana had disappeared. The lock was solid and the door thick, so Nimrod searched for something that would assist him in getting inside. After walking up and down the nearby halls, he finally found a small bonze nail. Clicking his tongue as he jiggled it in the lock, he clicked the latch and soundlessly walked inside.

He found that the room was a place of meditation, with alters and tables filled with all sorts of incenses, oils and lotions. There in the middle of it all was a table, upon which lay Enana in a deep sleep. Coming closer, Nimrod perceived that she was breathing easily and seemed unharmed. But just as he was about to turn around and make his way back, he turned on his spirit sight and noticed light from as eight pointed star inscribed on the floor surrounding Enana. Swiping his finger against it, he sniffed and tasted the substance to find that it was chalk. When he rose clicking his tongue to perceive Enana closely, he found that she had awakened and was standing right in front of him.

"Nimrod," she said, "I am so glad you came to see me!"

Nimrod immediately knew that the voice coming from Enana did not belong to her. As he reached for his mercy sticks, she raised her hand and a bolt of black light emerged, crackling into his chest. The last thing he perceived before consciousness left him was Enana's face, strangely contorted and speaking terrible words:

"I already have the women you love, Nimrod! Now the Flame Lord has you also and the phoenix bird shall soon be mine! Ha ha ha ha ha!"

The next thing Nimrod knew he was tied hand and foot, covered in some sort of cloth. By the jostling of his body, he knew he was being carried away in some sort of carriage. Clicking his tongue, he found it to be a normal merchant's vehicle stocked with grain, wood and other goods, all carefully placed to conceal him. There was a cloth stuffed into his mouth so he could not cry out, but he could feel the heat of the sun so he was confident that Allalu would be able to find him. Little did he know that the cloth covering him was festooned with sorcerous runes, blocking his link with his phoenix bird brother. Nimrod also did not know that at that very moment Allalu circled the town of Imsu looking for him in vain, while the Capturers also scoured the town fruitlessly. No one but his enemies knew that he was being taken back to the capital city Susa, back into the clutches of King Shamshi.

For several days, Nimrod was transported across the terrain and back up the mountains leading to the capital city. When Allalu had not come for him by the second day, he knew he was in trouble. Somehow the Flame Lord had not only managed to steal him away, but had managed to stop his link with Allalu. This troubled him a great deal, but not as much as the apparent possession of his beloved Enana by the vile demonic overlord. Despite his current predicament though, Nimrod had faith that the creator would provide a way for him to escape, to turn the tables on the enemies and make them pay.

At last the wagon rumbled to a stop. Nimrod then felt several hands seize a hold of him and carry him into a building. Then he felt himself being carried down several flights of stairs and through a creaky, heavy sounding door. There he was at last tossed to the floor in a dank, stale smelling place. No one had bothered to pull the cloth off his face, as they had on the journey to give him water and food at night, but after a while Nimrod managed to chew through the cloth stuck inside his mouth.

"Let me out! Nimrod shouted.

No one answered. Nimrod lay there in bound discomfort for quite some time before finally hearing footsteps approaching. Then the door opened and he heard a familiar voice.

"Ahh Nimrod!" King Shamshi said with delight. "So you have finally come back home."

"Untie me tyrant and we shall see whose home it is," Nimrod growled through grinding teeth.

"That I shall not do Nimrod," he replied. "But I will pull the cloth down so that I can see your face. It is night now, so your phoenix bird friend cannot perceive you."

As Shamshi pulled the cloth down, Nimrod turned on his spirit sight to look at him. Just as he expected, the king's aura was awash in dark tendrils that coiled around like snakes. The king was indeed damned and he knew he could expect no mercy from him.

"You know Nimrod, they tell me this room is where your family met their fate," King Shamshi said with a grin. "But then, you cannot remember can you?"

Nimrod clicked his tongue to perceive the surroundings in greater detail. The king was indeed correct. This was the very room where he had witnessed his parents being tortured and killed.

"I remember everything Shamshi!" Nimrod declared, wishing he could tear the king's head from his shoulders.

"A pity, that," Shamshi replied. "You know I have always liked you Nimrod, because you were a friend to my daughter!"

"Don't you dare speak of her!" "Nimrod snarled. "It was you! You sacrificed your own little girl for power to the Flame Lord! How could you

Shamshi?"

The king turned away for a moment and sighed sadly. Then he looked back at Nimrod with grim determination.

"It is a family tradition, Nimrod," Shamshi replied. "It usually falls upon the first born, but he was born crippled and had to be disposed of. This left the princess, so I really had no choice. It was a pact made by my great, great grandfather. Our family must remain powerful at all costs."

"You'll pay for it Shamshi! You are damned and shall one day pay!"

"Of that I have no doubt Nimrod," he replied. "But now let us discuss you paying. You will of course never leave this room alive. You will be killed the same way your relatives were. I am even going to take out your shiny new golden eyes. There is no escape for you, but the Flame Lord has agreed to let my daughter and your precious Enana go if you turn over the phoenix bird."

"Never!" Nimrod shouted. "You are a fool Shamshi, to think that you or even the Flame Lord could enslave Allalu! He and his brethren would tear you apart!"

"Not so Nimrod," answered the king gleefully. "We have a way to catch him and a way to control him. Then he shall be transformed into something we can use…"

"I won't do it Shamshi!"

"You will!" shouted the king. "You will because you love my daughter and you are in love with your precious Enana! And you will do it because if you do not, your teacher Elder Eshri is next!"

Nimrod was horrified and filled with rage beyond reason. Tugging at the tight bonds around wrists, he replied forcefully:

"But Elder Eshri raised you! She raised you and princess Hamash! Have you not one shred of gratitude, one shred of decency in you?"

"I think you know the answer to that Nimrod" the king said, pulling the cloth back over Nimrod's face. "I shall give you a day to think about it. After that I shall deliver Elder Eshri's head to you and then you shall join her in the afterlife."

With that, Shamshi turned and left. Nimrod heard him speaking to two guards outside, and then he walked away.

For a long time Nimrod turned everything over in his head. It seemed everyone he ever loved was destined to be hurt and for a second he suffered a crisis of faith in Yah. Then he put all that aside and began to meditate. After long minutes, he thought his emotions were clear enough for prayer. And pray he did. Nimrod prayed long and hard, in an effort to beseech the creator to send him a way out. Before long he was exhausted from praying and found himself nodding off to sleep, until he heard a familiar voice just outside the door.

"Breakfast!" the voice cried.

"About time!" Another voice replied.

"Dried pork again?" another said.

Nimrod could hear the men chewing and swallowing. Then moments later, he heard their bodies hit the floor. Then the key jiggled in the lock and the door swung open. Footsteps came near and a knife ripped through the cloth covering his body. Then the blade cut through his bound feet and hands and its wielder stepped back. Nimrod clicked his tongue rapidly. He could not believe his senses. There standing before him, holding a knife in much that same way he had seen him hold a killing blade many years ago, stood Albel. Suddenly flashbacks of his family being murdered and his own years of torturous enslavement took over Nimrod's mind and he lunged forward.

Seizing Albel's blade wielding hand by the wrist, Nimrod grabbed him by his crotch, lifted him and threw him against a wall. The impact was tremendous, the knife fell away and Albel lay there dazed. Looking up at his former slave bearing down upon him with murderous intent, Albel was strangely calm. Meanwhile Nimrod's conscious mind had flown from him, leaving only a lifetime of seething, overwhelming hatred and a thirst for righteous revenge.

"You…killed them!!!" Nimrod shouted as he dipped to pick up Albel's knife.

Albel looked up with tears streaming from his eyes.

"I'm sorry," he said.

Nimrod snatched Albel up by his throat. Pressing his former master against the wall, the former slave reared back with the blade.

"Is that all you have to say?" Nimrod screamed. "After doing what you have done? Is that all?"

Tears welled up even more in Albel's eyes, the droplets streaming down his face and over the iron gripped hand around his throat.

"I'm... I'm sorry." Albel croaked again.

"Well that's not good enough!" Nimrod screamed.

Just as he was about to plunge the blade into Albel's heart, Nimrod felt something between his hand and Albel's neck that felt familiar. Loosening his grip, Nimrod breathed for a moment and looked at Albel with his spirit sight. Suddenly he saw the light shining from the eight pointed star around Albel's neck. And Albel's spirit, instead of being wrapped in darkness as he expected, had only small streaks of negativity, which were being pressed upon by shining bands of light. Nimrod drew his hand away, but did not put down the knife.

"I'm sorry, Nimrod," Albel repeated. "I am a follower of Yah now. Elder Eshri has shown me the way. I work in the kitchen these days, and when I heard they caught you... I had to help. Nothing could make up for the wrongs I have done and I realized that if you had your memory back, you would surely kill me. But I came regardless... because I had to."

Albel then got down on his knees. Tears still streaming from his eyes, he tilted his head and offered his neck for the blade.

"Go ahead and do it. You have every right," Albel sobbed. "I just wanted you to know first...that I am sorry."

Nimrod gripped the blade tightly. Just one stroke and he would have vengeance for his family upon at least one of those responsible for their deaths. Just one stroke and he would avenge himself for so many years of humiliation and beatings. Just one stroke...

It was the hardest thing he had ever done, but Nimrod opened his clenching fingers and let the blade fall. Then he lifted Albel up and placed his hands upon his former master's shoulders.

"I forgive you Albel." Nimrod said. Then he embraced his former master and murderer of his family.

"Thank you!" Albel replied, sobbing on Nimrod's shoulder. "Thank you for forgiving me Nimrod, thank you, thank you."

Just then Nimrod felt a strange vibration going up and down his spine. Abel stepped back, his mouth falling open in astonishment. A golden light appeared above Nimrod's head, just as two similar beams arched upwards from his eyes. Uniting atop his head, the lights slowly formed a shining image of the Tree Of Life, the spiritual icon that Elder Eshri taught them about. For several seconds Nimrod then levitated in the air, his body bathed in a sparkling beam that shot upwards through the ceiling. Then, slowly and gently, the Tree Of Life sank down into Nimrod's head, his feet touched the floor and the golden light faded.

Enveloped in bliss unlike any he had ever known, Nimrod thought Allalu's name. Suddenly he could see the ground from far above, in another place, and knew he was seeing through the eyes of his phoenix bird brother. Meanwhile, many miles away near the town of Imsu, Allalu soared. Feeling a compulsion to look in a certain direction, the phoenix bird focused with his supernaturally keen eyesight. There in the far distance he saw a beam of light streaming toward the sky and flexed his wings in elation. For not only did the light pinpoint the location of his phoenix priest brother, it alerted Allalu that Nimrod had achieved a milestone in becoming who he was meant to be. With a tremendous melodious cry, Allalu looped once to express his happiness. Then he took off at a speed that only phoenix birds can achieve, becoming a silver and gold bolt of lightning across the sky.

Meanwhile back in the dank room deep in the bowels of the palace, Albel ceased crying and looked around warily.

"We must leave here Nimrod," he said.

"Fear not," Nimrod said. "My brother and I used to play in the secret corridors of this palace. Follow me."

Nimrod walked out into the hall, stepping over the unconscious men sprawled before the door. Clicking his tongue, he noticed his weapons near the men on the floor and snatched them up. Albel followed, and after a short walk down the hall, Nimrod tapped a few blocks of stone until one sounded different. Then he pushed it and part of the wall slid back. They went inside and it was pitch black. Nimrod hit the wall again and the secret portal closed.

"Keep your hand upon my shoulder Albel," Nimrod said. "Where is Elder Eshri?"

"At this time she would be tending to Princess Hamash in the princess' quarters."

"That would be the room where my brother and I used to reside. I know the way there. Let us hurry."

They hustled through the pitch black tunnels, which were no problem for Nimrod to negotiate, finally stopping at a wall that was familiar to Nimrod. Tapping on a block, he opened another secret door and they both stepped through. Light from a small torch on the wall dimly illuminated the room. Elder Eshri sat with her back to them before Princess Hamash's bed. The princess lay there, looking peaceful and serene. But Nimrod shuddered, knowing that her true self was anything but peaceful in the land of the demons. Elder Eshri got up and turned around, her arms and smile both open wide.

"Hello Nimrod," she cried. "Come to me my special boy!"

Nimrod rushed into her arms and they hugged for long seconds. Then Elder Eshri pushed him back to take a look at him.

"Look at you Nimrod, a grown man now, and a priest, a great and mighty priest. I just felt what happened to you dear one."

"It was unbelievable!" cried Albel. "Nimrod carries Yah's sacred tree within him now!"

"I knew he had the potential," the elder woman said, smiling.

"Elder Eshri, I have not come just to reunite," Nimrod said. "You need to leave, all three of you."

Then Nimrod told her of Shamshi's threat and other details she needed to know.

"I thought this day would come," sighed Elder Eshri. "I am prepared."

"Can you take the princess with you?" Nimrod asked with concern.

"Just get us to the rear of the palace. I have a wagon and provisions enough for all of us. The princess' mind is gone, but I have kept her body strong."

"I can get you to your wagon. Then you must get as far away from here as possible."

"But Nimrod, aren't you coming?" Albel asked.

"There is something that I must do first," replied Nimrod. "Do not worry. Flee as fast as you can. I will find you later."

Elder Eshri and Albel went back to their quarters to gather some small belongings, leaving Nimrod standing over princess Hamash's bed. Staring down at her spiritless shell with his spiritual sight, Nimrod remembered the day the demon had taken her away.

"I am going to find a way to help you princess," Nimrod said. "I promise you."

NIMROD THE HUNTER

Albel and Elder Eshri came back, and then they all entered the secret passageway. Nimrod carried the princess himself until they emerged near the stables. While Albel engaged the new stable master in idle shop talk in his former shed, Elder Eshri and Nimrod placed the princess in the wagon the elder used to pick up supplies in the market. With the princess well concealed, Albel joined her in the wagon and they set out.

Nimrod saw them off, and then crept back into the palace through the secret passageway. Without hesitation, he headed for the room he once knew as his parent's quarters. The room now occupied by King Shamshi. Just outside the secret entrance, Nimrod pulled his mercy sticks. Then he tapped a part of the wall and it slid over. Nimrod dove through, rolled and sprang to his feet. Clicking his tongue rapidly, he perceived Shamshi bent over a table studying maps. The king looked up with a look of astonishing surprise, and then reached for a sword lying on the table.

"I just got word that you had escaped Nimrod," the king said as he slashed his sword before him to loosen up. "I was just looking at these maps to decide how best to search for you. And here you are. Since you have not fled I assume you have come to get revenge for your family."

Nimrod took a moment to search his heart, finding the rage he felt towards the murderous king was gone, replaced by a feeling of peace. Imagining his family as he last saw them in the bosom of the creator, he smiled.

"I am beyond that now," Nimrod replied. "I have no hatred in my heart for you or any man. I have come to destroy the devices you would use to capture my phoenix bird brother. Where are they Shamshi?"

"You do realize that I am a renowned swordsman don't you Nimrod?" Shamshi replied. "And that even if you defeat me, there is no way you will make it alive out of the city?"

"I know you are going to answer my question," Nimrod retorted. "One way or the other..."

Shamshi leapt forward brandishing his blade.

"Make me then!" he cried.

"My pleasure!" answered Nimrod.

They came together, their weapons a flurry of wood and metal. Shamshi was sure that he would simply cut through Nimrod's inferior armament and slice the young warrior in half. But Nimrod was nimble and bold, deflecting the sword away at an angle each time, using both sticks to turn the blade. With a deft twist of his wrists, Nimrod flung the king's sword arm out wide. Ducking under Shamshi's returning riposte by coming down on split legs like a dancer, he simultaneously poked the tip of a mercy stick into the first power point above the king's groin. Experiencing numbing pain and weakness, Shamshi doubled over, right into a devastating strike that slammed the other mercy stick into the fifth power point above his right lung.

Pain exploded like lightning through the usurper's body and Shamshi let forth a blood curdling scream. Not only was it agony he could physically feel, but it was the emotional pain that accompanied a sudden burst of conscience after a lifetime of evil.

The blade fell and Shamshi dropped to his knees as the countless faces of those whom he had hurt or killed flashed before him. And the physical pain increased, becoming like the weight of a buffalo crunching down upon his chest and spine, causing him to writhe on the floor in agony.

Hearing footsteps approaching, Nimrod went to Shamshi's door. It was locked and sturdy, but he knew it was only a matter of time before the king's men broke in. As they began shouting and banging on the door, Nimrod seized the pain wracked king and propped him up. Waving the mercy stick in front of his face, Nimrod slowly pushed it back towards the spot he had just hit.

"Noooo!"screamed Shamshi, pointing at the wall. "There! It is there! A hidden closet!"

Nimrod walked over to the wall and tapped a few times. Suddenly a portion of the wall slid back, revealing a closet full of items. Clicking his tongue, he rummaged through them, pulling forth a long red crook similar to those used by the Capturers to control leviathan. Right next to it he found a folded net, again red colored. Wrapped within the net he discovered an inscribed tablet. Running his finger across it to read the words, he found it contained directions on how to use the instruments, complete with illustrations of a phoenix bird.

As Shamshi continued to writhe in pain and his men continued to pound on the door, Nimrod took the entire contents of the closet, which his spirit sight indicated reeked with evil energy, and placed it in the middle of the floor. In a corner he found a jug of pitch used to coat torches and spread the black substance all over the items, especially the red crook and net. As Nimrod plucked a blazing torch from the wall, Shamshi crawled over towards him. The king was in too much pain to say anything, but his eyes begged Nimrod not to do it.

Nimrod dropped the torch and the whole collection of infernal items burst into flames. Shamshi covered his face in despair as a lifetime of evil tools and cursed instruments burned to cinders. As the room began filling with smoke, his men finally burst in. There they saw Shamshi on his knees crying like a baby, shifting his hands through a pile of smoking ashes. Drool dripping from his mouth, the king had a distant, empty look in his eyes- the look of a man whose mind had been utterly broken.

On the sill of the large window across the room, Shamshi's guards spotted a Kushite warrior sitting calmly facing towards them. His arms extending straight up, the Kushite grasped two sticks with both hands as if he were climbing the rung of a ladder. Recognizing him as the escaped prisoner they had been searching for, the guards rushed across the room to attack.

In response the Kushite simply grinned and fell backwards.

The king's room was five floors up, and when the guards rushed to the window they expected to see the remains of the audacious arsonist dashed to pieces on the ground below. Instead they saw the warrior rising before them, wearing a smile of utter triumph. He still held the sticks above his head, only now they were clutched in the talons of a large powerful bird. With a beautiful melodious cry, the silver and gold feathered creature took the dangling warrior higher into the blazing light of the sun, leaving behind a legend that the astonished guards would talk about for generations: The glorious legend of the mighty Kushite who destroyed a powerful king and hunted monsters with a fabulous phoenix bird - the remarkable warrior named Nimrod!

Coming in 2013:
Nimrod The Hunter Book II
"The Tower"

NIMROD: THE HUNTER
Teaser Trailer Script
by
Jarrett Alexander and Brother G
Based on the Novel
by
Gregory "Brother G" Walker

FADE IN:

OVER BLACK: "'MAY THOSE WHO CURSE DAYS CURSE THAT DAY, THOSE WHO ARE
READY TO ROUSE LEVIATHAN.' – JOB 3:8"

EXT. ANCIENT COUNTRYSIDE – DAY

A bird's eye view of a sprawling countryside.

    NARRATOR   (V.O.)
In the mysterious land known as Elam in
the Old Testament, inter-dimensional tears appear, unleashing beasts capable of immeasurable
destruction. To combat them God sends an astonishing warrior saint...

A castle becomes visible. The POV swoops down towards it. ALLALU, a mighty phoenix bird,
soars above the castle. A bird's eye view indeed.

Far below the bird, a muscular, dark-hued African warrior sprints along a path. Although running
on the ground, he SEES flashes of the castle from above through the eyes of Allalu. This is NIM-
ROD.

    NARRATOR   (V.O.)(cont'd)
        He is a biblical hero, a subject of parable.
        Behold the tale of Nimrod, the Hunter.

INT. CASTLE – DAY

MINION, a slimy, sniveling ogre wearing a hooded robe cautiously closes the door to the chambers
used to interact with his hell-spawned master.

    MINION
At your service, my lord.

Minion bows his head in his master's presence. Minion's form is illuminated by an approaching
light source.

A roaring ball of fire nears Minion. He cowers.

The fireball shapes into the form of a man, the head and hands still flicker underneath his clothes.
This is the FLAME LORD.

    FLAME   LORD
        There is too much peace in the land.
        Your job is to create chaos. A job

Page 187

at which you are failing miserably.

MINION

> But my lord, our forces are causing
> mayhem all across the countryside.

FLAME
                  LORD
> Not nearly enough. Unleash the

Leviathan.

MINION

> Unleash the Leviathan? But my lo--

FLAME
                  LORD
> Silence! My decree already echoes
> within these halls. It need not
> be sullied by your paltry repetition.

MINION

> Yes, my lord. In less than a quarter moon
> it shall be done...

FLAME
                  LORD
> Nonsense. Make ready at
> once. Do it now. Or be consumed.

The flames rage once more.

MINION

> Yes, my lord. At once.

Minion unfurls a rug with mystical letters on it. Sits upon it. He takes a knife from his waistband and slices his palm. Three drops of blood fall from the wound. But they don't hit the ground – they suspend in mid-air. And grow. Into globes. Filled with swirls of mist. The globes fly out of the window.

The muted shriek of a bird echoes in the castle.

MINION

> (Panicking)My lord! He's found me!
> Please help me! What am I to do?

FLAME
                  LORD
> First, you are to stop your sniveling,
> you pathetic cretin. Next you are to
> face him. Alone. If you cannot
> defeat him on your own, you were never
> worthy of being my acolyte!

Flame Lord resumes his fire form and extinguishes. Leaving only smoke.

Minion is entranced by the sight, but quickly snaps out of it to prepare for Nimrod. He slices his palm once more, but holds it face up so the blood doesn't drip. The puddle of blood in his palm transforms into another translucent globe. He begins chanting to it in a mystical language. The globe illuminates.

The chamber door bursts open. The guard who was used as a human battering ram flies in behind it. Then another guard flies in landing on top of the first on. Nimrod stands in the doorway.

Minion backs away as Nimrod approaches, the globe behind his back. The globe gets brighter.

Minion tosses the globe up between them and a beam of light bursts from it, streaking towards Nimrod.

Allalu swoops in through a nearby window and deflects the beam. The deadly light is absorbed by the phoenix birds golden aura and is sent back to where it came from by the beating wings.

The beam shoots into Minion. Minion's body absorbs the light. His insides illuminate like a light bulb. He screams in pain. Collapses.

Nimrod kneels down and seizes Minion by the throat.

> NIMROD
> Where did you send them?
> Where are the leviathan?

MINION

You'll never stop us! The Flame Lord
shall   rule all!

Minion's eyes roll back. He dies.

Fade in:
Over Black: "HE WAS A MIGHTY HUNTER BEFORE THE LORD,
        WHEREFORE IT IS SAID:
        EVEN AS NIMROD, THE MIGHTY HUNTER BEFORE THE LORD"
        GENESIS 10

EXT. LAKE – DAY

Three ten-year-old African BOYS walk with fishing poles.

BOY   #1
No   way!

BOY   #2
I'm telling you, he's real!

BOY   #3
You still believe in Nimrod? That's
just a bedtime story for babies!

BOY   #1

NIMROD THE HUNTER

(taunting)
Baby,   baby, baby!

Boy   #2
Shut   up!

Boys 1 and 3 keep taunting Boy 2, who responds by chasing them with his fishing pole. As the boys horseplay, one of the globes filled with swirls of mist hovers above them.

The globe has an EYE. It watches the boys. Scans the surrounding area. Sees a bullfrog near the lake. The globe swoops down and envelops the bullfrog.

The frog croaks. Drunkenly stumbles about. Falls into the water. Its silhouette sinks.

The silhouette grows. Until it's as big as a hippo. Its head emerges from the water, covered in a Mohawk of horns.

The frog-beast leaps from the water into the air, blocking out the sun. The huge shadow catches the boys' attention.

They see the monster land into a squat before them. They look at each other in horror. Then scatter.

The frog-beast shoots out its tongue. Boy 2 runs towards a tree. The tongue lassos around his torso. He grabs hold of the tree. The other boys try to reinforce his grip on the tree as the tongue tries to pull him away.

Allalu's cry diverts the boys' attention upwards. Allalu swoops down with enflamed claws. The claws of fire burn through the tongue of the beast.

The boys unwrap the severed tongue and look up excitedly at the large colorful bird that helped them. Boy 2 sees something else and points excitedly.

Boy   #2
Look! It's Nimrod!

Nimrod charges towards the beast with a spear. Strikes.
The beast deflects the spear with its claws. Nimrod ducks and jukes the beast's attacks, strikes with the spear from different angles. All of the strikes are deflected by its huge, fast claws.

Nimrod jumps back. Overhead Allalu dives down, his talons aflame. Just as the phoenix is about to strike the leviathan Nimrod shouts.

Nimrod
Spare him Allalu! The beast is innocent!

Allalu pulls up at the last second, soaring back into the air. Nimrod drops the spear. Reaches for the bow at his back and retrieves an arrow from his quiver. The beast leaps into the air. Nimrod aims the arrow and shoots.
The arrow pierces the beast. Followed by another. And another. And another. Nimrod shoots arrows in rapid-fire succession, filling the beast's torso. Then Nimrod leaps out of the way as it falls to the ground in a slump.

The mist-filled globe rises from the fallen beast. The eye blinks and looks around for another victim to possess. The bullfrog shrinks back down to normal size. Leaps into the water.

Nimrod grabs a boomerang from his waistband, throws it toward the eye in the misty globe. As the boomerang passes through the mist a vacuum is created and the misty globe is sucked into the vacuum, leaving no trace. The boomerang swoops around and returns to Nimrod. He plucks it from the air and returns the boomerang to his waistband.

Allalu swoops down. Nimrod extends his arm. On which Allalu lands.

The boys watch in disbelief. Nimrod's golden eyes glow as he scans the water first with his radar sight, causing waves of sound that form images to bounce back. Then he looks with his spirit sight, which causes all the plant life to appear to him with a slight glowing silhouette. The glow is around the children also, who are standing a ways behind Nimrod. Still sweeping the area, he speaks to the children without looking at them.

> NIMROD
>
> Remain watchful in my absence.
> Yet know that I am always near.

The children smile at each other as boy #1 and #3 slap boy #2 on the back. Then a faint voice screams for help in the distance. Nimrod and Allalu simultaneously turn their heads towards the sound.

> NIMROD
> Fly,   Allalu!

Allalu shrieks. Flies towards us. His feathers fill the frame. The shriek echoes.

OVER BLACK: "'I SHALL DIE IN MY NEST, AND I SHALL MULTIPLY MY DAYS... LIKE THE PHOENIX.'"
Job 29:18   FADE OUT.   THE END

NIMROD THE HUNTER

Nimrod

Man, Maniac or Myth?

By Ekowa Kenyatta

http://www.essaysbyekowa.com/

Many Christians from scholar, minister, to the laity has pontificated on the blackness and evilness of the Biblical Nimrod. He has been used to curse and brand a people and is the ideal for all corruption and power that had ever been unleashed upon the earth. His name is only rivaled by Adolph Hitler in the minds of modern man.

Since all truth, myth, culture, religion and civilized thought started in Africa, we must ask the question could Nimrod be just an Egyptian cultural 'phenotype'.

"Phenotype is just a scientific word for: function or behavior and the outward manifestation of a thing."

There is no doubt that Nimrod was of African ancestry let's settle that once and for all time. The Bible is a retranslated and condensed copy of all African religious, cultural and iconographical events. Biblically and extra-Biblically Nimrod was shown to be a black man.

Nimrod:

נִמְרֹדNimrod, Tiberian Hebrew נִמְרוֹד In the Bible and in legend, Nimrod)Standard Hebrew" Nimrōḏ), son of Cush, grandson of Ham, great-grandson of Noah, was a Mesopotamian monarch and "a mighty hunter before Yahweh". He is mentioned in the Table of Nations (Genesis 10), in the First Book of Chronicles, and in the Book of Micah. In the Bible he is an obscure figure; in later interpretations, as recorded by Josephus and the rabbis who compiled the Midrash, he is the subject of innumerable legends. The most prominent of these was the story that he built the Tower of Babel …According to Hebrew traditions, he was of Mizraim[Egypt] by his mother, but came from Cush son of Ham and expanded Asshur which he inherited. His name has become proverbial as that of a "mighty hunter".[1]

Here is the Rabbis Midrash version from the 6th century AD medieval version of a story of Nimrod and Abraham:

"(...) He [Abraham] was given over to Nimrod. [Nimrod] told him: Worship the Fire! Abraham said to him: Shall I then worship the water, which puts off the fire! Nimrod told him: Worship the water! [Abraham] said to him: If so, shall I worship the cloud, which carries the water? [Nimrod] told him: Worship the cloud! [Abraham] said to him: If so, shall I worship the wind, which scatters the clouds? [Nimrod] said to him: Worship the wind! [Abraham] said to him: And shall we worship the human, who withstands the wind? Said [Nimrod] to him: You pile words upon words, I bow to none but the fire - in it shall I throw you, and let the God to whom you bow come and save you from it!

Haran [Abraham's brother] was standing there. He said [to himself]: what shall I do? If Abraham wins, I shall say: "I am of Abraham's [followers]", if Nimrod wins I shall say "I am of Nimrod's [followers]". When Abraham went into the furnace and survived, Haranwas asked: "Whose [follower] are you?" and he answered: "I am Abraham's!". [Then] they took him and threw him into the furnace, and his belly opened and he died and predeceased Terach, his father."

A lot happened between the time of the Biblical Nimrod and Abraham and the 6th century Jewish Rabbi's that dreamed up this scenario.

The name Nimrod has also become synonymous with a 'fool' as the American Heritage Dictionary says:

"The name Nimrod is either a hunter or a person regarded as silly or foolish." Many people have tried to correlate Nimrod with all the initial evils, idolatry and ills in the world. Many have taught the whole world rebelled against God because of Nimrod's rebellion. His name, they say, means rebellion and it is said he was the first Idolater."

But, what accounts of Nimrod came first? Mighty Hunter, Fool, Rebel? History is written by the victors and to him goes the spoils.

Some Rabbinical scholars have identified Nimrod as part of the first of a family (Cush) and ignorantly cast him as the first Homosexual who was licentious and practiced bestiality. It is also said that Noah wife was of the offspring of Cain (another biblical sinner) who transferred all of those hateful characteristics to her son Ham [but not Shem and Japheth?] and from this evil hatred of God and disobedience to his word was transferred from the line that was considered African.

But is that so? In a word… Hell No!

"In the absence of the real [truth] the counterfeit [lie] becomes reality."

Where did these racist notions come from? It came from a long line of those who wanted to control History and put fear in the hearts of men toward those who had the keys to all religions, the African. Rabbinic as well as Catholic and later Christian and Arabic leaders redesigned the nature of Nimrod to suit their racist paradigm.

Notes from the Church fathers:

> "Fallen angels taught men the use of magical incantations that would force demons to obey man. After the flood Ham the son of Noah unhappily discovered this and taught it to his sons. This became ingrained into the Egyptians, Persians, and Babylonians. Ham died shortly after the fall of the Tower of Babel. Nimrod, called Ninus by the Greeks, was handed this knowledge and by it caused men to go away from the worship of God and go into diverse and erratic superstitions and began to be governed by the signs in the stars and motions of the planets. Taken from Recognitions of Clement 4.26-29." [2]

The Church Fathers were the men who replaced the Apostles in authority of the CHRISTIAN church and were under the control of Rome, but did they all believe the same thing? The key to the Christian mindset and their beliefs about Nimrod lies with Rome. Rome became the site of Christianity and those who were not were killed were excommunicated, and others were branded heretics if the orthodox view of the Bible, and biblical events was not adhered to. This view was 'tweaked' added to, and built over the course of many ecumenical councils, the first major conclave in Nice.

Further commentary from the Church Fathers:

Some modern information on Nimrod was developed and recently with the well-used and often quoted book: The Two Babylon's by Hislop. Here is an excerpt from many of his semi-orthodox viewpoint:

> 'The Two Babylon's, was written by the late Reverend Alexander Hislop in pamphlet form in Edinburgh in 1853, greatly expanded 5 years later and has since appeared in many editions in both Great Britain and the United States. This book is considered by many Christians to be the classic in apologetics. See how a religion that was started by Nimrod and his wife spread to various regions, taking on different names, but keeping the same pagan rituals and trappings. These same rituals embody the Catholic church of today.'

Many have taught that Semiramus was the wife of Nimrod, and Tammuz was said to be their son, as was chronicled in the Two (2) Babylon 's by Alexander Hislop. But, is her personage really authentic? And if it is not, then can she have married Nimrod and had a son?

"Semiramis: (sĕmĭr´emĭs) , mythical Assyrian queen, noted for her beauty and wisdom. She was reputed to have conquered many lands and founded the city of Babylon . After a long and prosperous reign she vanished from earth in the shape of a dove and was thereafter worshiped as a deity, acquiring many of the characteristics of the goddess Ishtar. The historical figure behind this legend is probably Sammuramat, who acted as regent of Assyria from 810 to 805 BC." [3]

Sammuramat

Assyrian Queen, 9th Century B.C

Let us compare the two women.

Sammuramat is the subject of many myths about her reign as both the wife and mother of kings. She apparently accompanied her husband into battle, greatly expanded Babylonia's control over far-flung territories, irrigated the flatlands between the Tigris and Euphrates rivers, and restored the fading beauty of her capital, Babylon

Semiramus conquered the whole of the Middle East, invading Kush and India. Her consorts has little or nothing to do with government (she did not have a king as a husband), she was the daughter of a goddess [mighty woman because of the matriarchal reign in families] Some said she castrated the males of the royal household, suggesting that she was a goddess whose temples were served by eunuch priests. Most early Assyro-Bablyonian queens she embodied the spirit of Mari-Ishtar or (Isis) and later the image of Mary the mother of Jesus [italics mine]. [4]

But, is there archeological and extra-biblical proof that?

1. Semiramus the mother of Tammuz and Nimrod the great-grandson of Noah lived in the same time frame?

2. Nimrod was said to be Ninus and later Baal?

Some Rabbinic writers claim that Nimrod, because of his unrighteousness, was slain by Shem his great-uncle. Others say he was beheaded by Esau the son of Abraham.

How could that be? Did they live in the same time?

'Nimrod was slain by Esau, between whom and himself jealousy existed owing to the fact that they were both hunters (Targ. pseudo-Jonathan to Gen. xxv. 27; "Sefer ha-Yashar," section "Toledot," p. 40b; Pirke R. El. l.c.; comp. Gen. R. lxv. 12).W. B. M. Sel.'

Nimrod was slain by Esau? Nimrod was in Abraham's time? Obviously this is a game of confusion.

Here is the mythical story again. Please note the similarities between this story and the story of Daniel and the Hebrew boys in Babylon .

"The punishment visited on the builders of the tower did not cause Nimrod to change his conduct; he remained an idolater. He particularly persecuted Abraham, who by his command was thrown into a heated furnace; and it was on this account, according to one opinion, that Nimrod was called "Amraphel" (= "he said, throw in"; Targ. pseudo-Jonathan to Gen. xiv. 1; Gen. R. xlii. 5; Cant. R. viii. 8)."

Note the similarities of Crossing the Red [Reed] Sea and the Egg of the Creation story in Egypt

"Nimrod was informed that Abraham had come forth from the furnace uninjured, he remitted his persecution of the worshiper of the Creator of all things, Yahweh; but on the following night he saw in a dream a man coming out of the furnace and advancing toward him with a drawn sword. Nimrod thereupon ran away, but the man threw an egg at him; this was afterward transformed into a large river in which all his troops were drowned, only he himself and three of his followers escaping."

"Then the river again became an egg, and from the latter came forth a small fowl, which flew at Nimrod and pecked out his eye. The dream was interpreted as forecasting Nimrod's defeat by Abraham, wherefore Nimrod sent secretly to kill Abraham; but the latter immigrated with his family to the land of Canaan."

Wait there's more:

"Ten years later Nimrod came to wage war with Chedorlaomer, King of Elam, who had been one of Nimrod's generals, and who after the dispersion of the builders of the tower went to Elam and formed there an independent kingdom. Nimrod at the head of an army set out with the intention of punishing his rebellious general, but the latter routed him. Nimrod then became a vassal of Chedorlaomer, who involved him in the war with the kings of Sodom and Gomorrah , with whom he was defeated by Abraham ("Sefer ha-Yashar," l.c.; comp. Gen. xiv. 1-17)"

Wow...all of this is outside the Biblical cannon? Why? All we see of Nimrod is a few lines in the Bible, but before we cracked open that 'Holy Book' we were told that Nimrod was Black and the epitome of evil. So the ideas of those writings outside the Bible influenced our biblical perception and still do! So if the Bible is the inerrant word of God then why are we taking errant extra-biblical ideas from outside of the cannon? Humm...sound like a kettle of fish to me.

Here is what one writer said:

"Those who identify Nimrod with Marduk, however, object that the name of Izdubar must be read, as is now generally conceded, "Gilgamesh," and that the signs which constitute the name of Marduk, who also is represented as a hunter, are read phonetically "Amar Ud"; and ideographically they may be read "Namr Ud"—in Hebrew "Nimrod." The difficulty of reconciling the Biblical Nimrod, the son of Cush , with Marduk, the son of Ea, may be overcome by interpreting the Biblical words as meaning that Nimrod was a descendant of Cush."

Two other theories may be mentioned: One is that Nimrod represents the constellation of Orion; the other is that Nimrod stands for a tribe, not an individual and (comp. Lagarde, "Armenische Studien," in "Abhandlungen der Göttinger Gesellschaft der Wissenschaften," xxii. 77; Nöldeke, in "Z. D. M. G." xxviii. 279).

Orion and its seven stars

The possibility that Nimrod was a group of individuals is plausible. Nimrod may have been a title of royalty just like the term Pharaoh, Nebus [Babylon], Negus [Ethiopia], Shah [Iran], Tsar [Russia], Caesar [Rome], Rajah [India], Tenno [Japan], Ajaw [Mayan], Moi [Hawaii or King [European].

Another two prominent theories are now held in regard to Nimrod's identity;

"One, adopted by G. Smith and Jeremias, is that Nimrod is to be identified with the Babylonian hero Izdubar or Gishdubar (Gilgamesh).

The second, that of Sayce, Pinches, and others identifies Nimrod with Marduk, the Babylonian Mercury. The former identification is based on the fact that Izdubar is represented in the Babylonian epos as a mighty hunter, always accompanied by four dogs, and as the founder of the first great kingdom in Asia."

Others claim he was the builder of the Tower of Babel and because of his desire to 'Reach God' the languages of the world were confused, but the Bible does not exactly say that: Genesis 10.

"Cush became the father of Nimrod, who was the first potentate on earth. He was a mighty hunter by the grace of the LORD; hence the saying, "Like Nimrod, a mighty hunter by the grace of the LORD. "The chief cities of his kingdom were Babylon, Erech, and Accad, all of them in the land of Shinar.From that land he went forth to Asshur, where he built Nineveh, Rehoboth-Ir, and Calah, as well as Resen, between Nineveh and Calah, the latter being the principal city Mizraim became the father of the Ludim, the Anamim, the Lehabim, the Naphtuhim, the Pathrusim, the Casluhim, and the Caphtorim from whom the Philistines sprang.

Genesis 11:1-9

"The whole world spoke the same language, using the same words. While men were migrating in the east, they came upon a valley in the land of Shinar and settled there. They said to one another, "Come, let us mold bricks and harden them with fire." They used bricks for stone, and bitumen for mortar.

Then they said, "Come, let us build ourselves a city and a tower with its top in the sky, and so make a name for ourselves; otherwise we shall be scattered all over the earth."

LORD came down to see the city and the tower that the men had built. Then the LORD said: "If now, while they are one people, all speaking the same language, they have started to do this, nothing will later stop them from doing whatever they presume to do.

Let us then go down and there confuse their language, so that one will not understand what another says." Thus the LORD scattered them from there all over the earth, and they stopped building the city. That is why it was called Babel, because there the LORD confused the speech of all the world. It was from that place that he scattered them all over the earth."

Hey -Did the Bible say Nimrod built the Tower of Babel? NO! It said MEN. What men? - The men migrating in the East that came to the Valley of Shinar and settled there. In Genesis 10 it said the chief cities in his kingdom one was Shinar. But where was Nimrod? We are told he taught the people to rebel, but where is that story within the Bible? Nowhere! We got that from extra-biblical non-canonized writings from the 1st and 6th century AD after the death of Christ!

Ask yourself: Why during those centuries after Christ were they trying to re-write the story of Nimrod, Cain, Ham and all the rest of the so-called black folks in the Bible?

The key is in the statement "ALL the people spoke one language, and said the same words." was this before or after Nimrod? Genesis 11 seems to be floating and because the chapters are one after another it makes it seem as though the events in Genesis 10 and 11 are Chronological but are they?

Here in Chapter 10 we read this simple statement:

The sons of Japheth:Gomer, Magog, Madai, Javan, Tubal, Meshech and Tiras. The sons of Gomer: Ashkenaz, Riphath and Togarmah. The sons of Javan: Elishah, Tarshish, the Kittim and the Rodanim. (From these the maritime peoples spread out into their territories by their clans within their nations, each with its own language.

What language were they speaking? Was it before Nimrod and Babel? But in Genesis 11 it said ALL the people spoke the same language. Was that just the sons of Nimrod or ALL people that lived in that area? Was it the children of Shem, Ham and Japheth?

I believe the writers of Genesis [yes I said writers] put this story in as a separator to highlight the tribe of Shem to the reader and to add a codicil to the story Nimrod and Babel.

More myth:

"By the Arab, Nimrod is considered as the supreme example of the tyrant ("al-jabbar"). There is some confusion among Arabian historians as to Nimrod's genealogy. According to one authority he was the son of Mash the son of Aram, and consequently a Semite; he built the Tower of Babel and also a bridge over the Euphrates, and reigned five hundred years over the Nabatæans, his kinsmen."

But the general opinion is that he was a Hamite, son of Canaan the son of Cush, or son of Cush the son of Canaan (Ṭabari gives both); that he was born at the time of Reu (meaning: a bright idea), and was the first to establish fire-worship. What was fire worship? The eternal spark the atom the thing that quickens us.

Another legend is to the effect that there were two Nimrods:

1. The first was the son of Cush.

2. The second was the well-known tyrant and contemporary of Abraham; he was the son of Canaan and therefore a great-grandson of the first Nimrod. According to Mas'udi ("Muruj al-Dhahab," ii. 96), Nimrod was the first Babylonian king, and during a reign of sixty years he

dug many canals in 'Irak.

The Koran says:

"After these adventures Nimrod continued to reign wickedly. Four hundred years later an angel in the form of a man appeared to him and exhorted him to repent, but Nimrod declared that he himself was sole ruler and challenged God to fight with him. Nimrod asked for a delay of three days, during which he gathered a considerable army; but this was exterminated by swarms of gnats. One of these insects is said to have entered Nimrod's nose, reached the chambers of his brain, and gnawed at it. To allay the pain Nimrod ordered someone to strike with a hammer upon an anvil, in order that the noise might cause the gnat to cease gnawing (comp. the same story in connection with Titus in Giṭ. 56b). Nimrod died after forty years suffering."

Dang, he lived a long time! But I thought all that century old living was stopped at a certain time according to the Biblical account.

Others say he stole the 'animal skins' that God gave to Adam and Eve as a covering on their expulsion from the garden. But I believe that is code for the priesthood of Egypt/Africa.

"The origin of the importance attached to the spotted fawn and its skin had evidently come thus: When Nimrod, as "the Leopard-tamer," began to be clothed in the leopard-skin, as the trophy (Triumph) of his skill, his spotted dress and appearance must have impressed the imaginations of those who saw him; and he came to be called not only the "Subduer of the Spotted one" (for such is the precise meaning of Nimr--the name of the leopard), but to be called "The spotted one" himself.

In actuality the Leopard skin was a sign of the Egyptian Priesthood worn by the Sem [funeral] Priests.

This leopard skin is studded with golden stars and attached to a leopard head made of wood and covered with a sheet of gold. A representation of the leopard's paws is still in place. [see Tassels/Tallit]. The leopard head once decorated a garment that imitated the animal's skin through the use of silver stars in place of spots.

This representation can be traced to the ancient concept of the leopard as a symbolic representation of the sky.

The leopard skin was a distinctive garment of the Sem Priest who was charged with revitalizing the mummified body of the pharaoh in the ritual known as "Opening the Mouth."

[1]The Sem Egyptian priesthood wore leopard-skin mantles, or cloaks, while performing their official duties, marking them as high priest. Tutankhamun, who was in theory the high priest of every god, was buried with this mantle.[6]

The Tallit with the blue color from the Chilizon:

"The Torah commands us to wear a thread of blue, techeilet, in each corner of our tzitzit.[1] While tzitzit serve as a visual reminder to do the mitzvot, the blue thread reminds us of Hashem: "Techeilet resembles [the color of] the sea, and the sea the sky, and the sky the throne of glory".[2] The Gemara informs us that the techeilet dye comes from a bodily fluid (lit: blood)[3] of the chilazon. [4] At some point it becameforgotten which species is the chilazon. Exactly when techeilet ceased to exist is unknown. Though some have suggested this happened sometime between 500-700 C.E.[5], there is evidence that techeilet continued to be dyed in some places for another several hundred years.[6]"

Nimrod's other name was the spotted Leopard and became a spotted Fawn.

"We have distinct evidence to this effect borne by Damascus , who tells us that the Babylonians called "the only son" of the great goddess-mother "Momis, or Moumis." Now, Momis, or Moumis, in Chaldee, like Nimr, signified "The spotted one." Thus, then, it became easy to represent Nimrod by the symbol of the "spotted fawn," and especially inGreece , and wherever a pronunciation akin to that of Greece prevailed. The name of Nimrod, as known to the Greeks, was Nebrod."

What is the symbolism of the spots? Power and Authority.

The Bible fuses these two images of skin color and leopard or spotted fawn allusion:

"Can the Ethiopian change his skin or the leopard his spots? Then you also can do good who are accustomed to doing evil. Jeremiah 13:23.

Let's take a look at what the Bible says about Nimrod and compare it to the extra-Biblical information to glean what may possibly be the truth. Remember, we are dealing with an ancient story and in doing so, we must see what are truths and what is myth. We must also remember that the Greeks, Romans and later the Europeans used the actual [Kings, Queens , Priests, Sages] people of Egypt/Africa to make their myths and then embellished those myths and called it His-story.

The story according to the Bible:

'Kush fathered Nimrod, who was the first powerful ruler on the earth. He was a mighty hunter before the Lord (Adonai) - this is why people say, 'Like Nimrod, a mighty hunter before the Lord (Adonai). His (Nimrod's) kingdom began with Babel, Akkad and Calnah, in the land of Shinar.' Gen. 10:8-9

'Kush fathered Nimrod, who was a powerful ruler on earth.'1 Chron. 1:10

'They will shepherd the land of Ashur with the sword, the land of Nimrod at its gates; he will rescue us from Ashur when he invades our land when he overruns our borders. 'Micah 5:6

Nothin' negative ... not like what we have been told. Without any extra-Biblical information Nimrod was just a powerful leader and the son of Cush. We need to sift through the extra-Biblical information especially when it come from the Romanish, Greek, Medieval or European viewpoint because they have heavily influenced our thoughts about this man or group of men.

The Talmud is not helpful when it comes to the truth, it cast the same shadow on the Nimrod:

Possibly named "Nimrod" as the one who caused the world to rebel ["Limrod"] against HaShem: Eruvin 53a; Pesachim 94b

Possibly named "Amrafel" as the one who threw Avraham into a fiery furnace: Eruvin 53a Also related to Nebuchadnezzer. Pesachim 94a-b.

Yes, there was a similar story of Abraham like Daniel being thrown into the fiery furnace, and earlier we saw Nimrod suffer the same fate. But we see their explanations as possible an not probable. It is either a possibility or it is not. Which one is it? It depends on the message you want to convey to those who believe everything they read.

'A lie can travel around the world 1000 times before the truth gets it boots on.' Ben Franklin

Here is one Rabbi's opinion on Nimrod using the Medieval Midrash.

"Nimrod a mighty hunter before Adonai [Yahweh/God] - The description is both unique and obscure. What is the Torah trying to tell us when it says that he was the first "mighty one"? What does it mean to be a mighty hunter before the Lord? While the basic understanding of the text would imply physical prowess, Rashi opts for a more conceptual definition."

Rabbi Shlomo Yitzhaqi,(a rabbi born in 1040AD in(רבי שלמה יצחקי is an acronym for רש"י Rashi France famed as the author of the first comprehensive commentaries on the Talmud and Tanack. Acclaimed for his ability to present the basic meaning of the text in a concise yet lucid fashion, Rashi appeals to both learned scholars and beginning students, and his works remain a centerpiece of contemporary Jewish study. His commentaries, which appear in all printed editions of the Talmud and Torah (notably the Chumash), are an indispensable companion to both casual and serious students of Judaism's primary texts.

Rashi says that Nimrod was a manipulator who ensnared people with his words. Rashi is based on the following Midrash:

Was then Esau a Cushite? [He is so called] because he acted like Nimrod. Hence it is written, Like nimrod a mighty hunter before the lord (10:9): it is not written, Nimrod [was a mighty hunter], but like Nimrod: just as the one snared people by their words, so did the other [Esau, i.e. Rome] snare people by their words, saying, ' [True,] you have not stolen, [but tell us] who was your partner in the theft; you have not killed, but who was your accomplice in the murder.' (Midrash Rabbah - Bereishit 37:2)

He was a mighty hunter before the lord; wherefore it is said: like Nimrod a mighty hunter before the lord. Truly he was a man of might, because he was clad in the garments of Adam, and was able by means of them to lay snares for mankind and beguile them. R. Eleazar said: 'Nimrod used to entice people into idolatrous worship by means of those garments, which enabled him to conquer the world and proclaim himself its ruler, so that mankind offered him worship. He was called "Nimrod", for the reason that he rebelled (marad=rebel) against the most high King above, against the higher angels and against the lower angels.' R. Simeon said: 'Our colleagues are acquainted with a profound mystery concerning these garments.' (Zohar Bereishit Page 74a).

So you can be a Cushite if you ACT evil? Come on! So being a Black man was the standard of evil? When was this derived?

While Adam gave names to the animals, and Hevel cared for the animals, Nimrod and Esav are hunters of animals.

Another Rabbi from Spain born around in 1092AD:

also known as Abenezra(1092, was one of ,ע"ראב or אברהם אבן עזרא ראב"ע [Abraham ben Meir ibn Ezra the most distinguished Jewish men of letters and writers of the Middle.

"The Ibn Ezra explains that Nimrod took these animals and offered them to God, and therefore the text speaks of Nimrod as being a mighty hunter "before God." While later scholars have found difficulty attributing apparently positive gestures on the part of Nimrod, it has been explained that this was a part of his manipulation.

If others were impacted by the flood and now were in fear of God, Nimrod can show that he too is God-fearing. If we take this logic one step further, we can posit that his original stated intention of the Tower was to build a shrine for the service of God."

Huh????????? Where did they come up with this stuff? Some say oral traditions but from who?

Where did all this didaction (instruction) come from?

Part two of this essay coming in Nimrod the Hunter: Book Two

NIMROD THE HUNTER

greg.brother9@gmail.com